# SONG OF THE SENDING

## THE EXPATRIATES, BOOK ONE

ALSO BY
# CORINNE O'FLYNN

LEI CRIME SERIES NOVELLAS
*Half Moon Girls*
*Tell the Truth*

SHORT STORIES
*Suicide High*
featured in: *Tick Tock: Seven Tales of Time*

# SONG OF THE SENDING

## THE EXPATRIATES, BOOK ONE

# CORINNE O'FLYNN

*Find the Author on the Web!*
@CorinneOFlynn
www.corinneoflynn.com
www.facebook.com/oflynnbooks

They told him their world was destroyed.
And they were the last to escape.
They thought he was safe.
They were wrong.

For Conor, Rory, Liam, and Aidan
*Never stop dreaming.*

# ONE

I dodged Sam's sword by dropping to the ground and rolling away, then waited for the tiger to do the same. My best friend's blade fell in a wide arc beside me, but Cotton stood still, the spotlight overhead making his white fur like frosted glass. I got to my feet and glared at the tiger as if I could guilt him into complying. The walls of the old big top puffed in, then out as if the tent were sighing my frustration. Cotton watched me for another moment before he crouched and rolled, a belated mirror of my movements.

"He's too slow, man." Sam pointed out the obvious. Always had, since we were kids. He rubbed the sweat off his face, leaving light dusty stripes on his brown skin. I tried not to laugh as he leaned on his sword. The blunted point pried a triangle of packed dirt from the ground.

"I know." I let my sword fall and pulled off my gloves. The tang of diesel fumes choked the still air inside the tent.

"He's not in sync." Sam wrinkled his nose. "Can't you make him do it like Bak?"

"It's not the same, and you know it. Bak doesn't need me to teach him." I stepped over to Bak and scratched the fur between my tiger's ears.

I slipped my mind into his.

*You don't need me, do you, boy?*

Bak pressed himself into my side. *Bak need Jim.* My tiger's thought whispered through my head like the swish of canvas moving in the stifling summer breeze, and the sun wasn't even up yet. Way too hot.

*I need you, too, Bak. Me too.*

Sam loosened the straps of his dented chest plate and plopped on the ground next to Cotton. "He's gonna make us look stupid. We should scrap the new stuff." He tilted his head to indicate Cotton. "Maybe it's time we really change the show. You know, leave him out of it." He lifted his dark hair off his neck. "Freaking hot in here."

"Yeah, you try selling that to my Uncle. What would Sweetwater's be without the Dueling Knights of Mysteria?" I pictured the carnival without its signature event. With makeup and armor, nobody would ever guess a sixteen- and a seventeen-year-old played the two knights beholden to the powers of Heaven and Hell. Along with our trusty tigers, Light and Shadow, we settled the eternal fight over good and evil— nightly at 8:00 PM and 10:30 PM.

Sam snorted. "A monkey might do better as my sidekick."

I ran my hand down Cotton's shoulder and wondered if the animal could tell Sam was ripping on him. "Don't talk about him like that. You're supposed to be the good guy. The white knight." The big cat sat there, licking his paw.

"Dude. Then let's switch and you be the good guy. Besides, if Cotton knows what's going on, then he should be able to keep up. Right?" My friend turned to the tiger as if waiting for a reply.

"Give him a break. It's a new move. He'll get it." I connected with Cotton. *Watch me and Bak, boy. You know what to do.*

The tiger stopped licking his paw and locked his pale eyes with mine.

*That's right. Good boy.*

"Come on, Bak, let's show him how it's done." I pulled on my gloves and picked up my sword and turned to face Sam and Cotton. Bak took his place next to me. I mind-tapped my tiger.

*Get down low. Sword right.* I bent my knees and raised my sword over my right shoulder. Bak lowered his body and tensed as he lifted his right paw, claws extended.

*Slice.* My sword flew toward my invisible opponent. Bak raked the air in front of him with his paw. His tail whipped out behind him to compensate for the shift in his balance.

*Down. Roll right.* I dropped and rolled, pretending to dodge Sam's blade as I rose to my knees. Bak moved in perfect sync, coming to rest on his belly, paws on the ground.

*Up and*—I got to my feet, feeling like I'd been punched in the side of my head. My connection to Bak broke. I looked at my tiger, a little dazed and unsure what had happened. Bak's attention went upward, near the roof of the big top. But aside from the lights and the normal rigging, there wasn't anything to see.

"What's wrong?" Sam said.

"Don't know." I tapped Bak again.

A siren screamed through my head. I covered my ears, but it did nothing to ease the pain. It felt like my brain was trying to fly out of my skull. The pressure was unbearable. Bak rolled on the ground, swatting at his nose and shaking his head as if a swarm of hornets had attacked him.

*Bak. You okay?* I sent the thought to my tiger—but I couldn't get through to him. He lay on the ground, writhing.

It felt like a searing hot knife was being jammed between my eyes. I dropped to my knees. Sam gaped. Cotton yawned. Something warm hit my knee—a dark droplet of something wet. Blood. My blood. My nose was bleeding. I ran my hand over my mouth. It came away red. *What the hell?*

Sam grabbed my shoulders and said something. I saw his mouth moving but couldn't hear anything over the wailing siren and the crushing pressure. His lips formed my name and the muscles in his neck strained, but I couldn't hear a thing.

Bak rolled onto his back and threw his head into the dirt, banging it over and again. I screamed his name—well, I think I screamed—I don't know. I felt my throat vibrate with the effort but couldn't hear myself. I knelt down and grabbed Bak's face, tugging at his fur and forcing my tiger to look at me. His amber eyes were wide and wild. His mouth gaped open. He was scared. I wasn't strong enough to hold him.

*Buddy, look at me.*

And then it was gone. The sound stopped like someone switched off the volume. I squeezed my eyes shut in the new silence. Was I deaf? Maybe the sound was my hearing imploding in some colossal failure of the senses. Everything seemed frozen in the moment. Still on my knees, I looked at Sam and at Bak. My friend stood still, watching me as my tiger inched to his feet. Then the big top canvas sucked the air in and out in a soft wheeze, the sound like relief itself.

"I'm gonna puke." I dropped to my hands and knees, trying to steady my head.

"Jim! Dude, can you hear me? You alright?" Sam's voice was a million miles away.

Bak sidled up to me and nuzzled my ribs, urging me to tap him. I closed my eyes and connected with my tiger.

*Jim sick?*

*You okay, Bak? What was that, boy?*

*Bak good. Bak hungry.*

"Jim? Man, what happened?" Sam made to touch me but pulled back.

My head felt lighter than before. Like it was being pulled away from my body. "That sound." I squeezed one eye shut against a swelling headache.

"What sound? Didn't hear anything. One second you and Bak were doing moves, then you were both on the ground."

"You didn't hear it?" I asked.

Sam shook his head. "I could feel the two of you go totally off the rails, but the only thing I heard was you."

Of course, Sam would've felt the tension change in me and Bak. As an empath, he was always in tune with how everyone was feeling. Made it hard to keep things from him for sure. Still, the sound was so freaking loud. It didn't make sense.

Sam grabbed our gear. "You okay? 'Cause I'm freaked out. Maybe we should take a break."

Cotton sat there like nothing had happened. I tapped the tiger. He couldn't talk to me like Bak, but I could tell he was hungry and bored and wanted to sleep. He wasn't tense or nervous at all.

Sam held the door flap open. The pre-dawn sky was a wedge of deep blue over the neighboring tents. We followed as Cotton and Bak loped down the narrow alley formed by several eighteen-wheelers until the tigers got to their cages. The cats climbed up their ramps and waited for Sam to close the gates.

Sam pulled out his keys and moved to the back of the refrigerator truck. "Hey, go get a drink. Wash your face or something. See if Doc's awake yet. I'll get started here."

A drink sounded great. "Yeah. Okay. Be right back."

I staggered back to the RV and let myself in.

Mom had left the RV as soon as we parked at the fairgrounds this morning. She'd smiled as she left and pressed her thought into my head as she walked away.

*Have fun on your ride today. Promise me you'll wear your helmet.*

"I promise!" I'd called after her.

She'd be off making her rounds, checking in to see if anyone needed anything after the drive from Las Vegas. My big brother, Dan, had gone with Uncle Paul to get the rides up and running before Sweetwater's opened tonight.

I washed up, changed into a new t-shirt, and slugged down a few ibuprofen from the medicine cabinet. I had to get back to Sam and the tigers—feeding them was a two-man job. I sat in the dark for a few minutes to let the pain subside. Then I hopped down the metal steps and let the screen door slap closed behind me.

As I walked into the lane behind our motorhome, a falcon landed on the ground in front of me. It was all lit up in the headlights from a truck across the midway. I've never been a fan of falcons. Birds of prey gross me out. Mind-tapping a falcon was like stepping into a gory dream full of eyeballs and intestines. No, give me someone's pet canary or parakeet any day. Birds of prey are nasty. I would've ignored it, but its silver-white feathers glistened, and its eyes reflected the light—reddish sequins that raised goose bumps on my arms.

The falcon held my gaze as if waiting for me, pulling me to tap it. The tug in my head throbbed all over again.

With my mind, I reached into the raptor's. I braced my stomach for the gore. But instead of fleshy bird thoughts, light blasted my eyes. Super-white beams filled my vision and threw me off balance. I grabbed my knees to keep from falling over. My palms felt slick, and the taste of metal filled my mouth.

Letting go of the bird's mind, I watched it take off. I was still outside the RV, white-knuckled and sweating.

"What the hell was that?" I called after the bird.

"Dan, is that you?" Chef's voice called from the neighboring rig. I walked around to the cook shack. Orange juice. With ice. I needed O.J.

Something moved across the roof of Chef's RV as I made my way around. The bird was back. It hopped back and forth on its taloned feet, opening its beak and squeaking raspy choking sounds.

"Get out of here." I swung my arm at the thing. It hopped backward on the roof but continued sputtering. I squeezed one eye shut against the rising pain.

The bird never broke eye contact. It kept rocking and bobbing, working its tiny beak like it needed to cough. Then it hit me: Maybe it really was choking. Maybe it needed help. I tapped the bird again, expecting the explosion of dizzying light. Instead, the world tilted to one side and I fell back on the gravel. "What the?" I broke from the bird and tried not to puke.

The strange falcon hopped back and forth on its feet, staring down at me from the top of Chef's RV.

"You're creeping me out, bird," I said.

Then it opened its wings and took off, circling overhead. I watched it rise until I could no longer make it out against the darkness. "Good riddance." I rubbed the gravel off my hands.

Chef Andy came around his cook shack and stood over me, smiling. "Need a hand?"

"Hey, Chef," I grabbed his hand and let him pull me to my feet.

"You seen your brother? I need him to pick up some stuff when he makes his run into town," he said.

My knees shook, but I managed to stay upright. "Uncle Paul has him setting the rides."

We walked around to the yard in front of his rig. A camping lantern sat on the table loaded with drinks and a spread of breakfast stuff. His eyebrows drew together. "What's with you? You're white as a sheet."

"Headache." I squinted against the lantern's harsh glare. I nodded to a few of the roustabouts stretching out the thick canvas of the cook tent on the ground in front of us. "Morning, guys, did any of you see that weird bird?" I asked. "It just flew by here."

The two men nearest me shook their heads. They waved their arms in the air and a pair of long wooden poles floated themselves under the canvas and lifted the tent. The boss canvasman called, "Hup!" and as one, a dozen other men levitated the two king poles into the rigging under the canvas. In a moment, the tent top was up with a crisp smack of fabric pulled taut. Several of the crew paired off and began hammering huge iron stakes into the ground. The clangs crashed through my skull.

Another crew pulled the guy-ropes and rigging tight around the stakes as the others laced up the wall panels. Since some of them didn't have any special ability, and nobody used real magic when the locals were around, they did most of the work by hand. The rest of the canvasmen moved down to the next tent, setting up for another day at Sweetwater's.

"Take a seat, Jim. You look like hell." Chef smiled as he pulled a folded paper from his jeans and handed it to me. "I've mapped out our ride. First day on your new bike is gonna be a good one."

I opened the map. I could barely make out the lines of the road. "I'm sorry. Can I look at it later? My head is killing me." I felt bad as I shoved the map into my pocket. He'd been planning this trip for weeks, preparing for when I finally got my driver's license.

He stood and patted my shoulder. "Sure thing. Go see the doc. He'll hook you up with something. Gotta get better. Your big day."

I nodded and grabbed a paper cup. I filled it with orange juice and took a sip. My head felt like it wanted to detach itself—by force if it had to—and sail away into the sky.

"Here." Chef lifted the cooler lid and dumped a scoop of ice into my cup.

"Thanks, Chef." I got to my feet. "I have to go. Sam's waiting." After downing the rest of the juice, I tossed the cup into the trash and walked back across the midway toward the tigers.

Sam wasn't around when I got back. I leaned my forehead against Bak's cage, closing my eyes and letting the cold metal bars soothe my head. Bak came over and bent his face to mine. He seemed fine. He pushed his huge foreleg through the bars and wrapped it around my back. Tiger hug.

*You not right?*

I nodded and pressed my nose into the thick fur between Bak's eyes. "My head's killing me, pal," I whispered.

*Food for Bak.*

Standing up, I looked into his eyes. "Yeah, I know. Let me see if Sam's got breakfast ready for the two of you."

I walked toward the fridge car. The strange tugging in the back of my head returned and thrummed like an unseen cell phone vibrating nearby. I willed my stomach to settle down.

Bak roared.

I turned as the falcon landed on the roof of Bak's cage. Fixing its shiny eyes on me, it made a hollow chittering sound. The tugging in my head amplified, and the urge to tap the bird overcame me again.

"Not a chance." I waved my hand at the falcon. "I'm sorry if you're choking or whatever. I can't help you."

It bounced back and forth, its talons clicking and squeaking against the steel roof. Eyes bulging, it worked its beak open and closed, hacking.

Bak let out a low whine and reared up on his hind legs to swat at his ceiling. Cotton sat quietly in his cage a few feet away as if watching his companion and his trainer go insane happened every morning. I connected with Bak and got flat, white static. "What the hell?"

"What's going on?" Sam came running around the corner and stood there watching as Bak curled up in a ball and then rolled over, growling at the bird above him.

I reached for Bak with my mind, trying to ignore the buzz coming from him. *Relax, buddy. Settle down.* But I don't think he heard me. Whatever the bird was doing to him was making him crazy. "He's going to hurt himself."

Sam grabbed a long broom and swung it on top of the cage. The bird took off, and the pull in my head went back to the little tug. Bak stopped freaking out.

"Holy crap! What was that?" Sam wore coveralls and a pair of long rubber gloves. He flipped his hair out of his eyes and looked at the tigers. He was taller than me, almost six feet, but even he couldn't see over the top of the tigers' cages.

"Bak heard it, too." I felt ridiculous saying it, but I knew Sam saw what happened. "Bird's been following me. It's messing with my head. I can't tap Bak when it comes."

"Really?" Sam looked dubious. "You still look as bad as you feel—and that ain't good."

Sam loved to play emotional analyst. But I wasn't in the mood. "My head's killing me. Let's feed these guys and go," I said.

"Then take a few deep breaths or something. You're bouncing out of your skin." Sam turned back toward the fridge car.

I helped him pull the huge coolers full of raw beef and lamb around to the front of the cages. The tigers got one whiff, and then they were all pacing and pawing the bars. Bak was his old self again.

I let go of the cooler. "Hey, Bak, what was that about? With the bird?" I mind-tapped him and was relieved I got through, no problem.

*Food for Bak.*

"Yeah, we'll get you fed. What was wrong with the bird?"

*What bird? Bak hungry.*

The problem communicating with Bak was he had the vocabulary of a toddler. Even so, I knew he always understood what was going on. But it was like he had no memory of what happened.

I stepped into a pair of heavy rubber coveralls made to fit someone much taller and a whole lot wider than me and pulled on a pair of thick brown rubber gloves. The cuffs came up to my elbows.

"So you think it's been following you?" Sam asked. "The bird?" He threw the lids of the coolers open. The cold metal scent of meat and blood filled the yard.

"I don't know. I think it needs help. Maybe it's choking or it's sick or something. I can't tap it."

"Weird," he said.

"Yeah, it's been a weird morning. You ready?" I asked.

"Let's do it."

I dropped my hands to my sides and took a deep breath. Eyes closed, I willed the noise in my head to give me a freaking break. Once I connected with both tigers, I told them to move to the back of their cages while we fed them. Unlike Bak, Cotton's response to me tapping him was like most animals: he usually did what I told him to. It was like he was a puppet and I had the strings.

The big cats retreated to the far sides of their cages and lay down to wait. They never took their eyes off me as Sam and I hefted the huge cuts of meat through the small, hinged doors on the sides of their cages. There was no malice in them. Sure, Bak was special, almost like a person. But without the mind tap, Cotton would probably have succumbed to instinct at some point and mauled us to get at the meat. But he's a tiger, it's nothing personal.

When we were done, I pulled off my gloves and stepped over to Bak. I stroked the soft fur between his ears while he ate. The morning sun broke through the bars of his cage, making my tiger glow warm and orange.

*Happy. Jim. Happy. Thanks.*

Bak looked up at me, his mouth gruesome with dripping blood, and he smiled.

"I'm happy too, Bak. Don't worry about me."

"Morning, boys. You ready for this afternoon?" Hollis leaned against the refrigerator car waiting for Sam and me to finish cleaning up.

"You know it," Sam said.

Hollis held his hand out to me, palm up. "Let's see it."

I took out my wallet as the pulling-sound swelled again. Peering at him through one open eye, I laid my new driver's license in his hand.

Hollis inspected the card. "Fancy. Nevada official. Nicely done, Jim." He handed it back to me.

"Only a year late." Sam punched my shoulder.

"Whatever. At least now you guys can stop giving me crap for failing the driver's test."

"Two times." Sam smiled as he stepped out of his coveralls. "What time we going?"

"We leave at one." Hollis clapped his hands together and rubbed them up and down. "You excited to finally take your bike out, Jim? We got that baby purring just right."

"Oh yeah," I said, trying to ignore the growing sound.

"I need your help with something, guys." Hollis waved us to follow him. "Got a sec?"

We walked across the midway to where his trailer stood alone on the far side of the fairgrounds. As the horse master, he stayed near the stable. He knocked on the door and Charlie jumped out. The copper in her brown hair caught the light as she landed next to me. She held a large rectangular package, untidily wrapped in green paper with little snowmen racing on sleds. A shiny, gold bow was stuck on near the corner.

They all shouted, "Surprise!"

Charlie handed me the present and kissed me on the cheek. For a moment, everything was gone and it was the two of us. No Sam, no Hollis, no weird head-pull-humming. She smiled at me with her gold-brown eyes sparkling in the sun, and I smiled back at her. My ears burned.

"It's from all of us. Sorry 'bout the Christmas paper. It's all we had," Hollis said.

"Wow, thanks, guys," I said, feeling like I was having an out-of-body experience. Part of me was intensely aware of the exact square inch of my cheek Charlie kissed. Another part of me could feel the noise pressure in my head building, and the rest of me was about to unwrap my first-ride present.

"Open it," Hollis said. "We've been waiting weeks to give it to you. Been killing me."

Charlie nodded. "We picked it up back when we were in Montana. Chef said we had to wait."

"You knew?" I asked Sam, surprised he hadn't let it slip at all. Dude has never been able to keep a secret from me.

He nodded.

"Your bike's ready and you're finally street legal. So, there you go." The smile on Hollis' face made him look like a little boy—if you overlooked that he was six-four, two-eighty with a bald head and bushy brown eyebrows.

I tore at the wrapping and let it fall to the ground. As I lifted the lid off the box, my chest went tight. It was a black leather motorcycle jacket. It was beautiful.

"You like it?" Sam said.

Nobody had ever given me a gift like this before.

"You've worked so hard restoring that old bike," Charlie said. "We wanted to make it super special." She beamed her smile at me.

The jacket was custom with the Sweetwater Riding Club emblem on the back, the two silvery wings of the Sweetwater shield spread out behind my name. Glittery white wisps of thin curling light floated from the center and wrapped through the letters of my name, disappearing around the sides. Charlie once asked me what it was like to tap the animals, if I saw anything when I did it. I had described tiny threads of light.

"Hollis. You guys, I …" I ran my fingers over the stitching and smelled the thick leather. The metallic thread glinted in the morning sun. I was afraid to say anything, my throat went so tight.

"Put it on." Hollis lifted the jacket for me to slide into.

It felt heavy and solid. It felt great. Stretching out my arms, I turned around to let them check it out.

"Like it was made for you," Sam said.

"I love it! It even matches your hair," Charlie said, tracing the stitching on my back with her hand. The pressure of her touch was firm and constant, electricity down to my belt.

"Thank you … guys … really," I said. "You didn't have to—"

"We wanted to," Hollis said. "Besides, your brother's old one don't fit you right. You need your own."

"It really is perfect," I said, trying not to let the hum building in my head ruin the most perfect moment ever.

"I knew you'd like it." Hollis slapped my shoulder. "I told you guys he'd like it."

Charlie slid her hand down my arm and hooked her fingers around mine for a moment before letting go. "It looks good on you." She smiled.

"Thanks." I felt my ears go hot when a shriek made us all turn.

The bird was back. It landed on the edge of the green storage tent behind Hollis, its long talons sinking into the thick canvas like it was tissue paper. Its bright orange eyes looked different in the sunlight, smarter somehow, and it was looking right at me again. The hair on the back of my neck prickled.

"By the Sisters!" Hollis gaped at the bird. "No."

Charlie grabbed my arm.

"Not again," I said, watching the bird and waiting for it to make my head explode.

The bird opened its beak wide, and the pulling sensation behind my eyes disappeared. The vice grip on my head let go. The dizzy feeling, and the hum and tug of it were gone. Instant relief.

"I carry ..." the bird sputtered a tiny cough and shook itself before starting again. "I carry an urgent message for James Wales."

"Did that bird talk?" Sam pointed at the falcon as if there could be any way we might not know exactly which bird he meant.

The mention of my name sent a jolt through me. I thought it was a joke. I thought this freaky bird was another part of my surprise. "Cool guys, how'd you get it to speak?" I asked. But it only took a second to see they were as blown away as I was.

"Wow," Charlie whispered, "What is it?" She let go of my arm and stepped toward the tent where the weird falcon perched.

Hollis stared, his face totally pale. "I know that bird," he whispered.

The raptor stayed on the edge of the tent, peering down with its strange eyes. It settled, folded its wings against its body, and rocked from foot to foot on the canvas edge. Its leathery bird claws opened and closed.

It spoke again. Its high-pitched, scratchy voice sounded strangely human. Its beak didn't move—it hung open as if a recording were somehow playing through its body.

"James Wales, you are called to return to Castle Marren. We'll watch for you under the next crossing moon. James Wales. It is time. James Wales. It is tiiiiiiiiime." Its last word stretched out like a wheeze from a sagging accordion.

The bird continued rocking, its eyes never leaving mine. As I opened my mouth to ask it for something, anything more, it let out a short cough and fell to the ground. It landed on its back. It wasn't moving.

# TWO

"Holy crap, that bird talked," Sam said.

I steadied myself against Hollis' trailer. Part of me still felt like I was on some hidden camera show. As if my mom would jump out with her phone camera at any moment, laughing as she recorded my shock. But if that were the case, the guys had really taken the prank and their acting to a whole new level.

I tried to make sense of what the bird said. Though the words were clear enough, they didn't mean anything. Someone was calling me back to Marren? But Marren was gone. All of Bellenor was gone … I joined the three of them kneeling down to look at the bird.

"Is it dead?" Charlie asked, her voice shaky.

It certainly looked dead. Its eyes had glazed over and were now a cloudy white. A thin coil of yellow smoke rose from the two tiny holes in its beak. It reeked of burning hair.

"Oh, man," Hollis said, rubbing his hands over his face, which had broken out in beads of sweat.

"What's that?" Sam pointed where the bird's wing met its body. Our heads touched as we all moved in to see. A brown leather strap was tied around the bird's wing. I pushed the animal gently with my finger, and it rolled facedown. On its back lay a little brown pouch, like a miniature leather backpack, fastened between its wings.

Sam started to untie the minuscule knots holding the flap closed when the bird's head spun to the side. It looked up at us, its dead white eyes focused on nothing.

Sam jumped backward, pulling Charlie by the shoulder. She let out a squeak as they both fell back onto the gravel. I couldn't stop staring at the bird.

"Well, it's not dead." Charlie let out a nervous laugh.

"What should we do with it?" Sam asked.

Hollis took off his t-shirt and proceeded to wrap the bird like a burrito. "We need to protect her wings in case she thrashes. She'll wake soon."

I looked at Hollis, stunned. "How do you know that?" I asked. And what else did he know?

"This,"—he cradled the wrapped bird in his arms—"is a very important messenger. It's called a Sending. They don't do that sort of thing anymore—change an animal like that." He shook his head as if lost in thought. "It changes them. Their brain. Something big must be going on back home. There's only one person who could have sent her to you. And if I'm right, then something's really wrong."

"What kind of wrong?" Sam asked, his forehead wrinkled with worry.

Everything in me flashed to attention at what Hollis said. "Back home?" I asked. There was no way.

Hollis stared at me, saying nothing.

"Hollis, what do you mean *back home?*" I repeated. I'd always known we weren't from here, from the Modern World—the human world. All of us, everyone in Sweetwater's, were originally from a place called Bellenor, which used to be connected to this world by some magical force—until the bridge collapsed. Or so I'd been told. "You all said Bellenor was destroyed. Back when my mother was a kid. Before I was born."

"I'm sorry, Jim," he said. "We had no choice."

Sam's jaw dropped. "Wait a second." He pointed at Hollis. "He's serious. How did everyone fool *me?*"

"They apparently had lots of time to practice," I said. "And your empathy wasn't so good in grade school." Looking at the bird, I tried to get my head around the idea it came from Bellenor.

Sam looked at Hollis. "What about the catastrophic break in the way the worlds connected?" He'd been taught the same things I had. So had Charlie. All us kids had.

"Yeah, what about the Great Shift?" Charlie added. "Is all of that a lie?"

Hollis frowned. "The Great Shift happened. Long ago. Though the bridge didn't collapse, it's dangerous, unstable. We can cross only under certain conditions."

"You're joking, right? Hollis?" Charlie said.

I didn't think this was the least bit funny. Not at all.

Hollis shook his head.

"He's telling the truth. But not all of it." Sam rubbed his chin. "If crossing is so dangerous, why come here at all?"

Hollis' forehead creased. "Because we bring the energy. Having our people on Earth helps keep the worlds from drifting."

Understanding was a tiny knife down my spine, cutting me off from reality. I thought about my mom and the story she told of how she barely escaped with her brother, my Uncle Paul. Sometimes she cried while retelling it. Why would she lie? It didn't make sense.

Hollis glanced over his shoulder. "I never agreed with the clan's decision to keep you in the dark. But now, you need to know. We all stayed past our tour of duty to keep you safe, Jim."

Safe? I wanted to understand but all I felt was angry. "Safe from what? More lies?" It came out louder than I expected.

Sam put a hand on his chest. "Dude. Calm down."

"Shh!" Charlie stepped toward the midway, her head cocked to listen. "What in the world?"

I followed her gaze across the fairgrounds where the big top towered over the smaller event tents. Festive red, white, and blue flags atop each of them blew in the morning breeze.

"Do you guys hear that?" she asked.

"Hear what?" Hollis said, wiping sweat from his face. He held the swaddled bird against his chest.

The peaked canopy of the big top stood tall over the row of concession stands. The old marquee twinkled faintly in the sunlight, its red and yellow light bulbs spelling out Sweetwater's Traveling Show. Everything was quiet.

"Charlie?" I knew better than to question her ears.

"What is it?" Sam asked.

"Shhh." She closed her eyes and cupped her hands around her ears.

"I don't hear anything," I said. "Actually I don't hear anything at all."

Usually, on the day we arrived in a town, the fairgrounds were so noisy you could barely have a conversation without shouting. The roustabouts and canvasmen made a terrible racket erecting the tents and hammering the steel spikes into the ground. Then there was the constant hum of generators and cranes and trucks permeating everything as we all got things ready for the weeklong stay. Not to mention the animals screeching and squawking and the regular people noise. But from where we stood, it was eerily quiet. The whole place felt like a ghost town.

A mushroom of black smoke billowed above the big top in the distance. A rolling boom reached us a moment later.

"Whoa," Sam whispered.

"Sweet Sisters. They're here," Hollis said. He turned and grabbed me by the arm. "We have to get you out of here. Help me get the horses loaded up." He handed Sam the bird. "Gently. Keep her safe." He ran off without looking back.

I was about to follow Hollis when Charlie took off in the other direction, toward the explosion. "People are screaming," she said.

I couldn't hear anyone.

Sam chased her, looking like a football player with the bird cradled in his arm as he ran.

"Jim, come on!" Hollis called from somewhere behind me.

Hollis could get the horses without my help. I went after Charlie and Sam.

# THREE

As we got near the big top, Sam waved for us to stop. "Something's really wrong here," he wheezed between breaths.

"You think?" I said, huffing.

"Not kidding. I don't know. I feel—trouble," he said.

"Charlie? What do you hear?" I asked.

We hid behind one of the ticket booths, the first in the long row of concession trailers lining the midway. I bent over to catch my breath.

"I hear crying, but there's nobody here." She turned as if following the sound. "It—it sounds like a little kid." Her face went white. "Oh, no, guys, do you think Davey and my parents are alright?" Charlie's eyes welled up.

"It's going to be okay," I said, trying hard to believe it myself. I pulled out my cell phone and dialed my mom.

"Where is everyone?" Sam asked.

"Shhh." I couldn't hear a ring, so I pulled the phone away from my ear. "Not working. We're not that far away from town, are we?"

"About a mile or so, but maybe the bluffs are blocking the signal." Sam indicated the high hills surrounding the fairgrounds and pulled out his own phone. He tried calling and texting then looked up. "Nothing."

"I left my phone on my nightstand," Charlie said.

A huge cracking sound made us all jump. A sort of rolling sizzle followed it.

"What the hell was that?" I said.

"I don't know, but it was really close," Charlie whispered.

The side wall of the big top hung directly in front of us. As we watched, fire seared through the fabric, eating it away as it grew. Wood popped and snapped inside the tent. Heat and smoke billowed out from under the eroding canvas wall and floated toward us in a dark oily rush.

We huddled against the ticket booth. The ridges and folds of the aluminum siding pressed into my back through my jacket. The big top started to lean, bending toward the midway like a listing ship. The thick steel cables securing the big tent snapped, sending loud thwangs reverberating through the air. The vibration hummed on my skin.

We stepped around the corner of the booth and into the midway.

"Oh my God," Sam whispered.

Everything was on fire. Thick, black smoke stung my eyes. Flames shot out of some of the animal tents. The aviary tent was barely there. Fire had eaten the canvas, leaving only the burning king poles and charred birdcages standing like skeletons in the hazy mess. I recognized some of our birds flying loose, relieved at least some had gotten out in time. It felt like watching my own house burn down.

"Look!" Sam pointed in the direction of the fun house.

A flash of white. Cotton ran down the midway away from us. His paws dripped bright red.

"Is he hurt? Whose blood is that?" I was about to tap the tiger when Bak came flying around the corner, causing all of us to slam back against the wall. I was so relieved to see him it took a second to notice he was totally freaked out. He was all wide eyes and bared teeth, fur standing on end. His feet pedaled as his claws fought for a grip in the loose gravel. His back and tail bristled. He bounded straight past us.

I mind-tapped my tiger. He felt me immediately, his huge paws skidding to a halt. Pebbles and dust flew out in front of him. Once we connected, pure panic overcame me. It was all I could do to break our connection so I could breathe.

"What's going on, boy?" I asked my tiger, my heart racing double-time again.

*Bak afraid. Bad man.*

I reached out my hand. Bak drew nearer. He was visibly calmer as he pushed his muzzle under my hand, flipping it up to his ears like a dog. I dug my fingers into his thick fur and scratched. The panic was gone. He chuffed, and I tapped my tiger again.

*Danger.*

Another loud crack. Closer now. A thin stream of blue light shot past us and forked in a thousand different directions.

Every hair on my body stood on end. I looked at Charlie and Sam and saw they felt it, too. The blue light dwindled and faded with a strange extended sizzle—like a cartoon firework fuse burning down. We all crouched, even Bak.

"What was that?" Sam asked.

Charlie's voice shook. "It looked like—lightning?"

Lightning in the morning on a sunny summer day in California? Seemed about as likely as Sweetwater's being attacked by a *bad man*, as Bak had put it. And yet, here we were.

A woman screamed from somewhere on the far side of the midway, near the tiger cages. I wondered where my mother was and willed her to reach out to me with her mind. *Find me, mom. I'm here.*

The last of the cables supporting the big top gave way. The long poles inside the tent moaned under the weight of canvas and metal rigging. The tent tipped, plucking the iron stakes from the ground like toothpicks. Clumps of dirt flew at us. The cables whipped dangerously, and the big top collapsed in a gust of hot dirty air. It blew out from under the canvas as it fell and hit us like a sandstorm.

Charlie gasped and coughed.

Squeezing my eyes shut, I held my breath. We were all covered with soot and ash. I tapped Bak as he took off. *Stay with us.* But he wasn't listening. What the hell was going on?

"Where is he?" A deep-voiced man shouted. He sounded really close.

Sam dropped to the ground. Pushing the bird under the ticket booth, he shimmied sideways after it. I pulled Charlie down and shoved her in beside Sam, then scooted in next to them. We lay on our bellies looking out between the two front tires. The dust and smoke made it hard to breathe. Charlie blinked furiously, tears streaming down her cheeks, cutting clean lines through the dirt on her face.

Black boots stepped into view from the left and stopped. Gravel crunched as another pair of boots, these with thick silver spurs, arrived from the right. The two stood facing each other, the bottoms of long black coats came almost to their ankles.

"No one is telling of the boy, sir," one man said.

"Where are you keeping them?" The deep voice asked.

"We have them caged, sir, in animals pens on the far side of the field."

Charlie and Sam and I looked at each other. Charlie mouthed *caged* with a question in her eyes. The thought of anyone being trapped in the animal cages made my stomach turn. Who were these people?

"Have you found the Sending?" Deep Voice asked.

The bird lay stiff and bundled on the ground in front of us. Dust coated its feathers and crusted around its eyes. Sam pulled the bird closer to him.

"Not yet, sir. Mathan says he is certain she's here. He lost the signal only minutes ago. We have the boy's mother."

"You are not to leave without the Sending. I require the map it carries."

"Yes, sir. I'll see to it."

"Take me to the prisoners. And bring the boy's mother to me. We shall see who remains silent." The two men walked away, beyond the fallen big top and out of our view.

"What the hell was that about?" I whispered when they were gone.

"Shhh," Charlie said, "I am trying to listen."

I couldn't see anything. I slid out from under the trailer and brushed the pebbles and dirt from my clothes. My jacket was scuffed and scratched from the gravel.

"Jim, no," Charlie whispered.

I was still on my knees when a huge hand gripped me by the back of my neck and dragged me to my feet.

"Hey!" I tried turning and took a swing at him but my fist only found air.

"And who are you, boy?" The man's breath was hot on my cheek. I squirmed against his grip, which only made him squeeze tighter. He lifted me off the ground.

There was a grunt as another man came around from behind. His heavy steps pounded the gravel as if he were marching. When he turned to face me, I stared in complete shock. His hideous face had no lips. A hole gaped where his mouth should have been. He let out another grunt. The thick stump of his tongue rolled uselessly inside his mouth as he moaned. His rotted, yellow teeth showed through the ragged hole in his face. His black hood almost concealed his greasy, dark hair. His breath smelled totally rank.

The man holding me squeezed my neck and waved a knife in front of my face. He pressed the point into my throat, sending warm blood trickling down my neck and onto my chest. I kicked backward at him, but my feet swung free. Pulling at his hand, I tried to make a little room for air. He wore tight leather gloves. My lungs were on fire.

The man with no lips grunted and got down on his knees. He pointed a thin black rod under the trailer. The hole in his face pulled wide into the most grotesque smile I'd ever seen.

The guy holding me spoke, his voice clear and calm. "You lot will come out from under there if you value this boy's life."

"No, don't." My words were lost in the crush of my throat.

Charlie and Sam crawled out from under the ticket booth and stood in front of me. They didn't have the bird. The knife dug deeper under my chin. I flinched against the cutting blade, but there was nowhere for me to go. With my feet still dangling in midair, I had no leverage.

"Let him go," Charlie said through clenched teeth. No Lips pointed his stick at her, and it exploded in a flash of light. The burst hit her square in the chest and sent her flying backward. As she landed with a crunch of gravel, her face slammed against the ticket booth's tire.

Sam screamed, "Charlie!"

I fought to get free.

She lay completely still. Sam took a step toward her but stopped. No Lips pointed the lightning stick at Sam's face. Magic? Technology? Whatever it was, it seemed deadly.

Sam put his hands up. "Who are you? What do you want?"

No Lips poked his weapon at Sam and forced him back against the trailer.

"Settle now, Little William," the man holding me said. "We want to talk to them, not send them into oblivion."

I looked at Charlie. *Oblivion.*

No Lips took a step back from Sam, but he didn't drop his stick.

I watched Charlie's back to see if she was breathing. I couldn't tell. *Please, please be okay, Charlie.*

The man threw me down, and I landed on my knees. Blood rushed back into my head, making my vision all spotty. I took in a long breath. As my vision cleared, I looked up at the man who had been holding me. He was tall and broad, a really big guy, wearing a dirty black cloak with the hood pulled back, revealing brown hair and flat, brown eyes.

"We seek the Wales boy. Son of Vernius Wales and Jane Sweetwater."

At the mention of my parents' names, everything in my body raced. I felt like I was going to have a heart attack.

I was one of the Wales boys.

Sam looked at me, uncertainty on his face. "There's more than one—they're brothers," he said.

"We seek the scholar. The one who carries the mark of Lashte," he said.

"Lashte?" I asked, confused.

No Lips reached into his cloak and pulled out a roll of torn brown paper. He pulled it open and showed Sam and me a symbol made up of one vertical line crossed by four others. It reminded me of a lowercase "t", only with three extra cross bars, and all four of them tilted, pointing down to the right. Two dots hovered near the top bar and the bottom bar. Sweat ran down my back while my insides turned to ice.

I looked at Sam and saw him glance at my right shoulder. I had a scar in that exact shape right there, under my jacket. I never could recall the injury that led to such a strange scar. I figured it was because I was too young when it happened to remember. But it wasn't a scar—it was a mark, according to this guy.

"I don't know what that is," Sam said, covering for me.

"Master Eldred shall discover what you know," the big man said as he pulled out a short silver sword from his belt and forced Sam to his knees next to me. He slid a thin rope around my neck and shoved his heavy boot into my back. No Lips did the same to Sam. My rope was yanked so hard it started crushing my windpipe. I dug my fingers under it, but there was no room. I couldn't get any air at all, not a whisper. I kicked at the ground, struggling for air.

"Tell me their names, the Wales boys," the big man said.

"Dan," Sam said, "an—and Jim. But I saw them head into town this morn—"

"Silence!" The man backhanded Sam with his gloved fist. Sam went down clutching his cheek.

It's true what they say about your life flashing before your eyes when you're about to die. It took all of five seconds for me to catalog mine. Seventeen years didn't seem like nearly enough. White spots pulsed at the edges of my vision. The flames in my lungs threatened to burn right through my chest.

"Leave the girl. We'll take these two to Master Eldred," the big man said. He lifted his boot off my back and the rope loosened a bit. I sucked in huge lungfuls of air. Then he started walking, dragging me behind him.

My own weight worked against me. I struggled to my feet and had to walk fast to keep the rope from tightening again. My eyes felt like they were going to explode out of their sockets. No Lips hit Sam across the back of the head with his stick, and my best friend fell, hard. I turned around, trying to get a look at Charlie's face.

No Lips kicked Sam in the ribs. Sam rolled onto his back and looked at me—then his eyes flashed wide at something behind me.

My brother, Dan, flew over me in a blur and tackled the man holding my rope. The two men landed on the mounds of canvas of the fallen big top and rolled to their feet. The canvas puffed and bulged as the air trapped inside billowed out. The guy was big, about Dan's height, and built strong. But Dan was bigger. My brother was huge, like puffed-up body builder huge. And he was wicked fast.

Dan's hand shot out and punched the man right on the chin. The man's face snapped to the side, but he didn't go down. Instead, he pulled his hands up to fight.

Precious air rushed in and cooled my burning lungs. Air, even dirty, smoky air, had never tasted so good. The man's blade lay on the ground next to me. It had a thick black handle carved with silvery scrolls and intricate designs on the pommel and guard. I grabbed it and stood up, watching them fight.

The man moved like a ninja. All knees, arms, and flowing motion. He kicked and punched, dancing around my brother like something out of a movie. Amazingly, Dan matched him move for move. I had no idea my brother knew how to fight like that. They were on the ground now. Blood covered Dan's hands, and he kept on punching. Then he reached down and snapped the man's neck. A sick crunch marked the end of it. I didn't care. I wanted him to die for hurting Charlie.

The man with no lips was gone. Looking around, I found Sam back at the ticket booth huddled over Charlie, listening to her chest. I ran to them.

"She's alive." Sam cradled her head.

I felt my eyes well up. "Oh, thank you, God." I touched her hand, then pulled out my cell phone to try again.

Dan came over, wiping the dead guy's blood off his hands onto his jeans. "Don't bother. They pulsed everything. All our phones are bricked."

I put my phone away. "What? Where's mom?"

"I've been looking for you guys. What happened to her?" Dan indicated Charlie.

"Some sort of lightning stick," Sam said.

Dan bent down and felt her throat. "She's still here."

"What the hell was with the Kung Fu?" I asked. "Did that just freaking happen?"

Dan barked a humorless laugh. "Welcome to the real world, little brother. It's about damn time you knew the score. And it's Luon Ordo, not Kung Fu." He put a hand across his chest and bowed.

I crawled under the ticket booth and grabbed the bird, still stiff and wrapped snug in Hollis' shirt.

Dan looked at the bird. "Holy … that's …" He blinked, shook his head, and stared at the falcon. "Oh, man." My brother scooped Charlie into his arms like she weighed nothing. "Come on, we need to get you out of here."

# FOUR

**W**e crept along concession stands and game booths, taking cover behind the small buildings and sneaking across the spaces between. Dan carried Charlie while I followed with the bird. I stepped into the alley between the skee ball booth and the funnel cake stand when my mother's thoughts came over me in a wave. I stopped walking, letting her mind fill my head.

*James. Stay hidden.*

"It's mom!" I whispered. The touch of her thoughts was a familiar cold pressure like leaning my head on a frosted winter window. I looked around. She wasn't within sight. If I could hear her, she had to be close.

"No, Jim, this way," Dan whispered. "My truck's over here."

I didn't think my mom knew where I was—she was likely reaching out with her mind, trying to find me. I needed her to see me so she could read my thoughts in return. Ignoring my brother, I ran through the alley.

"Jim, no!" Dan hissed.

On the far side of the fairgrounds, I ducked behind the crane parked near the animal cars. The tiger cages sat where Uncle Paul had left them this morning, only now they were jammed with people. It looked like most everyone from Sweetwater's had been corralled and locked inside. A dozen men stood guard outside, their backs to the cages.

I felt like I'd been kicked in the stomach. Everything twisted and churned at once, the nausea from earlier bubbling up again. Though I searched for my mom among the wall of faces behind the bars, she wasn't there. I saw Chef and Uncle Paul standing with the schoolteacher, Mrs. Hood. She had all the little kids grouped together in one corner of Bak's cage. Most of the kids were crying. Charlie's brother Davey stood holding his mom's hand. I could still feel my mother's thoughts.

*James. Be careful. Stay hidden.*

Then I spotted her. She wasn't inside either cage. She was outside, held captive by a man in a black, hooded cloak. He pulled her arms roughly behind her, but she didn't seem to notice him. As she scanned slowly across the field, I closed my eyes and tried to reach her with my mind. I couldn't tap her like I could the animals. I had to hope she would feel me eventually and open a channel between us once she knew I was here.

Dan and Sam caught up with me. "You're impossible, you know?" my brother whispered as he knelt beside me. "We need to get you out of here." He placed Charlie on the ground with the bird. They were both out cold. We knelt behind the crane and watched.

"Whoa," Sam whispered, taking in the crazy scene.

I felt my mother's mind touch mine and take hold.

*James! Find your brother. Go with him to your father. Tell no one who you are. Stay hidden.*

My father? But how? My father was dead.

The man in the spurs paced between my mom and the cages. He put a hand on her shoulder. In his other hand, he held a huge golden longsword. She didn't cry out or even flinch when he raised his sword in front of her, showing it to her in the sunlight. There was surprise in my mom's face, but not fear. Like she expected it to hurt but was resigned, waiting. This couldn't be happening.

The guy with the gold sword motioned to the man holding Mom, and he dragged her backward through the gravel like a bag of trash. The leader bellowed, his deep voice familiar now, menacing, "I am Eldred. I know you are near, son of Jane Sweetwater Wales. Reveal yourself and I shall show your mother mercy." His square, fleshy face held thick bags under deep-set eyes. He turned toward me, searching. His brown hair hung loose and wild, wisping out behind him as he moved.

*Mom …*

*James, stay where you are. He's a monster and a liar. Stay hidden.*

"Have you no love for your dear mother? Come now, boy. I only want you." Eldred called, his words slow, deliberate.

Part of me knew I didn't stand a chance against more than a dozen armed men, but another part wanted to come out and save her. I still had the knife from the guy Dan had killed. I grabbed the hilt from my belt. Dan put one arm on my shoulder and forced me to stay down.

"Don't," he whispered through clenched teeth.

"But, Mom needs ..." I said.

He got in my face. "Your bravery is wasted here."

"But ..."

"You'll give us all away." He motioned to Charlie, still unconscious on the ground.

One look at Charlie and my insides churned. He was right. I'd never forgive myself if something happened to her—or any of us—because of me.

Eldred turned toward the people in cages. "Any of you who produces young Mister Wales shall be freed, and no harm shall come to you or your family."

Nobody spoke. Eldred turned away from the cages and shouted, "Reveal yourself. Spare your people. It is the only way."

*James, you must not. I forbid it.*

*Mom, he'll let you go—*

*He's lying. If he takes you, it was all for nothing. Please.*

Charlie rolled onto her back and coughed.

Sam bent and covered her mouth with his hands, but it was too late. Eldred and his men turned in our direction.

Dan grabbed my shoulders and shook me. "Go! My truck's by the front gate. Keys are in it." His dark eyes bored into mine. "Leave." He pushed me away, then crawled around the far side of the crane and out of view.

I ducked down and looked at Sam. "What do we do?"

"Help me get her up." He pulled Charlie by her shoulders. "We can run for it."

I grabbed Charlie by her ankles. There was no way we'd be able to run with her like this.

"I'm here!" A voice called. Dan's voice.

I dropped Charlie's feet and peered over the crane. My brother stepped out by the back of the trailers and walked toward Eldred and my mother.

"No!" my mother screamed.

The people in the cages started yelling for Dan to stop and run away.

"Take him," Eldred said. My brother let two of Eldred's men grab him by the arms. No Lips stepped out from behind them and pointed his stick into Dan's ribs.

*Mom, I don't know what to do.*

*Don't come out, Jim. My love, I'm begging you.*

One of the men punched Dan in the side. My brother doubled over. I don't know how often I'd wished I could beat the hell out of Dan. He was always so tough, using his size to push me around. Trying to get me to fight with him. Calling me little man or wimp.

Watching it happen like this—everything was wrong. Dan never backed down in a fight. Cringing, I watched as the need to do something built in me.

*Mom ...*

*JAMES. DO. NOT. COME. OUT.*

"What are you doing?" Mom cried to my brother. She reached out to touch Dan, but Eldred's man pulled her backward, out of reach. She started wailing. When the man shook my mom, she struggled harder, kicking and biting him.

"It's better this way, Mom. I love you." Dan's eyes were brimming with tears. I'd never seen my brother cry.

"So you are the one? The child Vernius and Jane Wales tried in vain to conceal?"

Dan nodded. "Let my mother go," he said.

"Oh, you will find you are in no position to make demands, young man." Eldred walked around Dan. "I feel nothing with you near me. Where is your mark? Show it to me."

"My shoulder. But it isn't visible here in the Modern World. It disappears more the longer we stay here," Dan said.

"Is that so? Remove your shirt."

Dan peeled off his t-shirt. His muscled chest was tan and strong. Eldred inspected Dan's arms and back. As he circled my brother, he looked like a pale old man.

"No matter, we shall know soon enough." Eldred stood in front of Dan and they stared at each other. The hatred in Dan's face was almost a physical thing. Eldred was a little shorter than my brother. "I have searched a long time for you. I must credit your family for hiding you here, in the Modern World. In a carnival caravan of all things." He snorted laughter. "It has only served to delay the inevitable, as you can see."

Eldred waved at his men. They pulled Dan's arms wide.

My brother closed his eyes.

"It isn't him!" Someone called from the cages.

"Don't do it. He isn't the one you want!" another voice shouted.

My mother was transfixed, staring at Dan.

*Mom, what's happening?* I sent the thought to her. She didn't respond.

Eldred swung his sword in a wide arc toward the cages. "Silence! I'll know soon enough if he is the one. Have no fear," he said. He stepped behind Dan and raised his sword. When he thrust it forward, I expected him to stop. I expected a warning, something to scare us all into telling him that I was hiding not ten yards away.

The point of the golden sword stuck out through the middle of Dan's chest. The way it protruded, it looked almost like a stage prop. There was no blood. My brother's eyes opened wide, and he looked down at the blade. The men let his arms drop. Dan touched the tip of the sword as if he couldn't believe it unless he felt it with his own fingers. He dropped to his knees. His arms fell to his sides. His eyes rolled upward.

Mom screamed.

All the people in the cages, people I've known my whole life, went wild with fury. They shouted, howled, and banged on the bars of the cages, but recoiled on contact. With each touch, the bars crackled as if electrified. There was nothing they could do, not without a blowtorch or a sledgehammer to break the locks. And even then, the damage was already done. They were calling to Dan and cursing Eldred and his men. It seemed like every one of them was crying now.

Stunned, I didn't have any tears. I couldn't look away. What was so important my brother would sacrifice himself for it? For me?

Eldred pulled the sword from Dan's chest as he fell. My brother's dark blue eyes stared at nothing. Pooling under him, bright red blood soaked into the gravel.

My brother was dead.

It was supposed to be me.

Eldred wiped the blood off his blade and sheathed it at his waist. "Curious, I feel nothing. Nothing at all." He looked at Dan's body at his feet. "Perhaps the effects are masked as well in this world."

Eldred turned. "Riders!" He rounded up his men. There were at least a dozen, some wore jeans and regular clothes. Others had long cloaks with swords and elaborately decorated scabbards. All of the cloaks were black.

The man holding my mom released her. She crawled over to Dan's body, cradled his head in her lap, and cried.

The four men dressed in modern clothes approached Eldred.

"Do not return without the Sending," Eldred told the guy wearing a navy leather jacket like a high school athlete's. The guy nodded at the three others. The four of them stepped away from Eldred and the others and waited.

I looked at the faces in the cages. Mack, one of the roustabouts, held his wife Leese. Mr. Hill, who cooked all our meals with Chef, reached through the bars, pleading to the men for mercy. As I saw Charlie's mom, I realized with a jolt she was looking right at me. I ducked lower behind the crane. She mouthed *Charlie*, her face a question aimed at me. I nodded and she closed her eyes, relieved. I was glad she couldn't see her daughter.

Eldred spoke to the crowd. "If this isn't the boy, I'll find him among the rest of you. Starting with the youngest." He smiled a wicked grin at Mrs. Gladstone, who clutched her baby son tighter to her chest.

I tried to memorize the faces of everyone I saw—as if I didn't know each and every one of them already. As if I hadn't grown up with each of them here in Sweetwater's my whole life. I knew exactly who was in those cages, down to the youngest baby, Peter Gladstone, who was born last month. I caught a glimpse of old Mrs. Umpleby, who liked to sew all of the costumes for the show.

Eldred pulled something shiny from inside his cloak. As it caught the light, it threw rainbows onto the ground. He slashed it through the air above him in a wide arc, tearing open a hole in the world. The sound it made was huge and hollow, like a fire hose streaming full blast into an empty metal barrel. Through the hole, the night sky shone bright with stars in another place. Reaching up, Eldred grabbed the edges of the opening and pulled the sky down like it was made of elastic. He covered himself and most of his men as well as my mom and Dan. The sky billowed down over all of them, and then it snapped back and they were gone. They disappeared into the air amid a swirl of smoke and dust.

Everything was silent. Sam and I stared at the place where they had been a second earlier, but all that remained were four of Eldred's men standing with their backs to the crowded cages. Everyone from Sweetwater's stood behind the bars, staring at the air in shocked silence. Only the baby let out a thin wail.

# FIVE

S am and I huddled behind the crane with Charlie at our feet. The bird lay across her belly like a stuffed toy, rolling slightly with Charlie's breathing.

"Find the Sending," the guy in the navy coat said to the others. They walked up the midway toward the fallen big top. They passed right by us.

"Mathan, have you had any sign of the bird?" another man asked. He had long blond hair pulled back and braided through with a thin silver chain.

The tall one with dark hair shook his head. "I hear the bird no longer. Perhaps she has met her end?" He scratched at the scruff of his trimmed beard.

"Then we shall deliver a dead Sending to Master Eldred." Silver Braid addressed the group. "The bird carries a parcel Master Eldred requires. Separate and search the caravans. The bird cannot be far." The four men split up in twos and started searching the grounds. They headed up the midway—away from us, toward the entrance to the fairgrounds.

"Stay with Charlie," Sam whispered. He crawled away and disappeared behind the remains of a tent.

Grabbing Charlie's hand, I wondered if she could feel mine trembling while she was unconscious. I wished she would wake up so I could know she was okay. Part of me wished I'd been knocked out. Then I wouldn't know my brother was dead and my mom was gone. I wouldn't have seen Dan's eyes as he fell: shocked and empty. I wouldn't have heard my mother wailing.

"Jim!" Someone whisper-called my name from the cages.

I popped my head up over the back of the crane. Chef was waving at me. I made sure none of the bad guys were around. When I was sure it was clear, I left Charlie with the bird and ran to the cages. The air felt different, heavier. Like my chest would implode from the pressure.

I grabbed the bars. Electricity buzzed through my hands but didn't hurt. The locks on both cages were partly melted.

Chef grabbed my wrist. "Get a tire iron, something heavy to break this weld."

I ran back to the crane and dug through the toolbox until I found a crow bar. Once I brought it to the cage, I stuck it between the lock and the bars.

Uncle Paul reached out and took the bar from me. His eyes were rimmed red. "Jim, you need to leave. Right now."

"What? No way. I'm getting you out." I pulled on the crow bar.

He pushed my hands away. "You can't stay here. Eldred will figure out Dan isn't the one he wants. He'll come back for you. You need to be gone when he does. Go!"

Mr. Hill nodded and tugged on his beard. "Yes, Jim. Chef's right. You best leave."

They grabbed the end of the crow bar and heaved it into the lock, working it and prying the metal apart. It was going to take them forever this way.

Sam pulled up to the cages in Hollis' RV, hauling one of the horse trailers behind him. He jumped out and ran over to Charlie. As he dragged her by her shoulders from behind the crane, the bird rolled off her lap and landed on its head.

"Charlotte!" Charlie's mom cried when she saw her daughter limp in Sam's arms.

Sam shouted over his shoulder, "Jim! They're coming back. Get in!"

Eldred's men ran toward us from down the midway. Sam struggled under Charlie's dead weight as he pushed her through the door into the back of the RV. He ran back toward me, yelling, shoving me into the rig. A bolt of light struck the ground between me and the cages. Pebbles vaporized. Rock steam burned the back of my hand and made the cuff of my jacket peel.

Sam ran over to the crane, snatched the bird, and sprinted back to the idling vehicle. I snapped into action and flung the passenger door open. Hollis' rig. He'd gone to get the horses. "Where's Hollis?"

"Get in!" Sam screamed. He jumped in the driver's seat and tossed the bird on the console between us. Holding the door open, I searched the field.

"Bak! Come!" I shouted.

Sam gunned the engine and we spun out, spraying gravel and dust behind us. My door slammed shut from the force.

"We can't leave without Bak!" I screamed. "Where's Hollis?"

"Dunno. Found the engine running."

"Bak!" I called out the window. He had to be here. He had to come with me.

A crack of electricity. The motorhome fishtailed. Looking back through the rear window, I couldn't see anything with the trailer in the way. A single horse stood inside the trailer. I tapped the worried mare. It was Tess, one of the dancing horses in the finale. As I told her to hang on, I scanned the field for my tiger. Bak was nowhere in sight.

Sam drove the RV across the field in a beeline toward the road. "Get your head down," he said. The trailer rocked on its axle as we exploded through an old wooden bench. Bits of broken wood and metal bolts hit the windshield like lethal rain. We bounced over a flowerbed, jumped the curb, and landed on smooth pavement with a screech of metal and a shower of sparks.

The four men ran hard toward the gate to catch us. They were fast, but even with Sam slowing down to let the trailer stop rocking, they wouldn't catch up.

I stuck my head out the window and shouted, "Bak!"

My tiger came barreling out from behind a fallen tent. He tackled Mathan and took Navy Jacket across the back with his paw. Bak barely stopped running as the men fell. He was trying to catch up with us. I tapped him.

*You can do it, Bak. Run!*

One of the men still on his feet pointed his stick at us, and a blaze of excruciating light filled the air all around us.

"Oh, man, I can't see," Sam screamed. "I'm blind!"

I still saw my fingers digging into the soft leather of the armrest. "It's just bright. Keep driving."

As the light faded back to regular daylight, Sam started weaving on the road. The trailer fishtailed, pulling us back at an angle and threatening to roll us on top of Bak as he ran alongside. Tess whinnied from inside the trailer.

One of the trailer tires blew with the quick flop-slap-flop of a flat. I was about to tap the horse when the hitch on the trailer snapped. The trailer broke free, skidding sideways as it slowed. *Please, God don't let it tip over. Please don't tip over. Please.*

The trailer slowed and tipped on two wheels. It looked like something from a stunt show. But the horse was too heavy and off-balance. She forced the trailer back onto the side with the flat. Tess' whine echoed from within the trailer. As the rim of the flat dug into the blacktop, the trailer flipped forward, end over end. It landed on its side, the scream of metal on pavement the only sound louder than the horse inside. It slid a moment longer before coming to a halt, blocking the two-lane road.

Bak ran hard. His head was down and his huge paws tore at the blacktop.

The man with the stick took aim again, and the knot in my belly wound up even tighter.

I hopped out of my seat and stepped over Charlie. I opened the door to the living room for Bak.

*Come on, boy, almost there.*

"Slow down for Bak!" I shouted. The blast of light from the man's weapon hit Bak on his left flank. My tiger let out a roar of pain, but he didn't stop running.

*Good boy!* "Come on Bak!" *A little farther.*

As Sam slowed the motorhome to a crawl, Bak hopped into the living room.

"Go, go, go!" I pulled the door shut and pounded the seat.

The road looped around the fairgrounds. We sped back toward the field and what was left of Sweetwater's. Animals were everywhere. Many were dead and some were dying, but a few still ran through the smoke. Flames consumed the ticket booths and concession stands. A few of the tents still smoldered. Sam coughed and rubbed his eyes. Mine watered too, and I gagged on the stink. Charred flesh overpowered burnt wood and cloth. An injured bird hopped on the ground, dragging its open wing behind it. Several horses galloped together toward the town. I didn't see Cotton.

I couldn't see the tigers' cages from here—they were on the far side of the grounds from where we were, obscured by all the smoke and flames. I wondered if anyone else had managed to not get caught. I hoped somebody was helping the others break the locks open on the cages.

My mother's words rang over and again in my head.

*If he takes you, it was all for nothing.*

"You okay?" Sam asked.

"Yeah. No. I'm not hurt." I tried to get my head around what had happened. "That guy, Eldred. You saw what he did ... with the sky, right?"

Sam glanced at me, his eyes wide. "You mean when he pulled out the rainbow thing and cut a hole in the air, and it was night time on the other side?" He nodded and rubbed his eyes. "Yeah, I saw. What the hell is going on, man?"

"Don't know." I leaned over the back of my seat and touched Charlie's leg.

Sam was quiet for a moment then asked, "Why do you think they were looking for you?"

"I don't know," I said, unable to stop the replay of my mother's words and the image of my brother, dead in my place.

*If he takes you, it was all for nothing.*

# Six

Emergency sirens whined from somewhere in the direction of the town. Sam turned the RV toward the sound.

He looked relieved. "Thank God. Music to my ears."

I gaped at him. "We can't go to the cops, man."

"You kidding me? We have to!"

I couldn't believe what he was saying. All our lives we were told to keep things close—within the clan. No outsiders, no hospitals or doctors, and never, ever, any police. They'd figure out something was up with us—that we were different—in no time. Then we'd have bigger trouble.

Sam gripped the steering wheel. "I'd rather be discovered alive than dead."

"Me too, but what do you think the police will say when we pull up in what looks like a stolen RV, with a tiger and an unconscious girl in the back?"

He glanced sideways at me, saying nothing.

"They'll take Charlie to a doctor. Away from us. They'll send Bak who knows where, and lock us up for questioning. You think Eldred's guys are gonna sit outside and wait for us? No way. We can't get stuck here. They'll find us. We've gotta go far away from here."

"What about the others? My parents?"

I pointed in the direction of the sirens. "Help is coming, right? If they're still in the cages, Uncle Paul and Hollis know how to sort it out with the locals. But I don't think we should be here when it happens."

He blew his breath out in an angry huff. "Damn it." He took the next turn away from town.

Sam drove aimlessly to throw off anyone who might be tailing us. The bird lay on the console between us, its white eyes staring at the ceiling, lifeless.

I watched out the window as the landscape morphed into a blurry backdrop for replaying Dan's death. I felt as helpless now as I had this morning. No, not only helpless—I was clueless. I didn't understand why Dan had given himself up. I tried to think of a situation where I would have done the same to save him. I felt like a coward, a total nothing for letting him die without even trying to fight.

It all happened so fast. I played it over and again in my mind, trying to identify the moment when I could have done something to stop Eldred—to save Dan and my mom. But I couldn't alter the past. And now my brother was dead. And my mom ... had Eldred already killed my mom, too? We had to find them.

"I don't think they're following us." Sam eyed the traffic through the rearview mirror. "We need gas."

He pulled into a gas station. I pulled out my phone and tried it again. "This thing's toast." I threw it on the console next to the bird.

Sam tossed me the keys. "I'll go in. See if I can borrow a phone."

I told Bak to stay inside, but it was impossible to be inconspicuous. The RV was trashed. Sam had driven the rig without closing it up. The screen door hung at a weird angle. The awning over the door dangled by one corner like a limp flag. I pulled the loose stuff off and tried to get the satellite antenna to fold up. It was hopeless.

After I pumped the gas, I hopped into the living room with Bak. The burn on his flank was weird. His fur had been seared off in a gash as long as my arm, exposing an angry welt on his naked, striped skin. But it wasn't soft like a blister. The skin was hard and swollen, and it had already purpled like a bruise. At least it wasn't torn open. I found Hollis' first aid kit under the passenger seat and rubbed some antibiotic cream on Bak's skin.

He nuzzled me while I worked.

I tapped him. *You're going to be fine.*

*Bak hurt.*

"It'll be okay. Just don't lick this stuff off." I ruffled his neck fur and knelt next to Charlie. Her breathing sounded normal. I moved her up onto the couch and shook her gently by the shoulder, but she was totally out. After seeing Bak's bruise, I was worried for her. I held her hand and willed her to wake up.

Sam hopped back in the driver's seat and handed me a bottled water. "Here, it's ice cold."

"Any luck?" I asked. I folded Charlie's hands across her lap.

"I called both my parents, Hollis, and Chef … Nothing."

"Damn. How did they manage to kill all our phones?"

"And… I called 911."

"What! Sam?"

He raised his hands up to me. "Don't worry. I told them I'd been near the fairgrounds when all the fires started. They said to stay away. That there was an emergency and the cell tower was fried. Said it was under control."

"Well, that's good, right?" I said.

"Yeah. I wish we could talk to someone, though. Make sure."

Sam pulled the RV away from the gas station and onto a side road. "I think we should head back." He slowed to the curb and put it in park.

I almost choked on my water. "And then what? We don't have any weapons to fight off their lightning gun. And I have to find my mom. If we get caught, we won't be able to help anyone."

Sam shook his head. "I feel how much you want to find your mom, I do. But my parents are back there, Charlie's, too. Everyone's back at Sweetwater's."

Everything in me said it was the wrong move. "What if we wait? Until it's dark, at least." I glanced back at Charlie. "And until she wakes up, it doesn't make sense to head back. If Eldred's guys are still there, she would be in even more danger. We need to go someplace else for a while. Someplace where Bak won't be a problem."

"And where's that, boss?" Sam snapped. He closed his eyes. "Sorry, it's just ... hard."

"I know, man. It's okay." I stared out the window, trying to think of where we could go. Then I remembered. "Wait." I pulled out the paper Chef had given me and unfolded the map of computer directions. "Look where Chef had us riding today." I showed Sam the map and traced the highlighted road up the coast to the park we sometimes visited when we came to Northern California.

"The lighthouse," we said together. Sam threw the RV in gear.

For the most part, the California coast runs north and south, but an area northwest of San Francisco juts out into the Pacific, creating this cool point. The first time we went there was years ago, before I could drive on my own. I rode on the back of Hollis' bike. That day, Chef wouldn't tell us where we were heading. We followed him west along the Coast Highway until he turned off onto an unmarked road.

Like before, the view blew me away. Instead of looking straight out at the ocean with the shore on either side, I could see around an almost three-quarters circle. The place was so completely isolated, and the wind never stopped as it blew over the rocky cliffs. It whistled like a mournful ghost wandering the point for eternity.

Sitting at one of the old picnic tables perched up on the cliff, I remembered Chef talking about the park's history. A lighthouse used to stand on the point until this monumental squall—like sixty years ago—pounded the shore for days. A mudslide washed the lighthouse and all the little outbuildings right over the edge and into the ocean.

Sam slammed down his cell phone on the warped wooden table, and I jumped.

"Dan was right, thing's busted." He stared at the bird on the surface between us.

I turned to watch Bak as he stalked the edge of the field, chasing after rabbits. It was good to see he wasn't limping anymore.

"We're going to have to get some meat for Bak."

"Yeah. But first I want to see what's in the pouch." Sam said.

I tipped my chin at the bird. "I don't think we should unwrap it. Hollis said she would flail when she woke up. We don't have any way to take care of it—of her—if she gets hurt."

Sam wouldn't let it go. "Come on. She hasn't woken up yet, and we've been moving her around a bunch. We'll do it quick. I'll unwrap her. You hold her wings down nice and gentle against her body in case she wakes. I'll open the pouch fast, and then I'll wrap her back up."

I looked over my shoulder at the RV. Charlie's hair caught the breeze through the open door. "We should go check on her." I really didn't want to touch the bird. Its eyes were frozen open, and the sharp beak was way too close to my face. And after the craziness it caused with my head? No thanks.

"Come on. We'll do it fast."

I groaned.

The bird didn't wake up. In fact, she didn't move at all. I held her in front of me and stared into her blank eyes the whole time Sam fiddled with the pouch. She was a really cool looking bird—mostly white feathers on her head, flecked with gold and brown and black. Her eyes had been orange when she landed on the tent. Before she spoke. But now they were so clouded they made her look ancient and blind. Sam finished and hurried to retie the pack.

"What kind of falcon is it?"

Sam concentrated on the tiny knots. "Dunno. Not sure. Her tail is long and she has a small head like one, but the coloring is off, and she's a lot bigger than any falcon I've seen. We'll have to ask my mom …" Sam stopped.

I didn't remember seeing Mr. and Mrs. Anker in the cages.

He cleared his throat and went back to tying up the bird's pack. When he finished, he wrapped the falcon back in Hollis' shirt. "Okay, done."

Sam spread out the contents of the pouch. We examined a piece of rough yellowy paper folded into a tiny square, a brown metal coin, and a small purple marble. I picked up the old coin. It was heavy and dull, with a worn imprint of a figure eight etched into one side and a braided circle on the other.

Sam held the marble up to the sun and peered through it. "There's something inside it, like an arrow or something. It spins when I move it." He turned the marble in the light.

I unfolded the paper. It was a note. The smooth handwriting filled the page. My mouth went dry and I tried to keep my hands steady as I saw it was addressed to me.

*Dear James,*

*I pray Oona has found you. There is no time for a proper letter—the moon is setting and Oona is finally ready for you. Son, you are needed here. Eldred has attacked. Marren City is under siege. The Keystone is gone, stolen. The Grove is burned. All of Bellenor is in peril. Use the map to find the nearest crossing. Cross with the full moon. Use the eternity coin once you arrive. Your mother and Dan can tell you what to do. Make haste. Reveal yourself to no one. You are in grave danger. I look forward to meeting you again after all these years.*

*Your father,*
*Vernius*

*P. S. Take special care of Oona. She belongs to you now.*

"Whoa ..." Sam said as he leaned over and read the letter.

My father. I tried to swallow, but my stomach pushed my heart into my throat. I read the letter twice and handed it to Sam. My father. The letter had my name. Without a doubt, now I knew this bird had sought me. She came to me. But still, it couldn't be my letter. It couldn't. My father died when I was five.

"You think it's really him?" Sam handed the letter back to me and rolled the glass marble around in his palm.

"I don't know." My head felt hollow. The wind blew off the ocean and rang deep in my ears. A lone gull hung in midair off the cliff, wings out wide, its body held aloft by the constant breeze. The sun was still hours from setting.

I have one memory of my father. In it, I'm very young, maybe four, and we're standing in a field. It's warm out. I'm wearing shorts, and the tall grass is tickling the backs of my knees. My father looks down at me and smiles, his blue eyes and white teeth framed by dark brows and the hint of a beard. A small scar cuts a white J into the edge of his beard under the right side of his lip. He takes my hand in his and squeezes gently. With his other hand, he points in the distance at something in the sky.

"Look. There, son," he says.

I turn to follow his gaze. That's where it ends. Where it always ends. I never get to see what he's pointing at, and I never hear him say or do anything other than this. I asked my mom once if she knew what he was pointing at. She said she didn't know.

I don't remember the fire that killed him. Correction: *Supposedly* killed him. Everyone at Sweetwater's said it was terrible. When I go back in my mind, I don't remember him dying. I don't remember him being there one day and not the next. I don't remember a funeral. It's not that I don't care—there's nothing there to grab on to in my mind. Nothing in my heart. There's nothing at all. Maybe that's because it never really happened.

Bak loped toward us until he met us at the table. He thrashed a rabbit in his mouth until he was sure it was dead. I saw him do that once in the big top. The poor thing squealed until its spine snapped in Bak's powerful jaws. When he felt the animal go limp, he dropped it on the grass and nosed it before taking a bite and tearing at its fur. I looked away.

Sam read the letter again and held up the marble. "I can tell this is a coin, but if this is a map, then we're in trouble." He tilted his head and squinted at the glass ball.

"Let me see." I held out my hand.

Sam dropped the marble into my palm, and as soon as it touched me, the glass expanded, becoming a transparent purple orb about the size of a baseball. My hand grew warm where it made contact with the glass. "Sam … tell me you see this."

"Whoa!"

Inside the glass, an image spread out and formed a tiny map. I recognized the California coast. A shiny gold compass appeared in the corner and spun until it found north, and then a small red dot appeared, blinking near the top of the map. A similar dot, in black, materialized near the bottom, right on the coast where it jutted out into the ocean.

"That's gotta be us," Sam said, pointing to the blinking black dot.

"Amazing," I said. "Then what's the other one?" I stared at the red spot pulsing to the north.

"It must be the nearest crossing, like the letter said."

A crossing into Bellenor. I tried to get my head around the idea.

Sam held out his hand. I gave him the map-orb, and we watched as the sphere shrank and became a little marble again.

"Dude, what did you do?" Sam shook the tiny glass ball.

Was I supposed to hold it until we were done with it? The map was no longer visible. I took it back and the glass expanded, the coastline reappearing with the same red and black blinking dots. "Cool." I laid the orb on the table. Over and over, I put my hand on it and took it off. Brief contact made it enlarge only a little—then it fell back into the marble until I touched it again.

"Now that's awesome," Sam said.

"Yeah," I said, laughing. I wondered if I'd wear it out if I kept playing with it. I felt like a little kid. But that reminded me of my mom, and my stomach clenched.

Charlie woke in a panic. Sam and I ran to the RV and I knelt on the floor next to her, grabbing her hands. Her breathing came in short gasps, and she looked around as if she wasn't entirely awake. I leaned in so I was right in front of her face, filling up her vision.

"Charlie, it's me. Jim. You're okay."

She covered her face with her hands and sobbed. I wasn't sure what to do. A crying girl was still too far beyond my skills.

"I had the scariest dream ever." She pulled her hair away from her mouth and looked around Hollis' living room.

"I'm so glad you're okay." I touched her hand.

"Charlie, girl, you totally got zapped by that guy." Sam leaned against the kitchen counter. "Are you hurt?"

She sat up and stretched her sides. "I feel like I got hit by a bus." She looked out the door. "Where are we?"

"The lighthouse," I said.

"Do you remember what happened to you?"

"I don't know." Charlie shifted and moved to get out of the truck. I stepped out and gave her my arm to lean on as she jumped down. Her feet landed on the dirt, and she doubled over in pain, hugging herself. "Oh my god!"

I thought about the weird burn on Bak's flank. My mouth went dry. Charlie had been hit straight on, at super close range. Didn't people die if a burn was bad enough? If it was bad, we would need to get back to Sweetwater's right away. Doc Gramble's trailer was full of medicines and bandages. A hospital was out of the question for us, always has been. You can't tell by looking that we're not from here, but any blood tests would raise questions. We always kept everything "under the tent," as Doc would say.

"Let me see it," I said. Charlie knew as well as I did—we had to deal with this ourselves. Sitting in the doorway, she unbuttoned her shirt. She started to lift her t-shirt and looked up at Sam, waiting.

He left, mumbling something about checking on Bak and the bird.

Charlie squeezed her eyes shut. "How bad is it? Is it bad? It's bad, right? Be honest."

One of the best parts about Sweetwater's was that we stuck to the warm weather as we traveled in order to stay open year round. This meant Charlie wore short sleeves and tank tops a lot that showed off her toned, tan skin. She had great legs. Solid arms. The best was when she pulled her hair back *and* wore a tank top.

And now, with her shirt open, and her eyes closed, I stared at her chest and felt ashamed for having wished for this very thing so many times.

The bolt of light had hit right in the center of her chest. The burn exploded outward from there, leaving behind a star-shaped blister that spread under her bra and looked like a bucket of purple and red paint had splashed her. I touched it lightly. It was hard, like Bak's bruise.

I lifted her shirt away from her shoulders until I found where the damage ended and her perfect skin appeared again. With the lines so defined, the burn looked like something stuck to her. I decided to go with the facts. "You've got a blister-bruise from your sternum to your throat. None of the skin is broken, and it's hard like the one Bak's got on his leg. But I think you need to take off your um—your bra and check it out yourself." I tried to keep my face from reddening, but I knew it didn't work. I felt myself flush.

"Okay." Charlie touched her fingers to her damaged skin. "It aches like I was kicked, but my skin doesn't hurt." She reached around to undo her bra clasp and gasped in pain. "I need your help with it."

I grabbed the first aid kit and handed the antibiotic cream to Charlie. Hollis stashed a small bottle of ibuprofen in the bin. I shook out three for me and three for Charlie. We both swallowed them dry.

She turned so I could reach behind her.

"Be careful tugging my shirt." She pulled her hair over one shoulder.

I tucked my hands up under the back of her shirt and felt her smooth skin. She was warm. I felt the rise and fall of her breathing under my hands. When I reached the clasp of her bra, I had to close my eyes and try to imagine what my hands were feeling. I'd seen a million of these in stores and on TV, but it wasn't the same as undoing one with my own hands. I fumbled a bit until the little hooks fell free.

"Thank you." She didn't turn to look at me.

I wiped my hands on my jeans. "Hey, back there … After you got hit. Something else happened." My mouth went dry. The guilt of it pressed on me like a stone. It was my fault.

"What?" She looked at me as if she knew already. "Is it Davey? My parents? Are they okay?"

I shook my head. "No. I mean, yes, I think they're fine. I mean … It was … Dan. He's dead."

"Oh, Jim." She grabbed my sleeve.

I told her what happened. How it was all because of me. I was glad to be sitting behind her so she couldn't see my face. I stared at the back of her head. I loved the way her hair caught the sun. "When you got hit, I thought you were …" My throat closed on my words. I moved so I could see her face.

She put her hand on my arm. "I'm still here, Jim. I'm a bit of a mess, but I'm here." She smiled.

I covered her hand with mine. "It's just that ... I realized ... I—we ... um. Look. I know the timing is freaking awful, I mean, it's not like we're dating, really or anything. But when I saw you on the ground, and I thought you were ... And I thought they were going to kill me too. I ... I don't know what I would have done if something happened to you." My ears were on fire. I couldn't stop looking at her hands. One of her nails was broken, and the glittery blue nail polish was chipped and scuffed on the other nails. When she didn't say anything, I looked up at her face. She was crying.

"Oh, man. I've gone and ruined it, haven't I? I'm sorry. I shouldn't have ..." *Crap. Leave it to me to blow it.*

She took my hand and smiled through her tears. "You didn't ruin anything. You're blind, Jim. Totally stupid and blind."

# SEVEN

Charlie gritted her teeth with every step away from Hollis' rig. I was glad to see Bak feeling better as he bounded over the hill and joined us. Sam waited for us at the picnic table, his gaze glued on the bird as it lay on its back, its blank eyes staring at the sky.

"She twitched," he said.

"Really?" I helped Charlie onto the bench and sidled in next to her.

"Watch her feet. I saw her talons close, just a little," he said.

I inspected the bird—Oona—according to the letter from my father. "She still looks the same to me." Dust and dirt covered Hollis' black t-shirt. The bird seemed unaware, stiff and frozen as ever. "I still can't believe the letter," I mumbled.

"Show me," Charlie said.

I handed her the paper and waited while she read it.

Her eyes went round. "You think it's him? You think it's really from your father?"

I shook my head. "It can't be. You know as well as I do, he's dead."

Sam pointed at the bird. "Dude, the letter named you and your brother. There's nobody else named Jim in Sweetwater's. And the bird definitely was following you this morning. It said *James Wales*. So, there's no doubt about it wanting you."

I threw up my hands. "If my father *is* alive and Bellenor still exists, why did everyone make us think otherwise? Why lie?"

Sam shrugged.

"Maybe they didn't know." Charlie glanced at me.

My mother's words from this morning rang through my mind again.

*Find your brother. Go with him to your father. Tell no one who you are.*

"No, they knew." I scratched my head. "Well, whoever wrote the letter seemed to think I knew, too. Like it wouldn't be that big a surprise to get a letter from him out of the blue. But I don't know anything about him."

Charlie put her hand on mine. I thought about all the times my mom had cried, saying she missed him. My chest tightened. Where was she now? And Dan. What did Eldred mean when he said he would know soon enough if Dan was the one? The one what?

"I want to see the map," Charlie said.

Sam dug into his pocket and handed her the marble, waiting to see if it opened. "Hmm, it only works for Jim," he said.

Charlie looked at the glass, turned it over in her hand, and held it up to the sky. "There's an arrow in it." She placed it in my hand, and we watched it become the orb like it had done each time Sam and I tried it before.

"That's incredible." She traced the line of the coast and touched the places where the two dots blinked their slow, soft pulse. "Well, this map isn't from here—from the Modern World—that's for sure. She looked at me. "Maybe it really is from your dad. I mean, who else would give you this stuff?"

Sam rubbed his face. "You know, I've never told anyone this, but I don't remember your father. I mean, I don't remember when he died."

"Me neither," Charlie said, looking aside.

"So? It's not like it's a fun thing to reminisce about." I pressed my hands onto my legs. I didn't want to admit that I didn't remember either.

"So? Denial much?" Sam sat forward. "So, what if it never happened? The fire. What if they made it up?"

I didn't want to have this conversation. "Why make it up? What would be the point?"

Sam looked at the sky as if he were begging God for some patience. He counted off his points with his fingers. "Look, that guy said they were looking for a Wales boy. He had a picture of your scar—your mark or whatever. Hollis said he recognized the bird. And the letter, and Dan. Right? Let's go back to Sweetwater's and ask them ourselves."

My mom's words weighed heavy on me. Pushing me toward her. To find her. To go back home. Man, the idea of Bellenor was too much. "I don't think we should go back. It isn't safe. Not with Mathan and those other guys around. And Eldred could pop through the sky at any moment. Besides, what about my mom, and Dan. Where did they go?"

Sam and Charlie's families were here, but *I* had to go. I had to find my mom. And I would make Eldred pay for what he'd done to Dan and to Sweetwater's. I had to get Oona away from the people who could track her. I had to figure out what was so damned important to make every single person I knew lie about everything. I had to find out why they wanted to keep me hidden.

Charlie rubbed my arm. "Do you think we should follow it? The map? Go to Bellenor?"

The thought gave me goose bumps. "That's like going to Atlantis. I mean, I feel like I have to, but I can't even get my head around it."

Bak startled and crawled out from under the table. He shook his head and swatted a paw at his ears.

"What's up, boy?"

*Noisy bird. Bad.*

I looked at Oona. At that moment, the weird hum and tugging sensation exploded in my head again. Loud at first, but then it got quieter until I could hear only a hint of it. Nothing like this morning.

"She definitely moved that time," Sam said.

Oona still lay on her back, the shirt wrapped tight around her. Then she shook like a vibrating toy, bouncing toward the edge of the table. I eased her over with my arm to keep her from falling. Closing her eyes, she bobbed her head and chirped a loud keek kek kek sound. At least she wasn't speaking words anymore. Or talking about me.

Bak raised his paw to strike at her.

"No!" I stood up and blocked his way. He could definitely hear her too. When he realized he wasn't going to be able to get at the bird, he bared his teeth at Oona and hissed. I tapped him again.

*Noisy bad bird.*

"She isn't bad." I shook my head at Bak. *She's with us now.* I ruffled the fur on his head. Bak let out a low grumble as if to say he wasn't happy with this arrangement. Not at all.

Oona opened her eyes and looked around at the three of us. The cloudy white film on her eyes was gone, replaced by clear orange irises. They found me and locked on. Sam picked her up and placed her on her feet. Turning her head, Oona kept staring at me. She wobbled a bit and tipped over onto the table again, still not breaking eye contact.

"She needs her wings. She can't balance," Charlie said, steadying the bird on her feet again.

Sam unwrapped the shirt and let it fall to the table. As if testing her wings, Oona opened and closed them. They spanned the length of the table. Their undersides were white with a single black band down the center of each. She rocked back and forth on her feet and then took off flying. The wind from her wings was like a gust as she lifted off.

"No, wait!" I stood and shouted after her. The farther away she flew, the smaller the sound in my head became. I didn't want her to leave. Not after all this.

A shudder of relief ran through me when she circled back and soared overhead, spinning and twirling in the sky. When she finally returned to us, she landed on the grass next to the table. She wouldn't stop staring at me.

"Hello, Oona," I said, leaning my knee on the bench next to Charlie.

The bird hopped up and down on her feet, chittering. Well, at least there was no doubt about her name. When she flew up onto the edge of the picnic table, I squeezed my eyes shut. Sure, she was a special bird, but she was still a falcon. I didn't need her poking out my eyes. But nothing happened. I opened one eye. The falcon sat there, staring right at me.

"What are you supposed to do with it?" Sam said.

"I don't know." I stared back at the bird.

"The letter says she belongs to you," Charlie said. "What did you say Hollis called her?"

"A Sending," I said.

Keek kek, Oona chirped.

"Whatever that means," Sam said. "I can't believe nobody told us Bellenor was still there."

"I can't believe everybody lied about your dad." Charlie touched my hand.

Oona's eyes changed color. They were now a pale blue and almost looked lit from within.

"Can you understand me?" I asked the bird. Oona hopped back and forth and made a short keek.

"Her eyes are freaky," Sam said.

"They keep changing colors," Charlie said. "Look, they're going green now, and blue again."

Oona watched me.

Keek kek kek.

"What do you need, bird?" I mind-tapped Oona. I didn't even think about it, really. It was more of a reflex than anything else. I half expected her to fill my head with images of bloody flesh and eyeball strings. Then I remembered the blinding light from this morning and braced myself.

What I did see was so unexpected, I disconnected and fell backward off the bench, landing on Bak.

He turned and looked at me. *Jim see? Bird bad.*

"What was that?" I asked the falcon. I tried to make sense of what I'd seen.

"What happened?" Charlie said.

"I tapped Oona." I stood up and got ready to tap her again.

"And?" Sam asked.

I slipped my mind into the bird's again. This time I gripped the edge of the table and stayed connected. The falcon looked directly at me. And I saw myself through her eyes. I waved hello to her and saw me waving back at myself. I saw Charlie sitting on the bench next to me, looking back and forth between me and the bird. Every time she made eye contact with the falcon, it felt like she was making eye contact with me, only Oona's vision was so sharp and clear, the details popped from everywhere.

Through Oona's eyes, I could count Charlie's eyelashes and the pores on her face. I looked at my own hands and saw dirt in the lines of my skin. A tiny bug moved through the forest of splintery old wood of the picnic table. A mouse moved through the blades of grass in the trees over Charlie's shoulder. How in the world was this possible?

"I see what she sees," I said. I disconnected from the bird and looked into her eyes. They were back to the fiery orange. "Oona, how'd you do that?" I asked.

The falcon bent her head as if taking a bow.

Charlie giggled.

The sun hung low in the sky when we decided to head out. Since it would be dark by the time we got back, we compromised and settled on a drive by. We'd see what was going on at Sweetwater's from a distance and then decide what to do from there.

After piling into the RV, Sam drove us back on the narrow road toward the highway and town. Oona sailed overhead. I kept one eye on the sky, relieved to see her circling back, keeping pace with the truck.

We stopped at a strip mall with a convenience store so Sam could run in and buy a paper map. He parked on the far side of the lot near some grass and bushes. I helped Charlie down the steps, and I tried our phones again. No luck. While Sam was inside, I waited with Charlie. Bak skulked through the small patch of green before settling in and lying down behind us. I could feel Oona close by, somewhere, but couldn't see her.

There weren't many cars on the road. The few that did pass us pulled into the gas station on the other side of the two-lane. Using Bak as a pillow, Charlie lay down, hugging herself the whole time.

"How does it feel?" I asked.

Charlie grimaced. "Like I tried to self tan with a blowtorch."

"I'm sorry." I squeezed her hand. "Look at Bak. You're going to be okay. We have more cream and bandages. Do you—you, um—want me to help? With that?" My ears were on fire.

Charlie's cheeks flushed. "I got it, thanks." She leaned up on her elbows, staring at the road.

"What?" I looked around, worried I'd said the wrong thing.

"Shhh." She raised her hand to block the setting sun and squinted. "There." She pointed up the highway.

One of them rode Hollis' motorcycle. The other one rode mine. The rumble of the two bikes was as familiar as the sound of my voice. I sat up straighter. They were riding slow, coming toward us, watching the sky. They didn't seem to notice us across the way.

"Oh my God." Charlie got up and opened the door to the RV.

I tapped my tiger. *Bak. Get in the rig.*

Bak obeyed, and I scanned the sky for Oona. I thought back to what Eldred's guy had said earlier about being able to find the bird. "One of those guys must be able to hear Oona like I can," I said. "Must be how they found Sweetwater's in the first place." I strained to listen, but I could barely hear the bird—it was more like I could feel her. I knew she was around here somewhere.

The riders slowed on the other side of the highway when one of the men pointed up into the sky. They pulled over and watched.

Then I spotted her. Oona circled and began her descent. She was coming right toward us.

Charlie held the door open. "Get in."

I slid in the door and climbed across the console to the driver's seat. Sam had left the keys in the ignition. *Bless you, bro.* I started the engine and inched us forward, toward the front of the store. I willed Sam to step through the doors. The RV's engine ticked. He didn't come out.

"Hurry up, Sam," Charlie whispered.

With a glance across the road, I tapped the horn once and cringed. I tried to get a look inside the glass storefront. Advertisements for hearing aids, cheap prescription medicines, and an old poster for a local school bake sale blocked my view. A picture of a deli sub on a plate with a side of chips and a drink obscured the top half of the door. A tiny *We I.D.* sign covered the one little rectangle left near the door handle.

At last, the door swung open and an elderly woman emerged, carrying a newspaper. She thanked the "nice young man" holding the door for her. It was Sam.

"Sam. Get in." Charlie stood and pushed the side door open.

He smiled at the woman as she shuffled past him. Then he turned and started walking toward the side of the building where we'd been parked.

I felt Oona getting closer.

Their calm faces skyward, the men watched from across the road as Oona sank slowly, gliding down.

"Sam." Charlie was louder now.

"Hey, what's …?" Sam said, climbing up the stairs. Charlie slid back to the couch.

Oona swooped low and gave the motorhome a fly by. One of the men kept following her movements with his eyes. The other stopped watching Oona and stared right at us. They might not have recognized any of us in the cab, but there was no way to hide Hollis' RV, with the Sweetwater's banner painted on the sides.

"They're coming." Charlie gripped the back of my seat.

The men rolled the bikes to the edge of the road, looking for traffic, preparing to cross.

Sam followed Charlie's gaze across the highway. "Damn."

I gunned the engine and peeled out onto the highway, the rig skidding on the pebbles and dirt lining the shoulder.

Bak slammed into the kitchen cabinets.

*Hang on, buddy.*

# EIGHT

Eldred's guys sucked at riding motorcycles. The two of them were all over the road like a pair of circus clowns doing a comedy routine under the big top. Except these guys weren't clowns, and this wasn't pretend. The guy on Hollis' Harley was the bigger of the two, maybe even as big as Hollis, and still the cruiser seemed too heavy for him. He kept putting his feet down to balance only to have the pavement snap his boots back and make him wobble some more. The tall, dark haired guy—the one named Mathan who could hear Oona—rode my bike. He was peeling out then braking hard and stopping short. Each time the rear wheel bucked, the guy looked like he might sail over the handlebars.

When I'd first started riding, Hollis spent a whole day teaching me how to accelerate smoothly and stop without flying off. It was definitely a learned skill, and these guys were getting smoother by the second.

I caught glimpses of Oona as she circled above us, but I didn't dare try to mind-tap her while I drove. I wanted her to fly far from here.

"They've got one of those guns." Sam slid his seatbelt down and clicked it in place.

Charlie went back into the bedroom and climbed up on the bed to watch through the rear window. Bak wedged himself into the dining nook, squinting at the wind whistling through the bent door, ruffling his fur.

*Get down, boy. Low.*

Steep hills rose up on our left, and the shoulder dropped off into the ocean on our right. The two-lane road moved with the rolling terrain, curving through the state park and veering off into small dirt lots for scenic overlooks. The sky was on fire with a blazing sunset reflecting off the ocean, which seemed to go on forever. I'd been grateful for the open road before, but now I wished for some traffic to get lost in. It would give these guys more trouble riding, too. Maybe we could lose them once it got dark.

"We're too open here," I said.

"Get down!" Charlie ducked as a bolt of blue-white light rumbled past the passenger window in a wide arc. It struck an evergreen tree, which burst into fiery splinters that rained onto the windshield. The next blast hit the driver's side window, blinding me for a moment as cubes of safety glass exploded into the cab. I fought to keep the motorhome on the road. The wind screamed in through my broken window. Bak yowled in fear.

"Everybody okay?" Sam shouted over the wind.

"I'm here." Charlie's voice came from the bedroom far behind me.

*You okay, Bak?*

*Bak scared.*

Tapping him made my heart race. Between fear and fury, the tiger was all over the place. He'd never had a killer's instinct. He knew concern and worry and all the other feelings people had. Adrenaline surged through both of us.

Oona swooped down, her talons back and her head low in a hunting stance. She whipped past the broken window and flew directly at Mathan, despite his lightning gun. Spreading her wings, she pushed her talons out in front of her, going right for his face. She flapped once and flew over his head. But the damage was done. He lost control of the bike—my bike—and crashed sideways onto the pavement. Mathan slid off and rolled onto the shoulder. My bike flipped end over end until it lay in a heap on the blacktop. I cringed. I'd worked for six months restoring it. When Mathan crashed, the other rider jammed the brakes to a stop—Hollis' bike bucked and threw him off as it landed on its side. Metal screeched as it slid onto the shoulder.

"Go, Oona!" Charlie whooped.

Mathan sat up as the other guy ran toward him.

The two-lane spilled onto the highway, and we slowed down with the flow of traffic.

"You think we lost them?" Charlie asked.

"It bought us some time, I think." I could barely sense Oona above us now. I wondered how sensitive Mathan's bird-sensing ability was.

"We need to lose the bird." Sam craned his neck and peered out the window, trying to find Oona in the sky.

"She doesn't seem to want to leave." I flipped on the turn signal and moved into the slow lane. "We have to keep moving and try to get Oona to stay away until we figure something out."

I pulled over and let Sam drive so I'd be free to connect with Oona. My hands ached from gripping the wheel so tight. I rolled down the passenger window and leaned my head out. Oona was a dark spot in the twilight. She circled overhead in a lazy spiral, riding an updraft around and around. Closing my eyes, I tapped her, and she brought me into the sky, flying. The air pushed up from below, and we hung there, resting, watching everything.

*You need to stay farther away from us. The bad man can follow you.* I told the bird.

Oona didn't react to my words. She sailed around the slow arc and didn't make a move. Through her eyes, I watched her track a small bird as it crossed the sky below us. It seemed oblivious to the danger hovering above.

*Can you understand me? Can you blink or something to let me know I'm getting through?*

Oona dove.

I gripped the leather of the seat where I sat in the RV while my eyes were Oona's. She tucked her wings and rocketed toward the earth. The sensation of flight was wild but this—

this was incredible. I could see the individual feathers in the smaller bird's tail—gray and white and tipped with black. It was a gull.

The gull grew larger as Oona descended. The hunt was on, only the other bird didn't have a clue death was coming at such speed. We sailed in behind it, talons up and open. The impact broke the smaller bird's neck with a tiny crack. Clutching its body in her claws, Oona circled again, looking for a place to land. She dropped the bird in the grass beneath a stand of oak trees, circled back, and touched down next to her prey. I didn't want to stay for her meal.

*Oona, can you hear me?*

She hopped back and forth on her feet.

Keek kek.

*One of those men back there can track you. It isn't safe for you to be seen.*

Keek kek.

*Keep out of sight.*

Keek kek.

I hoped it was her way of saying she understood. When she found me this morning, it was dark and they managed to track her anyway. So it probably didn't matter if it was day or night. But it was worth a try.

When I disconnected from Oona, I found myself back in the motorhome with Sam at the wheel and Charlie seated on the couch behind him.

"Welcome back," Sam said. He'd pulled off the road and parked on a residential street. Lights came on in the houses, and the street was quiet except for the occasional car arriving home—presumably from a normal day at a regular job—and disappearing behind silent garage doors into seemingly quiet lives.

I tapped Bak. He was asleep in back. I felt Oona coming close. She landed in a tree behind us, sounding a short keek as she settled. So much for her keeping her distance.

Sam handed me the paper map he'd picked up at the store and pointed to an intersection near the middle of the page. "It looks like we're here. The fairgrounds are here." Probably half an hour away.

Before I could open my mouth, Charlie spoke. "You said the police were on their way to the fairgrounds when we left, right?"

Sam nodded.

She looked at me and then at Sam. "Yeah, okay, but you said there were more of Eldred's guys. What if they're waiting for us to go back?"

"Exactly," I said.

Sam slammed his hand on the wheel. "Don't you guys care at all about our families? Don't you want to make sure everyone's alright?" He sounded exasperated.

Charlie touched Sam's shoulder. "Of course I care. We all do. But think about it. This morning, nobody was able to fight them off. We don't have any way to beat them. If the police got there this morning, then I'm sure everyone's okay. Right?"

He shook his head. "What about my parents? What about yours, Charlie? What about your little brother? We have to go back. We have to make sure everyone got out of the cages. See who else got away. Help get the animals rounded up ..."

I sighed. Someone had to do all of those things. But my mind kept going back to my family. "I have no idea where Eldred took my mom. I don't even know if she's still alive. And Dan ..." I couldn't say it. I still couldn't get my head around it. Dan was dead. But maybe he wasn't really gone. Maybe bringing him to that other place could revive him somehow. Maybe that's why Eldred took Dan's body with him.

Feeling Charlie's hand on my shoulder, I realized my friends were waiting on me. I said what I'd been dreading. "Look. We've all got family in trouble. Maybe it's time to split up."

Charlie snorted. "No way."

"I'm not going back alone," Sam said.

Oona sailed through the sky above the RV, tugging at my mind. I closed my eyes and felt her grow nearer. "What if we could check on everyone without going back? Without going in person, I mean.

I flew back with Oona to do reconnaissance. It felt better flying in the dark, and figured with her vision I'd be able to see everything when we got to the fairgrounds. The dark didn't matter though—a bunch of searchlights lit up the place bright as day. Oona landed on one of the spotlight rigs.

Police cruisers, fire trucks, and all sorts of emergency vehicles filled the lot, each with their strobes swirling red and blue and yellow and white.

Animal Control trucks blocked the driveway near the entrance gate. A woman stood behind the kennel truck with a hawk on her hand. She murmured to the bird as she eased a hood over its head and gentled it into a cage. At least she knew what she was doing. Another man had Cotton on a wire lead at the end of a long stick. The tiger wasn't fighting as he was coaxed into the back of another truck. Relief drained through me. He was safe.

The fairgrounds were busy. Hopping with activity. I scanned the chaos below and located the tigers' cages.

The cages were empty, but people were everywhere. *Everyone's here. They're all fine.*

Through Oona's eyes, I stared at the spot between the cages where Dan had died. His blood stained the gravel. I could still see Dan's face as he reached up to touch the blade sticking out the front of his chest. Total surprise. I wondered if that was how death came for everyone—you can't accept it's over, you can't accept you're going out like that. I could still hear my mom wailing as she cradled my brother's head in her lap. His face and hair were clean and perfect. He could have been asleep if you didn't look down at the wound in his chest. And then the blood. There was so much blood. My mother's words moved through my mind.

*If he takes you, it was all for nothing.*

As I watched, I realized I didn't recognize any of the people below. The entrance gate hung open to allow all the vehicles to come and go. The darkness covering the road seemed thick compared to the searchlights beaming over the remains of Sweetwater's. I spotted a man talking to a policewoman. When he turned, I got a look at his face and the dark blue letter jacket he wore.

*Wait. He's one of them.*

What was he doing talking to the cops? I looked again at the cages. They were definitely empty. But where was everyone? They had to be okay now. Maybe they were all taken away by ambulance and were stuck thinking of ways to get out of having blood work done at the hospital. But what was that guy—Eldred's guy—doing talking to a cop?

A familiar rumble made me look toward the gate. The big guy rode in on Hollis' bike with Mathan sitting behind him. Blood covered Mathan's face.

Navy Jacket turned away from the policewoman.

Mathan looked up into the spotlights, to the top of the tall metal rig. Even through the glare of the lights, he found Oona. We made eye contact.

*Oona, fly!*

I let go of her mind as she took off and I was back in the RV. Sweat dripped down my back and under my arms. I couldn't get my hands to stop shaking.

I looked at Sam. "They're gone."

"Who's gone?" he asked.

"Everyone. Except the bad guys. And they'll follow Oona straight to us."

# NINE

With no clue how to find anyone from Sweetwater's now, we drove north up the highway. Toward Bellenor, if the orb map was right. Bak circled and lay down at Charlie's feet behind me. I held the orb, and marveled as the now familiar warmth spread up my fingers. Holding it brought an odd sense of relief that we had somewhere else to go.

"I can't tell how far, but we're getting closer." I traced our progress on the paper map, trying to figure out where the orb was taking us. "We need to head east soon."

Oona moved in a figure eight above us, the hum of her presence growing full and then weak and then full again as she looped through the sky. The black dot on the orb map crept ever closer to the red one, which stayed in position as if patiently waiting for us.

With a few wrong turns and a lot of doubling back, we navigated that way for hours. Following my directions, Sam drove until the red dot pulsed directly north of our position. He parked in a rest area on the top of Donner Pass, near the California-Nevada border.

I analyzed the paper map. "There's no road north of here. It's all National Park."

I still had my jacket, but none of us were dressed for hiking. Charlie went back to Hollis' bedroom to look for warmer stuff we could wear. I found his backpack stuffed in the cabinet by the kitchen and raided the pantry for food again. I loaded up on chips, crackers, and a bag of chocolate raisins.

Sam had found a couple of water bottles in the pantry and filled them at the kitchen faucet. "Make room." He dumped them into the bag.

Charlie poked her head through the doorway from the bedroom. "Hey, guys? Come look at this." Her voice sounded muffled from the back of the trailer.

I followed Sam to the bedroom and joined Charlie in front of the open closet. She had pulled on one of Hollis' sweatshirts. It fit her like a dress.

She tipped her chin at the closet. "It must have come loose with all the crazy driving." She'd pushed aside the clothes hanging on the rod, revealing a plywood panel that had fallen from the back wall. Hollis had a tall, rectangular safe built into his closet. Its brass lock required a big, thick key.

"One sec." I ran to the front of the cab and grabbed the keys from the ignition. I'd thought it was a decoration for his key ring, but sure enough, the oversized brass key looked like a perfect match. I ran it back to the bedroom, but when I got there, I couldn't do it. I couldn't bring myself to open the lock.

"Well, what's the problem? Open it." Sam crowded in between me and Charlie.

"It feels wrong without Hollis here." The last time I saw Hollis he'd been running to get the horses rigged up. He must have known we'd be hiking through the woods. He knew about Oona. He must have known what the red dot was. Using his key to open his safe seemed disrespectful somehow. As if we were writing him off. *Please be okay, Hollis.*

"Oh, please." Sam snatched the keys from me. "I don't think he'd mind a bit." He slid the key into the lock. It sounded smooth and heavy as it hit home. The safe swung open on silent hinges. Blue lights blinked on within the safe, shining an eerie museum glow on the gleaming silver longsword hanging inside.

"Whoa." Sam stepped back.

Blue velvet lined Hollis' safe. The longsword looked almost as if it were floating in the light. A pair of matching short swords hung crisscrossed on the inside of the door. Below them hung a set of three daggers. Every weapon was honed to a razor's edge.

The white stone hilts of all the blades were carved with a design that looked like the moon phases with two short crescents, a full circle, and one longer crescent.

"What's Hollis doing with this?" Charlie reached up for the longsword, wincing as she stretched. I took it down and handed it to her.

I thought of all the afternoons of sword training the three of us had with Hollis through the years. Sam and I joked all the time how the Dueling Knights of Mysteria were the best-trained fake swordsmen in the world. It never occurred to me to ask how Hollis knew so much about blade fighting and sparring. He'd always just done it.

"Why didn't he ever show this to us?" Sam asked, moving a short sword slowly through the air.

For as long as I could remember, Hollis sought out medieval sword fighting competitions whenever Sweetwater's was near a town with a chapter of the Society for Creative Anachronism. We thought it was the height of nerdville. I mean, a bunch of people pretending to live in medieval times, having tournaments and melees? We made fun of him as he left Sweetwater's dressed up like Sir Lancelot.

That was until Sam and I went with Hollis one time and watched him at it. Hollis' skills and knowledge of the art even awed the SCA members. He was a natural with almost any sword. But he'd never taken these to a tournament. I would have remembered if I'd seen these weapons. They were incredible.

Sam hefted the blades in his hands. "They're so light. What kind of metal is it?"

Belts and scabbards for all of the blades had been stacked on shelves in the lower portion of the safe with a duffel bag stuffed into the bottom. We took turns trying them on. Sam and Charlie each took one of the short swords. I tossed the knife from the guy who grabbed me at Sweetwater's into the bag and pulled on a belt with a scabbard for one of the daggers.

We matched the rest of the blades with their sheaths and loaded them into the duffel, which Sam slung onto his back long-ways like a backpack. Charlie couldn't wear the food pack over her shoulders because of her burn, so I strapped the longsword onto my back and slung the food pack over it.

We left the paper map behind. Outside, we checked the glass map again. The orb glowed in the dark with a purplish light, bright enough to read by.

"It's directly north of here." Sam pointed into the dark woods looming in front of us.

Keek kek kek. Oona watched from a nearby branch.

"Whatever *it* is," Charlie said.

I looked back at the RV and wondered if we were doing the right thing. We could probably keep moving and live in the motorhome for a long time. I had a couple thousand dollars saved, and I bet Sam and Charlie did too. There were ATMs everywhere, and we knew how to drive. Feeding Bak would be expensive, but we could get jobs.

Keek kek.

*If he takes you, it was all for nothing.*

We had to move forward. For my mom, and for Dan, and to get Oona—and us—far from Mathan. But now I also wanted to go for my dad. I wanted to find him and hear him explain why my whole life had been a lie.

We followed Bak through the woods. Charlie found a flashlight in the glove box, but the battery died before we'd gone twenty yards. It wasn't possible to walk side by side anyway, and the flashlight had only served to ruin our night vision. Bak didn't have a problem seeing. His eyesight and keen sense of smell led him to a game trail cutting through the underbrush and making the going a little less treacherous.

I kept my eye on the orb, making sure we stayed on course—not an easy thing without a real trail to follow through the dense woods. About half an hour in, the two dots were almost touching. "It's not much farther."

Sam leaned in for a look at the map.

Charlie poured some water into her hands for Bak to drink. He tried to lap at it but instead wrapped his giant tongue around her wrist. She looked up at me and smiled. I smiled back. Then she looked away and seemed distant, serious. She dropped the water bottle. "There's someone coming. Behind us," she whispered. She cocked her head to the side, listening.

"What?" Sam said.

"Shhh," she whispered.

I couldn't hear anything but knew better than to doubt her ears.

She turned back to us, eyes wide. "There's a bunch of them. They're back a ways, sounds like they're getting stuck in the brambles and stuff. Making a racket. Let's go. Hurry up."

*Bak, lead the way.*

My tiger padded along the trail.

When the dots in the map overlapped. I stopped. "This is it."

As we stepped out into another clearing, I looked around. "There's nothing here." There was no blinking red anything telling us we'd arrived. It was still dark, but my eyes had adjusted enough to see the wall of trees standing like a black sheet on the far side of a grassy meadow.

I looked at the map again. "It's gotta be here." We were in the right place.

Sam scanned the tiny meadow. "What are we looking for?"

I shrugged. "No idea. Split up."

Charlie followed me around the tree-lined edge of the clearing, listening. "Turn off the map before they see it."

I shoved the glowing orb into my jacket pocket and felt it shrink.

The full moon rose above the mountains around us, illuminating the little clearing.

Keek kek kek. Oona perched on a rock near Sam. She rocked back and forth a few times and then took off into the trees.

The meadow was roughly oval with knee-high grass and wildflowers growing all over the place. Water trickled somewhere nearby and a single lightning bug glowed, its green-yellow belly pulsing lazily as the revving sound of cicadas filled the air.

"Guys, I think I found it," Sam's words carried easily in the still air.

"Shhh!" Charlie hissed.

When we reached the rock where Oona had perched, I saw it wasn't an ordinary rock. It was overgrown with field grass, but it was man-made and stood about three feet tall. The gray stone was roughly rectangular with rounded edges. Definitely man-made. It looked like an ancient headstone from a forgotten grave so old any inscription had long since worn away.

"You feel it?" I held my hands out in front of the stone.

"Feel what?" Sam said.

"It's vibrating."

Sam touched the stone. "I don't feel a thing, man. Now what?" he asked.

"I don't know." I ran my hands over the smooth, flat stone. Lichen grew on one side. Parting the grass, I looked at the lower half and found a symbol cut into the stone, down near the ground. It was a single vertical line crossed by a curved one, like an ornate hook, with a dot inside the curve and two smaller lines on either side. The sight of it gave me the chills.

Sam knelt next to me. "That kinda looks like your scar."

I remembered what the man who caught me this morning had said. Not a scar. A mark. "They called it Lashte." I pictured the paper No Lips had shown us. It was similar, but mine wasn't the same. My mark had four intersecting straight lines with dots on either side. The one on the stone was curved. But Sam was right. The combination of lines and dots felt related.

Charlie crouched next to us. "We need to hurry. They're almost here." Her voice shook.

Oona sailed down and perched on the stone again. Folding her wings, she tossed something on the ground in front of me. It was a small sparrow. Its head rolled as I turned it in my hand, its neck broken.

"For me?" I asked Oona.

The falcon bowed her head and spread her left wing out in a flourish. I didn't want to hurt her feelings by tossing her gift away. I tucked the dead thing into my pocket with the map. "I'll save it for later."

I stared at the standing stone, wondering what to do. In the letter, my father assumed we'd have help with this.

Charlie touched my arm. "Maybe we need to hold hands or something." She reached out and took my hand and Sam's. Then we waited. "Maybe you two should hold hands, too. Form a circle." Sam shrugged and gave me his hand. It was warm and solid in mine. We made a circle around the stone.

This was stupid. "Nothing's happening," I said.

A branch snapped in the woods behind us loud enough for me and Sam to hear it, no problem.

"They're almost here, guys." Charlie dropped my hand.

"Hurry up, Jim," Sam said.

"Don't look at me. I have no idea what to do!" I whispered. Sweat ran down my back.

Men's voices sounded through the trees, getting nearer.

I looked at Oona. "Leave, now," I whispered, hoping she sensed my urgency.

Oona took off. I tapped Bak.

The first man to step into the clearing wore a makeshift splint on his foot. I looked at Sam, and he recognized him too. It was Mathan, the tracker who crashed my bike on the two-lane. He limped right over to the standing stone and called the others.

Bak lay flat on his belly, obscured by the trees and the tall grass. Sam, Charlie, and I were doing the same thing right next to my tiger.

Mathan's eyes were on the sky, searching. "They won't be far ahead, the engine on their caravan was still warm. Make haste."

"Do you hear it?" asked Silver Braid.

These were the four Eldred left behind to find Oona.

Mathan shrugged. "Can't be sure. The stone has a song of its own. Blocks out the Sending's song. But they must have crossed." He never stopped looking at the sky.

I clenched my teeth. It was as if he knew Oona was still here. I couldn't tell if she was close by or not. And without seeing her, I couldn't tap her, so I willed her to stay away.

Silver Braid stepped aside. "I leave it to you, then."

Mathan hobbled over on his splinted foot and touched the stone. He placed his hands against its flat face and smoothed them down the sides with a surprising gentleness. He pushed the tall grass aside, exposing the front of the stone and revealing the symbol in the rock.

"Roush." Mathan traced the carving with his finger. He knelt down in front of the stone and touched his forehead to the ground. Silver Braid knelt with Navy Jacket, and the big guy did the same. The overgrown grass almost hid them. Mathan spoke in a low voice, words I couldn't make out at first. Then he repeated himself, and I realized he was chanting. Gooseflesh prickled all over me as he spoke the words louder the third time, then a fourth.

"Harken, Roush! We are humble before you. We summon your power to open the way. Harken Roush ..." His voice grew even louder as he continued to repeat the words.

The air around us hummed, a deep vibration ringing in my bones and in my teeth. Bak shifted on the ground next to me. To calm him, I pressed my hand on his paw, but I'm sure he knew my own heart was about to jump out of my chest.

*Don't move, buddy.*

*Bak not like this.*

Sam covered his ears with his hands, but his eyes were wide open and staring at the stone. Charlie looked awestruck. We all watched, waiting for something else to happen.

The trees surrounding the meadow shook, rustling without the help of a breeze. Leaves rained down onto us. Hundreds of birds tweeted and cawed, fleeing the quaking branches and scattering like bats into the night sky. Even the grass began to shiver. All the while, Mathan continued his chanting, even louder now to carry above the rumble rising from the air itself.

"Harken, Roush! We are humble before you. We summon your power to open the way! Harken Roush ..."

A fine, pale mist rolled out of the woods all around the meadow. When the gauzy cloud obscured my sight, my heart froze in my chest. The air filled with the smell of rain and wet leaves. The fog moved away from us, toward the stone.

Mathan rose. Facing the stone, he stood calm, waiting. Everything grew quiet. The aching pressure in my chest remained constant. It was hard to breathe.

Moonlight shone behind the stone, casting its glow upon the mist. What looked like a flat patch of fog took form—of something. At first, it looked like a cave, its entry yawning slowly open as it stretched into a tunnel. I watched as it settled and shifted, and finally turned itself into a bridge. It was completely detailed with small abutments, vertical shafts, and even a decorative trellis. The floor of the bridge looked like it was made of misty cobblestones. The bridge began behind the standing stone and disappeared into the darkness of the forest beyond. The whole thing glowed ethereal white in the moonlit meadow.

I fought to catch my breath. It felt like walls were squeezing me. The others looked equally uncomfortable. Bak's panicked eyes darted from place to place. He dug his claws into the dirt though—bless him—he didn't get up.

*Good boy.*

Sweat dripped from Sam's nose and ran in rivulets down the side of his face. His breathing was really fast and shallow.

Mathan turned to look at his group with a huge smile on his face. "Men, welcome home." He raised his arms, letting his companions go ahead of him. All the while he watched the sky, searching.

They filed one by one onto the bridge, actually stepping up onto the mist. As they walked, the men faded and disappeared where the bridge did.

Mathan lingered at the opening for another moment or two, his ear tilted up toward the sky.

My heart dropped when I felt Oona coming. She flew in fast from somewhere to my left. By the way he shifted his gaze in that direction, I knew Mathan could feel her too. Damn it. I worried then if this tracker was able to see with Oona's eyes like I could. I imagined him seeing us huddled in the trees only a few yards away. I imagined myself invisible. If he called his men back and they looked for us, there was no chance we'd get away.

Mathan smiled as Oona flew into the clearing. "Left you behind, did they? Well, you want to catch up then, yes, little one?"

Oona's white wings flashed the moonlight as she twirled in the air.

I tapped the bird and saw it all through her eyes.

*Oona, we're still here.*

She circled the meadow, her falcon eyes zeroing in on the three of us and Bak. Through her eyes, we stood out despite the cover of trees and grass. She flew over us and then around the clearing again. Oona's uncertainty washed over me. She wasn't sure what to do. Relief welled up that Mathan couldn't see through her eyes. He'd surely have seen us hiding if he could. Instead, he kept watching Oona as she circled.

"Come, your young friends await you, winged beauty." Mathan stepped off the bridge and onto the grass to make room for Oona to pass by him.

*No. Oona, stop!* I sent my thought to her, willing her to fly away.

She flew down low, heading right toward Mathan who smiled as she got closer. Through Oona's eyes, I noticed he had a dark metal earring pierced through the top part of his ear, and a pair of fresh thin gashes that tore through his eyebrows and continued up his forehead and into his scalp. Oona must have been going for his eyes when she flew into his face this morning. I didn't realize she'd made contact. Too bad she missed.

Keek kek kek. She trilled as she flew past us one final time. I felt her settle on a plan. She knew we were here and also knew he thought we were gone. She knew if she stayed, he would stay too. Tucking her feet, Oona swooped onto the bridge.

Mathan turned as if to follow as she entered the misty opening. Then he whipped his arm down fast as she shot past him. Shrieking, Oona banked hard to the left.

I lost my connection to her. Everything went white. I didn't feel him make contact. Everything in me wanted to run to Oona, to find her and make sure she was alive. Charlie clutched my hand, holding it down on the ground. Shaking her head, she pleaded with her eyes and mouthed, "No."

Mathan stepped up onto the bridge, which hung there, glowing white. He took one last look at the woods before turning and walking across the wispy stones, disappearing into the mists.

# TEN

We waited for an eternity to make sure Mathan had crossed.

"Oona's gone." I felt breathless.

"Did you see how fast he moved?" Sam stood and helped Charlie to her feet.

Bak sidled up against me. I leaned into him for a moment, pressing my face to his neck.

*Bad bird gone? Sorry, Jim. Sorry gone.*

"Thanks, buddy," I whispered. I knew he was only saying it for me.

Charlie walked over to the misty bridge and ran her hands through it. The mist parted, then took form again. "Did you feel him actually hit her?"

I shook my head. "Everything went white." I stood in front of the stone, looking into the bridge to see if maybe Oona lay there, injured.

I stepped up onto the bridge. My foot went right through and landed on the grass. "What the ..."

The mist lost its shape. "No!" The bridge melted away. It evaporated before our eyes, becoming low-hanging fog that glowed in the moonlight.

Sam watched the fog disappear around his ankles. "They think we crossed ahead of them. That's good, right?"

"Yeah, but it cost Oona her life. That's why she crossed," I said. It surprised me how proud I was of the stupid bird. "She protected us." I wanted to know why. I needed to know what the hell was so important it demanded so many sacrifices. What could be worth all this?

We waited a while longer, giving Mathan and his men more time to put distance between us.

Sam and Charlie joined me in front of the stone. After parting the grass, I fingered the symbol engraved deep into the rock. I felt the stone's vibration in my chest.

Charlie moved close to me. "You remember the words he spoke? To open the bridge?" She slipped her hand in mine, intertwined our fingers, and gave me a reassuring squeeze.

I leaned against her, grateful the night hid the heat in my face when she touched me.

"I think so." I got down on my knees and bent to touch my forehead to the ground. The grass was wet with dew and smelled faintly metallic. I closed my eyes and hoped I remembered it right. "Harken, Roohesh, we are humble before you. We ask you to open the way." I held my breath.

"He didn't say *Roohesh*." Sam's voice sounded too loud in the silent meadow. "It was *Row-oosh*."

"Really?"

"Yeah, and the last part goes, 'We summon your power to open the way.' Jeez."

"You want to do it?" I sat up on my knees and glared at Sam.

He threw up his hands. "Just saying."

"He's right, Jim." Charlie's voice was soft, soothing. "It was Row-oosh."

As I leaned my forehead on the ground again, I inhaled the earthy scents of dirt and moss. My face was wet with the all the moisture condensing. "Harken, Roush, we are humble before you. We summon your power to open the way." I said it again, and a third time.

Nothing happened.

"You got it right that time," Sam said.

Charlie nodded. "I think so too."

"Then what's wrong?" I asked. The fear we'd never find Oona again, never find out what happened, never find my mom, was thick in my throat.

"Try it again." Sam rubbed his hands together.

I said it over and again, like Mathan had, but couldn't feel anything like I did when he'd done it. Air pressure stayed the same. The trees were totally still. I didn't want to think about Oona being gone or Dan being dead and us stuck here. Sweetwater's was gone. I had to find my mom. I had to. There had to be another way. Charlie and Sam stood beside the stone watching me. I glanced up at them and pushed the panic back down into my belly.

Then I remembered.

"You guys need to kneel. All of Mathan's men got down when he did."

"Duh." Charlie grinned.

They got on their knees. Pressing my head to the ground, I stretched my arms wide. "Here goes."

"Good luck," Charlie whispered. She reached over and touched my hand.

I took a deep breath. "Harken, Roush, we are humble before you. We summon your power to open the way." I repeated the words louder and faster, over and over until my throat dried, and my chanting became a croak.

I pictured the bridge of mist. At last, the air around us began to hum. Cool, misty fog poured in from all sides of the forest, burying us and the clearing under a blanket of white.

Bak pounced onto the fog rolls as they wafted from the woods. He reared up to swat and capture the cloudy masses, but each time they blew apart. As if being reeled in by invisible string, they continued to flow toward the forming bridge.

I fought to catch my breath under the growing pressure. It was like the bridge was pushing the air away, squeezing us. On our feet, we watched the fog connect itself into the bridge made entirely of misty stones.

Sam clutched at his throat. "I can't breathe," he said, his eyes wide with panic.

"It's okay. It isn't getting any worse. Sam, breathe." My voice sounded tinny.

Charlie called to me. "Jim! Listen!" She laughed as she watched the bridge. I couldn't hear anything at first.

Keek keek kek kek.

Oona was a flash of solid white among the translucent fog as she burst into the air from over the bridge. She chirped and trilled as she spun in circles and loops above us. I felt every muscle in my body relax at the sight of her.

*Glad you're back, Oona.*

We waited until the bridge seemed complete. Directly overhead, the moon was full and white, illuminating the span of fog, making it appear like glowing white cotton. We gathered up our packs and made to leave.

"Wait." Sam grabbed my arm, pulling me away from the bridge. "What if we can't get back?" He wiped the sweat off his forehead. "What if this is a one-way thing, and the bridge doesn't open from the other side?"

I looked at the bridge. "Well, clearly there's a way back here. Eldred and his guys came over, right?"

"Yeah, but ..." Sam wrung his hands. "We have no idea what's waiting for us on the other side."

Seeing Sam afraid unsettled me. I dropped my pack. "The way I see it, everyone back at Sweetwater's ... they're together, right? If they got out, then they'll be coming this way. And if somehow, something went wrong, and they ... didn't, well, I don't know how the three of us going back will help."

Sam looked away as if to say he didn't agree.

But I knew he could feel it in me. And just in case he couldn't, I stepped toward him and got in his face. "I care about them as much as you do, you know that."

Charlie touched my arm. "Don't be upset, Jim."

I shook my head. "I'm not upset. I won't hold it against you—either of you—if you decide to stay. I get it. I'm scared out of my boots, man. I know you can feel that in me, too. But you have to see why I can't go back. I carry the weight of Dan's death. Right here." I pressed my hand against my racing heart. "I don't know what's coming. I don't know where this map leads. I only know I can't ignore this. I can't throw away my debt. A lot of people gave up a lot of themselves to protect me from—whatever this is. But now that I know, it's my turn to step up."

*If he takes you, it was all for nothing.*

Charlie took my hand and pressed up against me. The heat of her made my heart race even more.

"I think my parents would want me to stay away. I'm going with you." Charlie leaned her head onto my shoulder. "Sorry, Sam."

Sam threw his hands up. "What if it's a trick? What if Mathan is waiting for us on the other side? They've been over there for a while, but they could have waited. What if we get lost?" He paced between the trees. "Crap! Oh, man ... It's just ... I have a bad feeling about all of this."

"If that's your empathy talking, you should go back, Sam," I said.

"What? By myself? Thanks a lot. What if the rest of those jerks are waiting back at Sweetwater's?"

I didn't know what else to say. "Dude, you know I want you with me. We both do. You're my best friend. But I'm not going to ask. I can't. It's too much."

Sam blew out his breath. "I know. You don't have to ask. I ... I just don't like it."

Charlie put her arm around Sam's shoulders and pulled the three of us together. She whispered, "I'm scared, too."

She stepped onto the bridge. Bak went after her. I followed Sam. I could actually feel the smooth rounded cobblestones under my feet. Oona flew onto the bridge, her wings brushing our heads.

I raised my arm, a reflex to having Oona so close to my face. She grabbed hold, her talons gripping the thick leather of my jacket. "You should have told me you needed a perch," I said.

Oona clicked her beak and peered at me. She didn't break eye contact as she stood on my arm. With any other bird at this proximity, I'd be looking for protective glasses, but with Oona, I now had no worries about her ripping off my face. She felt light on my arm, yet firm and strong.

The bridge seemed as solid as any real stone bridge might have been, and yet I could see through the mist to the forest floor as well as the trees and underbrush through the cloudy stone half-walls on either side.

Up ahead, Charlie, Sam, and Bak were covered in dew. Tiny drops of moisture glowed in the moonlight, twinkling. Sam was still breathing hard, even though the pressure was lessening. "Hang in there, Sam. It's letting up," I said. "I can feel it. Keep going."

Sam nodded fast, droplets showering from his hair as he bobbed his head. Stretching out my free hand, I swept my fingers through the top of the bridge wall, causing a gap to appear as the mist wafted out of formation. I pulled my hand away and the wall was whole once more.

"It's … it's like walking in a dream." Charlie's voice sounded small and far away.

The bridge was a lot longer than I'd thought it would be. I could no longer see the entrance behind us—or the forest below. I shivered. There was no wind or noise from outside— it sounded more like a tunnel with our own footsteps being the only sounds.

"How long do you think it is?" My own voice sounded hollow and echoless.

"I don't know, but it's amazing," Charlie said.

When we finally stepped onto solid ground, we were back in the clearing again. The moonlight still shone brightly, only now we stood opposite the standing stone, on the far side of the little field. Our shadows stretched out before us. Everything looked the same.

"Didn't it work?" As I stepped onto the mossy grass, Oona took off for the trees.

"Oh, thank everything that is good in the world, I can breathe again!" Sam dropped to his knees. His face looked pale. "Actually, I've changed my mind, I don't want to do that again. Not ever." He gave me a weak smile. "Thanks," he said. "For talking me down back there."

"No problem." I eyed the stone across the meadow. "I don't think it worked. We're back in the same place." I took off my jacket and shook it out.

"Man, I'm soaked!" Sam said, flicking his arms and trying to brush the water droplets from his clothes and his hair. It only made him wetter.

Charlie pulled her wet hair back into a ponytail, her gaze upward. "Oh, it worked." She pulled an elastic hair tie off her wrist and wound it around her hair. "Look at the moon."

Sam turned. "Ho-ly crap." He gaped at the sky.

I followed their gaze. The night sky was a swirl of purple and navy blue, like liquid smoke as it flowed. The moon looked ... different. The face wasn't there—the man in the moon was gone—replaced by an array of smaller craters and lines that seemed moon-like, only the arrangement was wrong. And beyond the moon ...

"Look." Light clouds slid away as I traced the object's arc in the sky. "Behind the moon, you see it?"

Charlie gasped. Sam plopped onto the ground, his mouth hanging wide open.

There was something else—another planet or another moon—out there, floating in the sky. A thin rim of it was visible. It looked gray and blue. And really close.

"Where are we?" Charlie whispered.

I couldn't believe I'd thought the bridge didn't work. The more I looked, the more I realized things weren't the same here at all. We were still in a clearing surrounded by trees, but that was about all that matched. The trees here were huge—bigger than the old redwoods in California. Their leaves hung like sheets from heavy trunk-size branches. Overhead, the stars were a spray of white, and there were so many more of them crowding the familiar ones. I could pick out the constellations Orion and Ursa Major, although I had to really concentrate to do it with all the swirling air and other stars closing in.

Everything was totally recognizable, yet different somehow—magnified, maybe. Closer.

"It's … incredible," I said.

Charlie shivered.

"Where to now?" Sam sat in the grass near where we had hidden in the clearing on the other side, only here wildflowers surrounded him. They swayed lazily on thin two-foot-long stems. A lightning bug—a big blue one—lit near Sam's face and flew by in a slow hum.

I pulled out the marble map and waited for the image to appear. Again, the coast took shape, only now it was clearly not California. The map zoomed out a few clicks. The black dot that represented us pulsed a little bit east of the strange coastline. Tiny words appeared, naming the features on the map. A label appeared, marking the crossing stone as *Sierra Crossing*. It was no longer pulsing. A new red dot, far east of us, blinked slowly. The word *Marren* came into view below it. A groan escaped my throat as I tried to calculate what that distance might be as compared to the well-worn road atlas in my head.

"What's wrong?" Charlie came over to look. "Where is that?"

"I don't know. Far."

Fog pooled around our feet. We turned and watched as the bridge melted into a hazy mass that spread on the forest floor and disappeared.

Looking around, I tried to get a glimpse through the trees. "We shouldn't stay here. Mathan and those guys could come back." I studied the map and tried to get my bearings.

Oona keeked from the branches above and swooped down toward me. Out of reflex, I raised my arm, but I wasn't wearing my jacket. As if she knew my arm was unprotected, Oona tapped her open feet down and took off again. She settled on a nearby tree branch and hopped from one foot to the other.

"What's gotten into you?" I asked the bird.

She lifted off the branch, circled quickly, and keeked again, this time landing on my arm and grabbing hold.

The pain of her talons sinking into my flesh was so fast and so hot, it felt more like I was being burned than pierced. I let out a shriek of my own as her talons tore at my forearm. Oona took off again. She perched on the branch once more, hopping back and forth like she had in the fairgrounds. Keek keek kek kek.

Biting back the blinding pain, I held my arm against my chest, pressing the wounds into my shirt. "What is it, girl?"

"Bird's gone crazy," Sam said.

Bak came over and sniffed my arm.

*Bad bird. Bak told Jim.*

Oona danced on her perch.

I closed my eyes and tapped her. As soon as we connected, she shrieked and took off. I felt myself falling backward onto the grass. I heard Charlie shout my name. Someone squeezed the cuts on my arm. But as Oona flew high into the weird night sky, the sounds of my friends faded with the pain.

The view was spectacular and so much more incredible through Oona's eyes. Like every other kid, I'd always wished I could fly, but nobody could possibly have imagined this. The Bellenor sky was stunning. Around the moon, everything was a deep violet that spread and swirled into navy blue as it stretched beyond the reach of the moonlight. Along the horizon, the swirls were lighter—auroras of phosphorescent green and turquoise. Oona shot straight up into the cloudless air and sailed us over the mountain.

It only took a moment before I saw the campfire. From this height, it was a tiny twinkle in the trees. Even so, the golden flicker of flame was easy to pick out and the smell of wood smoke unmistakable.

Oona dove. My stomach flipped, and it seemed like my own skin would peel away with the speed. A group of about two dozen people milled around a campfire not two miles from Charlie and Sam and me. Oona sailed down and perched on a branch high in an evergreen with pinecones the size of footballs. The people were cooking something over the fire. One of the men turned a spit with several small animal carcasses skewered and roasting on it. With Oona's senses, I saw fat drip and watched it sizzle as it hit the flames. A couple of men talked together off in the shadows. Another stood facing a tree, relieving himself onto the trunk of an enormous oak while he laughed at something someone behind him said.

Oona turned and with a single flap of her wings, we sailed on. She looked down occasionally, and I realized we were following a dirt road cutting through the forest. A few moments later, she circled back and perched high in another evergreen. We looked down at the road where it crossed a small clearing before disappearing again in the woods.

I counted two women and one man on horseback, pulling at least twenty more horses through the woods behind them. I could barely see their faces from this side angle, but they were heading right to the camp.

*Oona, back to the campfire.*

Oona dutifully flew us back to the people around the fire. It was hard to count them when they were all moving around, but there were at least fifteen. Oona circled, around and around, letting me get a good look. One of the men sitting around the campfire whittled a stick to a sharp point with his knife. When he turned his face up into the sky, I noticed his leg laid out straight and awkward. He had a splint supporting his ankle and foot. Mathan's smile spread wide across his face when he saw us. His white teeth shone bright in the moonlight.

*Get out of here, Oona.*

Keek.

Diving abruptly, Oona, flew low, using the trees as cover. But I knew it wouldn't do any good to hide. Mathan could feel the bird as well as I could. Hell, even better than I could—he'd tracked her all the way to Sweetwater's from wherever they started. I could barely tell when she was nearby, let alone know which way she was going. As long as Mathan was near, we had to keep moving.

# ELEVEN

I let go of Oona and found myself back in the woods with Bak curled up next to me and Charlie squeezing the cuts on my arm.

I sat up. "Eldred's men are on the other side of the mountain. There are more of them, and Mathan is there. He saw us—saw Oona." The sudden change from free flight to being back on the ground made me dizzy. My arm throbbed. I gritted my teeth. "We need to get out of here."

Grabbing my good hand, Sam pulled me to my feet. We gathered up our things and followed Bak through the woods, heading east and away from Mathan. We stopped from time to time so I could fly with Oona and see what was ahead.

After a while, Bak found a small stream winding out of the mountains. We stayed with it until it joined another stream and snaked through a wide green valley. By the time we stopped, the moon was directly overhead.

"We've been walking for hours." Sam opened the food pack and pulled out the water bottles, passing them around. An owl called from somewhere close by, its low bellow almost like a foghorn.

Charlie leaned against a tree and closed her eyes. "What time you think it is?"

I looked at my watch. "That's weird. The hands are frozen at nine forty-seven. First my phone, now my watch is dead?"

"We're definitely not in California anymore," Charlie said.

I was too tired to laugh. We were all exhausted—even Bak started to complain. The only one who seemed to have limitless energy was Oona. She chirped as she flew over us and sailed into the open, a black silhouette against the painted Bellenor sky.

Sam gulped down the last of his water and belched. "Hey look, there's a house." He pointed straight across the stretch of open field at a low wooden building with a steep sloped roof and warm light pouring from every window. It looked like some kind of bar or pub. We approached slowly, hugging the tree line. As we passed the stable, I noticed every stall was in use. More horses stood at troughs outside.

Voices rose inside the main building. I told Bak to stay out of sight behind the stables and watched him until he disappeared into the trees near a fallen log. I took off the longsword and hid it in the woods with our bags.

The carved wooden sign above the door showed a fat pig with rosy cheeks and a zebra-striped hide. The pig stood on top of a pair of mugs that bubbled over with foamy beer. Beneath the sign, an oil lamp glowed, its flame warm behind the glass.

I quieted my mind and listened for Oona. She wasn't nearby—her telltale hum was gone, replaced by the trill of crickets and other night bugs and the music pouring from the bar's open windows. I took a peek inside, checking the faces in the crowd. I didn't expect to see Mathan and his guys. Afraid to bring attention to us, I'd only flown back with Oona twice since we got underway. Both times we found Mathan's group at their camp. Not seeing any familiar faces, I nodded to Sam and Charlie.

Sam stepped up and grabbed the door handle, then hesitated. "You think they'll card us?"

Charlie rubbed her hands up and down her arms. "I smell a fire. Be nice to sit down someplace warm."

Warm sounded really good to me. "Something tells me they won't ask to see our driver's licenses," I said. I pushed the door open and we stepped inside.

Dozens of men and women sat around wooden tables that took up most of the space in the crowded room. A man in the back strummed an upbeat tune on a high-pitched guitar. A woman behind him plucked the strings on a long, skinny instrument that sounded like the high twinkling notes of a piano. A third musician slapped a rhythm on a single drum nestled between his knees. The stuffy room felt overly warm and smelled of people, horses, and food.

Most of the men wore tunic shirts belted over pants tucked into heavy leather boots. The women all wore skirts and dresses. I felt out of place in jeans and my leather jacket. Charlie crossed her arms in front of her as if to hide the fact that she was wearing Hollis' giant blue sweatshirt.

"We should have come dressed as the Knights from Mysteria," Sam said under his breath.

He was right. It was like we'd stepped across the bridge and back in time several hundred years and landed in a medieval town. Oil lamps and candles filled the room with a golden glow, but it wasn't dark at all—stark white moonlight shone through thick glass prisms that looked like they'd been dropped from above through holes cut into the roof.

A woman walked over to us, drying her hands with a rag. Her face was flushed with the heat of the place, and her long brown hair was piled up on her head. "Moderners, welcome to The Striped Sow. Take a seat." She led us to a table in the corner and cleared away the plates and mugs left by the people who sat there before us. "Are you arriving or departing?"

"Uh… arriving," I said, stunned at the realization that crossings seemed to be a regular thing.

"Aye, you crossed over this night?"

I nodded, unsure what to say.

"Welcome home, then." She looked at each of us as if making an inspection.

"Do you have water? We don't have any money." Charlie smiled at the woman and pleaded with her eyes.

The waitress put her hands on her hips and scowled. "No coin, no seat. This is no giving house. Up with you! Go! Or I'll get Cob to throw you out." She swatted the three of us off the chairs, and we stepped back against the wall.

The song ended and the fire crackled, spitting embers onto the stone hearth. For a moment, it seemed all the conversations in the room found a lull. Faces turned to us as we moved toward the door.

No *coin* … something about the way she said it made me think of the eternity coin. I reached in my pocket and clutched it in my fist. "How much for three meals and some drinks?"

The waitress glanced at me then shot Charlie an eyebrow. "Ten waypens. You'll pay up front now, and no fakes, or you'll explain yourselves to Cob."

"Ten waypens?" My fingers, which had been closed tight around the eternity coin, were forced open to make room for the bulge of new coins filling my pocket. I pulled my hand out and looked at the money. The copperish coins were heavy, with some kind of shield stamped into the face. I counted each one as I placed them in the waitress' open hand. There were ten. She bit one, sniffed, and led us back to our seats.

"There you are." She wiped the table down with her rag. "Why'd you say you had no coin, girl?"

"I, um, forgot he still had some." Charlie looked at me askance.

The waitress rolled her eyes at Charlie.

I shrugged at the waitress, smiled, and tried not to worry that I'd wasted a magical coin on dinner for the three of us.

The waitress smiled back. "Roast mutton or eel stew?"

At the mention of eel, Sam pursed his lips and Charlie shuddered.

"Three muttons," I said, stifling a grin.

Once the waitress returned with our order, she handed me a single silver coin, thinner than the others and square. "'Twas only nine waypens half." She winked as she pressed the coin into my hand. "Have your returns."

Sam poked me with his fork handle while we ate. He didn't look up from his plate. "Hairy dude at nine o'clock is staring."

Looking casually around the room, I brought my gaze to the group of people seated to my left. Three men sat talking over the remains of their meal. One of them, a dude with a wild mane of blond hair and a greasy rat's nest for a beard, stared right at us. We locked eyes, and he didn't look away. Instead, he muttered something to his two companions and got up. He made his way to the back of the room, staring at me as he stepped through a door.

I felt my dinner churn inside me. "Let's get out of here," I said.

The hum of Oona's nearness was a comfort as we got up from the table. I'd taken care earlier to watch whether a couple seated next to us left a tip. As they stood, the man had tossed three of the square silver coins on the table. I dug into my pocket for the coin the waitress had given me. At least we could leave her something. But the silver coin was gone, replaced by the dark brown eternity coin. "No way."

I cupped the eternity coin to my chest and turned to face the wall. "Two waypens," I whispered into my hand. In a blink, the eternity coin disappeared and two coppery waypens glinted in my palm.

Outside the inn, Sam whooped. "That was amazing! Let me see that coin."

We stood outside waiting for Charlie, who had gone to ask the waitress if any of the horses were for sale. I gave Sam the eternity coin.

Two men stumbled through the door, leaning on each other as they walked around to the stables. They laughed as they swayed together and didn't pay any attention to us. Once they were out of sight, Sam cupped the coin to his mouth. "Three waypens." He smiled, and we watched the coin in his hand. Nothing happened. "Maybe it's done," Sam said.

"I hope not. We really need some horses." I took the coin and stuck it in my pocket.

Charlie came out the door and motioned for us to follow. "She said we needed the stable master. His name's Aldon."

Of the three of us, Charlie was the superior horseman. Sam and I knew how to ride and handle the tack, but Charlie worked with Hollis keeping the horses for Sweetwater's. She'd been around them since she was little. We decided she should be in charge of negotiations.

We found Aldon around back of the stable, fitting a large brown mare with a shoe. He tried one and then tossed it aside for another, the heavy metal clanged as it landed in a pile of discarded shoes.

"What d'ye three want?"

"Lizzy said you've got horses for sale." Charlie tilted her head back toward the inn.

"Aye, but they'll cost you." The old man smiled at Charlie and winked a brown eye. "What do you have for me, girl?"

"Well, I, um ..." Charlie looked at me, pleading.

"We'll pay fair price." I stepped forward, making the stable master look at me. "But we'll need to see the horses first."

Oona was close. I left Charlie and Sam under the guise of going to get our money while they negotiated. I really went to check on Bak and find Oona and get our stuff ready to leave. It wasn't like we'd know a fair price when we didn't even know the currency here. Besides, if the eternity coin worked again, it wouldn't matter how much the man wanted.

I walked around the edge of the woods until I reached the fallen log. The splintered trunk stuck out into the grassy embankment, its silver-white wood like a finger pointing to Bak's hiding place. Fog had collected in the low bushes and ferns.

I whistled, a short, single note that echoed through the trees. A moment later, and without a sound, my tiger appeared at my side.

"There you are. Everything okay?" I scratched the short fur on the top of his nose.

*Bak eat.*

"Sorry, boy." I felt a twinge of guilt that I hadn't thought to bring any food for him. I followed my tiger deeper into the forest. Finding where I'd stashed our stuff, I gathered our bags and the longsword. I hauled them back to the fallen stump on the edge of the woods, stuffed our backpacks into a hollow in the log, and laid the swords in the shadows.

"We'll be right back with horses. Wait here." I scratched Bak's ears.

*Bak wait for Jim.* He settled onto his belly inside the tree line, hidden by the tall ferns and wildflowers growing thick on the ground.

Keek kek kek.

Swooping low, Oona buzzed the top of my head. I was too close to the inn and the stables now to risk tapping the bird, but I sensed that she was telling me she was back.

Stepping around one of the stable master's outbuildings, I saw a couple making out against the side of an empty corral. The man had his back to me. The woman pawed at his waist, her skirted leg wound around his thigh. As he moved his head, light glinted off the thin silver chain worked through his blond braid.

I froze, my heart throbbing in my chest. I backed up, pressing myself against the wall, trying to figure out how Mathan and his men had beat us here. I'd checked. We were always ahead of them. I had to find Charlie and Sam and get us all the hell out of here.

I crept against the wall of the little outbuilding, stepped around the corner, and moved toward the main stable. Through the thin plank wall, horses whinnied only inches away. A hand reached out and covered my mouth as I crossed in front of the barn door. I thought it was Sam playing a joke. Until I heard the voice.

"I knew your bird wouldn't stray far from you," Mathan whispered. His breath was warm on my cheek and smelled of beer. I elbowed him. He moved his arm around my neck and pulled me tighter. I struggled to get out from his grip, but he pulled a knife and held the blade under my chin. "Call her to you."

"I can't. I don't control her." My fingers found my dagger. I pulled it out. It slipped from my hand.

"You insult me. I knew the moment she was made. The song from her heart is constantly pining for *you*. Can't you hear her? Or is that yet another thing masked by your time in the Modern World? What else can you not do yet?" He lowered his blade a fraction of an inch. I took advantage of the moment and smashed my head backward into his nose. Bones crunched. He dropped the knife. As I turned to kick him, he saw it coming and moved. My foot swung through the air and I lost my balance. I hit the straw-covered ground. I felt around for the knives.

Mathan kicked my side. I rolled onto my back. Slamming himself down onto my chest, Mathan straddled me, pinning me to the barn floor. I fought to breathe. He punched my face. My tooth cracked.

He sat up and wiped the blood from his face with his sleeve. "I knew when I heard your bird's song come alive again that my Master killed the wrong boy. Quite a trick to play, eh? And what a price." He arched his brows at me. "Who was he then? Your mother's tears were real enough. Was he your brother?"

Shifting my weight, I tried to get my hands free.

Mathan reached over my head and picked up his knife.

"You don't have to answer. I can see it on your face. Well, your brother was a fool." Mathan's voice was nasal and wet. I'd broken his nose. Good.

Holding his blade to my face, he huffed though his mouth. "Lord Eldred will be quite pleased when I bring you to him, eh? I'm sure he's pacing the cobbles at old Blackstone right now, wondering how he got the wrong boy. 'Tis a shame he needs you dead by his own hand, as I'd do the honor gladly." He smiled.

I thought of Dan. The image of him falling on the gravel filled my mind. Getting caught now and Dan dying for nothing sent a surge through me. Bending my legs, I heaved my back off the ground, forcing Mathan sideways onto his splinted foot. A horse in a corral across the way snorted and stared at us.

I got to my knees. Mathan rolled up to his feet. Standing, I backed into the stable. Thick black shadows sliced dark bands in the moonlight falling through the wood slats. It was near impossible to see.

I reached behind me, willing the wall to appear. When it did, I felt my way to the back, hoping for a door. Mathan's ragged breathing filled the barn. There was no way he could see into the darkness. I bumped against a wall of tools. The clanking wood and metal gave away my position. Mathan charged, letting out a low hiss that grew into a growl as he closed in.

Grabbing the nearest tool, I swung it in front of me, hoping it would give me a second to get away. I couldn't even tell what I was holding. I wished for something pointy. The sudden impact sent a jolt up my arm and into my shoulder. Mathan ran right into the tool. The brittle handle snapped as a weird strangled moan escaped him. He fell at my feet, landing in a wedge of moonlight. A pitchfork had impaled him through his left eye. A single tine stabbed into his eye socket while the rest of the fork hung in the air near his ear. Mathan's eyeball lay glistening in a beam of moonlight on the straw. As he clutched for his eye, his hands explored the fork in his head. Then his arms dropped limp to the floor.

I wanted to feel sorry for him, to feel bad about having done this to another person. But all I felt was relief. The one man who could track us by following Oona lay dying at my feet.

Laughter outside snapped me back. I pulled his body through the straw into the darkness at the back of the stable. As I dragged him, Mathan pawed at my arms. He tried to say something, but it was all babble. Was he going into shock? I didn't want to hear anything he had to say. I wanted to get away from him, away from here. I wanted to see Charlie and Sam and make sure they were okay. I wanted to run away with Bak and Oona and figure out what the hell was going on.

The wet sucking sounds of Mathan's breathing stopped. I checked for his pulse, but my hands were shaking so bad I couldn't find it. As I stepped out of the stable, I nearly walked right into Silver Braid, still grinding on the woman against the corral. I turned the other way and rounded the corner of the main stable, facing the inn.

"There you are!" Charlie covered my shaky hand with hers and arched a question at me with her eyes. "Mr. Aldon and I have made a deal for three horses and tack and some riding gear." She smiled brightly, as if nothing were wrong with me.

Sam gasped when I got close to him and he felt me freaking out. "What happened?"

I took a breath and wiped the sweat from my face as I tried to think. Had I moved Mathan far enough away from the barn door?

The horse master motioned to the stable at his back. "I've three strong horses for you, two mares and one stallion. The one brown mare is sweet as they come, name's Honey, but the stallion, now he is a snapper. You'll do yourself a favor to keep your fingers away from old Deacon's mouth unless you have something for him to eat, if you see my meaning? The other mare here is—"

"How much?" Every second spent talking about the horses was another second closer to somebody finding Mathan's body. I didn't give us good odds to get away if everyone started looking around for suspects. We had to leave quietly and now.

Aldon licked his lips. "A hundred forty gold flags, but you'll want—"

"That's fine." I reached into my pocket. Anyone could walk into that barn and find Mathan.

"Jim?" Charlie squeezed my arm.

I smiled. "Sorry, we should get moving. That's all." Taking a deep breath, I tried to relax my shoulders.

"Give us a second, please, sir." Charlie grabbed my arm and led me away to talk near the wall.

My heart was going to leap from my chest. "We have to leave, now. I saw Mathan." I dug into my pocket for the eternity coin.

"Give it. You're a wreck." Sam snatched the coin from me.

"What the … Sam?" I started, but he'd turned and walked back to the stable master.

"One hundred and forty gold flags, did you say?" Sam put the coin into the front pocket of his sweatshirt and crossed his arms underneath, no doubt preparing for the deluge of that much money.

"Aye, and that includes all the tack and riding cloaks, water skins, and I've added a nice pair of worn-in boots for the lass."

Sam paused, waiting, his eyes on his pocket. Nothing happened. He spoke again, louder this time. "I need one hundred and forty gold flags?"

Aldon looked confused. "Aye … as I said."

This was taking too long. I braced myself, waiting for shouts from some unsuspecting person as they discovered Mathan's body. Or Silver Braid, who was right around the corner. He might hear Sam—he was talking so freaking loud. I wiped my palms on my jeans.

"You alright?" Charlie touched my chest, her fingers like feathers on my skin.

What if she thought less of me for what I did? I shook my head. "Mathan's dead. I—I killed him."

She glanced over my shoulder, her eyes wide. "What? How? Where?" she whispered.

"Not now. We need to leave." I walked over to Sam.

Slapping the coin into my hand, he hissed, "Let me guess. It only works for you." He sulked away as two men walked out of the pub and headed toward the barn where I'd left Mathan.

Closing my eyes, I willed myself to focus. Charlie moved to block the stable master's view, and I whispered to the coin how much we needed. As soon as the words left my mouth, the eternity coin transformed into a pile of gold. The coins were angular, six-sided things about the size of a silver dollar with a little flag stamped on the face. The back of the coins featured a circle of stars. As they fell in a jingling heap, Charlie held out the bottom of her sweatshirt and caught them. I scooped them up by the handful and shoved them into my pockets. By the time we finished, I felt like I was wearing a lead coat.

"I've got no idea if we're getting a good deal or not," Charlie whispered.

I jammed my hands on top of the coins to keep them from spilling out of my pockets. "Does it matter? The coin keeps coming back." And thank God it did. I counted the money for Aldon. The stable master smiled wide as he stacked the coins in front of him like a poker player counting a big win. I felt the eternity coin reappear in my pocket while Aldon was still counting the coins at his table, so at least that wasn't a trick. We'd have a lot more to run from if all the money we spent suddenly disappeared from the people we paid.

A stable boy brought out the horses and the other stuff we'd bought. This was taking too long. I helped Charlie up on one of the mares. She pressed her lips tight through the pain.

Oona hummed closer now, and Bak waited for us in the woods. Now if Sam would get back here, we could go.

As if he heard my thoughts, Sam hurried around the corner toward us. "There's something going on in the barn back there."

"Oh, man." I tossed Sam the stallion's reins. "We have to go. Like now."

I didn't wait for him to mount. I coaxed my horse toward the field. Charlie followed. A brown wool cloak lay folded on my saddle. As I pulled the coarse fabric around me, I felt instantly better. We'd be much less obvious dressed like locals—as if three woolen cloaks could make riders on horses with a tiger and a falcon inconspicuous.

A crowd gathered at the barn. At least the people were all staring inside the dark building, not out at us as we walked our horses by—casual as you please. I held my breath and pressed my heels into my mare.

# TWELVE

The moon was about to set. The horses stepped gingerly through brambles and thickets of ferns and undergrowth until Bak found a little road. Then we trotted for a while to give us some distance from the village. My nerves had me jumping at every noise from the forest. I kept expecting a posse or a mad mob to come racing through the woods after Mathan's killer. Every branch snapping under a hoof and each leaf rustling rang in my head, a sure sign the law or Mathan's crew were coming for me.

The swirling night sky was so thick with stars, it gave off a light of its own. It was bright enough to follow the narrow path winding through the forest. The packed dirt road muffled the horses' hooves. The road had been worn smooth except for wheel ruts cut into the edges on either side. I tapped each of the horses, and they all seemed well enough. Charlie's mare,

Honey, was afraid of Bak. Sam rode Deacon, who was determined to be in front. He nickered and shoved at Honey whenever she tried to come alongside him on the road. My mare, Darla, flinched every time I tapped her. She was content to follow along with the others and wait for me to lead her.

Charlie was in pain with the jostling, and we didn't want to tire the horses, so we stopped a couple of times to rest.

Whenever we stopped, I flew back with Oona to see if we were being followed. After a third check where nobody came, we took it easy. But I still couldn't relax. The woods were so thick with growth that whenever Bak took a few steps into the brush, he seemed to disappear completely. We stopped at every fork and crossroads to check the map and confirm our direction. Though we made small progress, at least we were always heading toward the blinking red dot.

The map was different here in Bellenor. Before we crossed, it had shown a single line for the California coast and the two dots floating in empty space. Here, the forest bloomed inside the orb, a dark mass that filled the glass. Three-dimensional mountains stood far off to the east and a river split the range of peaks down the middle. Hundreds of tiny roads spread out like spider webs. Our marker still pulsed, tracing our movement at every turn along the network of tiny lines.

In order to tap Oona, I had to stop, so I flew with her only a couple of times to see what was ahead. And after missing Mathan and his guys the last time, we spent more time backtracking, making sure we weren't being followed. So far, it looked like we were alone. What I saw from the sky matched what the map was telling us—the forest rolled ahead for miles before the land opened up onto a valley with a small city the orb labeled *White Tor*. Beyond that distant town, the forest grew thick again, spreading into white-capped mountains rising in the distance.

"We need to stop. I have to sleep." Sam had been complaining since we'd arrived at the first small village on the road. It had started with his cloak, which was too itchy. Then we were riding too fast. And any time Charlie and I spoke to each other, he would grumble about something and kick Deacon to speed up.

Charlie and I rode side by side, our horses keeping pace behind Sam's. I practiced tapping Oona while riding, but I kept losing my saddle. Charlie held my arm to keep me from falling.

"I'm sick of this." Sam dismounted and stood in the road.

I disconnected from Oona and focused on Sam. "Sick of what?" I glanced over my shoulder, feeling conspicuous standing there in the open. "We can't stop here."

Deacon turned and tried to bite Sam. He swatted at the horse and held the reins away.

"We're not far enough from ..." I couldn't say it. I didn't want to own Mathan's death. As if saying it aloud again would condemn me further. We'd stopped near a group of little shacks nestled into the forest around a larger house with a sign out front that looked like another inn.

"What's really bothering you, Sam?" Charlie asked. "I don't believe for a minute that you want to stay here." She pointed to the closed-up houses, her voice soft and soothing, trying to get Sam to loosen up. The smell of wood smoke hung in the air.

Sam glared at me.

"What'd I do?" I said.

He didn't answer.

I threw up my hands. "There aren't any lights on inside those little shacks. Besides, I don't want to stop at one of the first places we come to."

"Who made you the boss?" Sam spit his words at me.

*Tell no one who you are. Stay hidden.*

I jumped off my horse and got in Sam's face. "In case you haven't noticed, these guys are after me. After us. I don't plan on announcing our presence here—or anywhere. We need to stay under the radar."

"Jim, don't," Charlie said.

"Fine." Sam pulled Deacon around and mounted again, but he didn't ride. He sat in the road, with his arms folded across his chest.

I glared at him while I hopped back on my horse. Charlie and I moved on. Sam eventually followed, staying far behind us. We waited for him whenever the road branched off so he wouldn't get lost.

"I think Sam's jealous," Charlie whispered when we stopped at a crossroads. Bak had taken off into the woods after an animal. At least he was taking care of his own food. I tried to ignore how hungry I was.

I didn't look up at her. "Jealous? Of what? He's my best friend."

She sighed. "Of you, of all this. Of the coin, of Oona ... of *us*."

I knew Sam was upset about something, but the mention of "us" sent my heart racing double time. I'd asked Charlie to go out with me two days ago. We had the day off in Vegas. I'd finally got my license, and there was this movie playing that she wanted to see. Nothing happened, really. Afterward, I wasn't even sure there was an *us* to speak of. I mean, we were always together before and after. It wasn't easy to avoid anyone at Sweetwater's.

That night, I helped her walk the horses after Sweetwater's closed. I'd tripped in the dark and she knelt next to me, moving my ankle to make sure it was okay. Then she kissed me. On my mouth. It all just … happened. We hadn't officially called "us" anything, yet. I hadn't even told Sam. But of course, he knew. He probably felt it and knew before I really was sure.

And now he was jealous? Of what? He saw what happened to Dan.

"I didn't ask for any of this." Anger swelled inside me at the thought. I shook my head, no way. Charlie was wrong. "Dan's dead. We have no idea what's happening with my mom or with anyone back home. Your family, his parents, everybody. He knows the score. How could he be jealous?"

Charlie shrugged. "I don't know, it was a feeling."

"Well, you're wrong. That's not Sam."

We passed the rest of the wait in silence. I noticed how the forest had come alive after dark. Owl calls and night birds' songs filled the air. Tiny flowers opened up all over the ground, glowing and giving off pale pink light. They flashed as they moved in the breeze or as the horses brushed against them when they grazed. A pair of small white animals ambled along the edge of the forest, single file. The lead one had at least six babies piled on its back, clinging there for the ride. They didn't even look at Charlie and me as they passed. A black butterfly floated down from the trees, the edges of its wings glinting green as it flapped by in the starlight. Lightning bugs glowed blue, red, and green as they settled on tree leaves big enough for us to wear as hats.

When Sam caught up, his scowl had deepened. We rode on. I tried to ignore his huffing. At the next fork, we stopped and checked the map.

Sam yawned. "Can we stop now, master?"

I swallowed my anger. "Look, if anyone comes looking for us, we can't be asleep in some inn. How do we know the people wouldn't give us away? We should probably camp in the woods and stay out of sight." I was fighting to stay awake myself. Charlie hummed agreement, swaying in her saddle under heavy eyes.

I wanted as much distance between us and Mathan's body as possible. Did they have police in Bellenor? What would happen if they found out I'd killed someone? I tried to muster up some shred of feeling for Mathan, but it wouldn't come. What the hell was wrong with me? I didn't like thinking that it didn't matter, but really, I didn't feel anything. I wondered what my mom would say, what Charlie would think.

And what about Dan? Didn't Dan deserve something? Did what happened to my brother justify killing Mathan? Did anything justify killing another person? Was it okay if I did it to protect myself? What if I was protecting someone else?

I thought about my mom, she could be dead too, for all I knew. Maybe with Mathan dead I was even with my karma scale. If murder even got measured on karma.

Maybe I was numb. The shock would wear off and it would hit me in the morning. The weight of taking a life would settle on me tomorrow. I wondered if I'd ever get used to it. How do you carry the weight of something you can't take back and didn't mean to do?

We left the road and made camp deep in the trees. Bak found a small creek dribbling through, so we watered the horses and tied them up for the night. All we had were the clothes we were wearing and the cloaks we'd bought with the horses.

"We should have hit the camping store before we left." Charlie smiled as she laid her cloak on the ground, curled up in it, and went to sleep.

"And the grocery store." Sam yawned. "We're going to be hungry in the morning." He pulled on the hood of his sweatshirt and lay down near Charlie's feet.

I hadn't thought about food. But there seemed to be people living along the road, and there was a big town up ahead. Eating wasn't likely to be an issue as long as the eternity coin held up. Watching Oona circling above, I lay on my back and tapped her. We sailed in the night sky as the moon finally set. Bak curled up between the three of us, his warmth radiating and welcome. I pressed into him and slept.

Charlie's scream shocked me awake in the middle of the night. Her cries echoed through the woods, unsettling some birds in the trees above us. Screeching, they took flight in a scatter of dark wings. Bak shot to his feet, stepping away from Charlie's sobbing.

"Char?" Sam rolled up on his elbows, groggy.

I crawled over to her, my hands grabbing for her in the darkness. She was trembling. "What is it? Charlie, what's wrong?"

"Oh, Jim, it was awful. Horrible. Your brother." She sat up and covered her face with her hands.

"What, a bad dream?" I asked.

Charlie nodded and wiped her face on her sleeve.

I blew out my breath. Only a dream. A dream. No big deal. I could handle a dream. "You want to talk about it?" I moved next to her. As I put my arm around her shoulders, she nestled into me. Her hair smelled faintly of strawberry shampoo. "You're shaking."

"It was awful. It was like you said. We were back at Sweetwater's hiding behind one of the cranes, and everyone was jammed into the two cages like a bunch of animals. Then Eldred was there and he stabbed Dan, and the sword ..." She clutched at the exact place on her chest where the sword had come through Dan's chest. "And then Eldred pulled out the Keystone and sliced the sky. Your mom was screaming for Dan and holding his head in her lap and telling you to go find your father and that if Eldred finds you, it was all for nothing. And then—like that—they were sucked away into space."

Everything in me went cold. "Yeah, it's like Sam and I said, exactly." Except I hadn't told her all of those things. I nodded and rubbed Charlie's arms, trying hard to hide the chill that came over me. I hadn't told them what my mom said to me. Mom hadn't actually spoken at all. She'd shouted those exact words, though. Problem was my mom shouted them into my head—with her mind.

Charlie wrung her hands together. "And then they landed inside this ruin like a crumbled stone castle made of super-black rock, and he dragged your mother by her hair down a hall and into this awful dungeon. And she screamed and screamed for Dan the whole time. 'Dan! Dan!' ..." Charlie reached her hand out in front of her as if miming my mother from her dream.

I wiped Charlie's tears. "Don't cry." Now I was shaking. I looked over at Sam. He stared at Charlie.

"What did Eldred look like, Charlie?" Sam knew as well as I did that she never actually saw Eldred herself. She was unconscious then, on the ground with Oona, next to the crane.

She looked up at Sam, blinking. "What? I don't know, um ... he was tallish, taller than your mom, Jim. And he had brown hair, long and greasy looking. He looked like a puffy old man. Not fat really, maybe out of shape. Like a male version of Mrs. Crandall. You know?"

I did know. Eldred actually looked like he could be related to Mrs. Crandall. Our English teacher at Sweetwater's had white hair and was much older, like seventy where Eldred had to be in his forties. But she had full fleshy cheeks and a thick wattle under her chin that shook when she talked. And she had the pasty look of someone used to sitting indoors. All the kids used to joke that it was a good thing not to read books all the time or we'd get a case of the Crandalls when we were older. Never to her face though. Mrs. Crandall was great. Come to think of it, I didn't remember seeing Mrs. Crandall in the cages. I felt a pang of worry for her. For all of them. But I knew they all had gotten out of the cages. The cops and EMTs were all over the place. So, even though the guy with the varsity jacket was there too, our clan had to be safe—somewhere.

"Eldred's voice was really deep though. Like it didn't fit him at all." Charlie's words brought me back to the woods and her dream that I didn't think was a dream.

I turned to Sam. "Did you tell her any of this?"

He stared at Charlie. "No, I didn't."

"Tell me what?" Charlie asked.

"Did anything else happen? In the dream?" I wasn't sure I really wanted to know.

She shook her head. "No, that was it. When your mom started screaming like that, I woke up. Oh, Jim, it was so real."

Could it have been real? How else could Charlie have known those things? I replayed the few conversations we'd had since she woke up, and I didn't remember ever describing Eldred to her. The only time we were apart for any length of time was when I was fighting with Mathan in the barn, and then she was with Sam and the stable master, buying horses. I doubt Sam was talking to her about Eldred then.

I'd talked a lot about Dan though. I told her how his death was cemented into my mind in slow motion. Every detail. How he gave himself up, sacrificed himself. For me. I'd told her about Eldred's theatrics, trying to scare everyone into giving me up. Dan's surprise. The blood. Mom's screams. How none of this made any sense at all. I'd told her all of that, but none of the other stuff.

Charlie's breath came in stutters and sighs. She'd fallen asleep with her head on my lap. I leaned sideways against the tree. My hand had fallen asleep. I could almost imagine us home and sitting in the back of her parents' RV watching a movie, and we'd dozed off like this, with nobody dead, and no lies, just our hands wrapped tight around each other's.

Hollis saw us kissing that first night with the horses. *Hollis. Where did you go, man?* I hadn't seen him in the cages either. He'd been with us when all hell broke loose and the first explosion happened near the big top. He'd recognized Oona. He'd run off to get the horses ready—which means he'd known we would cross over. I wondered if he'd crossed there before. Then Sam showed up with Hollis' rig and no sign of Hollis. Charlie never asked about that, how we were in Hollis' motorhome without him. Did she remember he'd been with us when they gave me my jacket? I decided to wait for her to bring it up before I told her we had no idea what happened to him.

From the branch above, Oona gave a soft chirp and sailed into the air. Sam snored softly, and the weight of Charlie kept a part of me grounded while I flew with Oona, free and alone in the swirling and alien Bellenor sky.

# Thirteen

etal clinked next to my ear, pulling me from sleep. Opening my eyes, I found a face directly above mine, uncomfortably close. I flinched back and smacked my head against the tree. A green-eyed kid leaned over me. He held two of Hollis' daggers—still in their scabbards—together in one hand. His other hand hovered near the open duffel bag by my ear.

"Hey!" I grabbed for the daggers. He ran into the bushes and disappeared.

"Stop!" I ran after him. Once I cleared the shrubs, I found two little boys no taller than my waist. They ran like crazy through the woods. The second one dragged Hollis' longsword behind him. He had one of the straps strung over his shoulder. It slowed him down, but he was totally booking—running all out. The sword was easily twice as tall as he was. The other boy was in the lead. Over his shoulder, he kept calling something I couldn't understand to the one with the sword. I hopped over thickets and bushes, trying to keep an eye on both boys without getting shredded by the thorny shrubs that suddenly seemed to be everywhere. The one dragging the sword was slowing down. The wide hilt kept getting caught on vines and branches.

I jumped over a fallen tree, pushed through a thick patch of ferns, and almost fell off a cliff. A wide canyon cut through the forest. The almost vertical drop made it impossible to see the bottom. To keep from going over, I grabbed onto an exposed root. The little thief wasn't so lucky. He hung upside down over the chasm, caught in the straps of the longsword's scabbard, which twisted tight across his chest. He'd managed to get his leg tangled with it, too. The same roots that kept me from falling had caught the sword hilt. It lay wedged tight against the ground beyond my reach. The leather strap at the throat of the scabbard that locked the sword into the sheath was a simple thong pressed over a metal bead. It had torn and was stretching dangerously close to tearing completely. If that happened, the scabbard would slide off and the little guy was toast.

"You lucky devil." I knelt down and reached my hand out. "It's alright, I won't hurt you. Come on." His green pants were cut off at the knees, ragged and frayed at the bottom. He had huge hairy feet, like an ape's with a thumb instead of a big toe. I realized with a start that this wasn't a normal child. Hell, I couldn't tell if he was actually a child of any kind.

Hissing at me, he kicked out his legs, making the sword shift a little, and sending a rain of dirt down onto his head. The creature let out a little whine. I raised both my hands in the air, palms up. "Look, see? I want to help you." I got down on my belly and reached my hand out again. "It's okay. Grab my hand."

"Gatoo!" The creature barked. The sword tilted downward. Clumps of dirt bounced off the wall and away, into the cavern.

I pointed to the falling dirt. "That's gonna be you soon. The scabbard's going to slip. You're going to fall."

I slid forward a little more. Holding the roots with one hand, I stretched to grab hold of his free ankle with the other. But he swung his leg away from me. A branch snapped behind me. The sword tipped down a few more inches.

I reached out again. "Please. It's not worth dying for."

The leather clasp snapped, and the scabbard slid down off the blade. The shifting weight forced the hilt from its roots and into the air. As the sword tumbled behind him, the creature grabbed my hand in an iron grip. His eyes never left mine. He had the same green eyes as the other one, wide and round, centered above a small pointed nose. His breath came in rapid puffs as he climbed up my arm and over my back. Hollis' sword was gone.

I got to my knees and turned to stand, but the other little man was there. He had both of the stolen daggers, blades out, pointed at me.

Scowling, he poked the knives into the air. "Oon gatoo!" The blades were razor sharp, but he was nowhere near close enough to be a danger. His brown hair was thick with mats. Pine needles, twigs, and dried leaves stuck out in all directions, and his tan pants were torn. He hissed again, revealing a mouth full of tiny white teeth with two long fangs.

I got to my feet and took a step to the side, away from them. "I was only trying to help your friend."

The creature's eyes grew wide as Bak stepped out of the trees and sat down next to me.

*Strange little people.* I felt my tiger slip himself into my mind.

*Yes, they are.*

*They are small.*

*That's true. Really good to see you, buddy.* I ran my hand down Bak's neck.

The one with the daggers spoke to his friend, "Chikoo renda. Renda!" The one I saved scurried and hid behind the one with the daggers. Keeping their eyes on me and Bak, the two of them backed into the trees. I stood there with my hands at my sides. Bak licked his paw. The one with the knives turned to me. "Oon Gatoo!" Two daggers threatened me if I dared to follow. Hoping I looked harmless, I raised my hands in surrender. I didn't go after them.

When I got back to camp, Sam was gone.

Charlie walked over and grabbed my hands. "Good morning." She kissed me, a quick peck on my mouth, and walked away. "Come help me. Sam's horse won't let me lead him."

She kissed me. Just like that. Like it was nothing. But my heart was doing flips.

"Come on." Charlie came back and grabbed my hand, pulling me over to the horses. "I woke up and nobody was here."

I let her lead me down the path. "I was chasing a pair of wild munchkins," I said.

Her hands were warm and soft. She laced her fingers between mine and squeezed, sending a thrill up my spine. I squeezed back.

"Munchkins? Are we in Oz?" She thought I was teasing.

I untied Deacon's reins from the tree and tapped Sam's horse, urging him toward the stream with the others. The stallion was stubborn, and I could tell he was going to bite me if I got close enough. "Munchkins. Barefoot wild ones. Two of them. They stole some of our stuff. I lost the daggers, and Hollis' sword." Charlie hadn't let go of my hand.

"Oh, no, really?" She turned to face me and wrapped her arms around my back. Her body was so warm. "You think Sam is off chasing wild munchkins too?" Her amber eyes smoldered in the light. Then she leaned in and closed her eyes. Closing mine, I kissed her. It was so natural and easy, like we'd done this a million times before. Everything in me was heat and rushing and heartbeat racing. I stood there kissing her, my one hand in hers and the other on her hip, willing this to last. Her lips were perfect and soft. She sighed.

I'd kissed a girl before. Her name was Marcie from some small town outside of Indianapolis. She wore super short cutoffs and a hot pink bikini top as if that was how everyone dressed for the carnival. Wherever I worked all day, she'd followed me and hung around Sweetwater's until well after we'd closed down for the night. She kept asking me to let her pet the tigers. Even if it was against the rules, I knew it was totally safe with me there. So I sneaked her into the yard after dinner and brought her to Bak. She said it was like she'd died and gone to heaven, running her fingers through Bak's fur. Afterward, she'd pinned me against the ticket booth and kissed me. It was nice, I guess, but later I tasted bubblegum and waxy lip gloss and had to wash my face.

Kissing Charlie was sweet and clean, with the hint of her strawberry shampoo. Kissing her, I never wanted to wash my face again.

"Hey guys, what's going—" Sam stepped out of the thicket.

Charlie stepped back and blushed. I didn't let go of her hand.

She pulled her hand free. "Hey, we're uh, watering the horses."

I shoved my hands in my pockets. "Have you seen Bak?"

"Yeah, he's upstream. Caught a fish." Sam wouldn't look at me.

Oona was nearby. I went back and checked through Hollis' duffel with the knives. The daggers were gone. We'd eaten all the crackers and candy and drunk all the water, so the backpack was empty now. After stuffing it and the empty water bottles into one of Deacon's oversized saddlebags I wrapped the empty duffel around the blade I'd taken from the guy at the carnival and tucked that in as well.

A dead rat landed at my feet. On closer inspection, it wasn't a rat, exactly. It was more like a ferret or weasel, brown and tan with a long body and pointed nose.

Keek kek kek.

"Thanks, Oona." I pushed the dead thing off my boot. Oona rocked back and forth on a branch above me, waiting. She was like a cat bringing dead things to her owner. "Go ahead and eat. We'll get something later." In a flash, she was on it, and I turned away.

I pulled out the map to see how far we'd come overnight. The image seemed to move with us. Somewhere beyond the edge of the map, the crossing stone and the little inn at the bottom of the valley were cut off behind us. I didn't like that. My head instantly envisioned Mathan's crew, hell-bent and right there on the edge of the orb, a fiery orange dot that burned through the road and gained on us with every moment. The town still lay ahead of us, and the map showed more villages on the way.

We decided to stay on the road as long as we could. When we came to the next village, it was almost midday.

The sun blazed as Oona flew low over the village, the lack of trees giving her the space to come close. I raised my arm and she settled on it. I was getting used to the feeling of her there. Nice and close.

Charlie urged her horse ahead. "Oh good, I'm starving. Come on, Honey."

The village was much larger than the others we'd seen so far. This one had shops, two-story houses, and a well in the center of a square. As we got closer, it was clear something wasn't right. There was no activity in the square, nobody coming or going from the shops. Windows were shuttered and shop doors were locked. But it didn't feel like the place had been closed up for long. Flowers in window boxes were drooping but alive, and everything looked neat and clean. There were no broken windows or broken shutters—nothing looked like it was in disrepair or overgrown. It was like the whole town packed up and left at once.

Sam hopped down from Deacon and walked over to one of the shops. "Where is everyone?" He tried the handle and knocked twice on the door. Nobody answered.

"The stable is empty." Charlie led her horse around the lane between the buildings. "I don't like this."

The well had a pump and a water trough. I filled the trough and we tied the horses to the post to drink.

"I'm going to take a leak." Sam walked off behind one of the houses.

A kitten skulked out from where Sam had gone. Mewing at us non-stop, it walked along the wall of the candle shop and crossed the square. It looked like someone's pet—fat and clean. Curling around Bak's leg, it pressed itself into his fur and purred. Charlie reached down and picked it up. It let her cradle it in her arms. Definitely used to being held by people.

During the night, we'd passed another smaller village that had been super quiet as well, but I assumed that was because it was the middle of the night. Could it have been abandoned too?

"Guys, over here," Sam called.

*Bak, with me.*

We followed Sam's voice behind a group of houses and into a small yard edged with trees. At the far end, Sam stood waiting for us.

"Look." He pointed into the band of trees lining the yards like a perimeter fence.

We walked through the trees and came out the other side into a huge crop field cutting into the forest. Everything was green and gold, ready to be harvested. There were straight plow rows, a silo for storage, animal pens, and a big wooden barn. It had the look of an active, organized farm. But there were no animals corralled and the crops looked almost past ready.

Charlie turned back toward the houses. "Nobody's here."

I tapped Oona and urged her to fly. I was getting better about keeping my feet under me while tapping her and no longer had to sit down when she took off. We sailed over the crop fields. On this side of the village, I counted six of them and another five across the other side. Everything was still and empty. Oona circled back over the square and the houses, then the band of trees past Charlie and Sam. Smiling, Charlie watched Oona. I saw myself standing there, my arms at my sides, eyes closed.

*Higher, girl. Let's see what's up ahead.*

The large town, which the map named *White Tor*, spread out in the distance, maybe half an hour's ride away. The land rolled upward and grew hilly. As Oona and I got closer, I saw it was more of a city built around a tall white castle that sat on top of the highest hill. On all sides, pale stone walls surrounded it, snaking through the valley at the base of the hills. The castle's center tower was square but twisted, the top disappearing into the clouds that hung low over the mountains behind the city. Smaller watchtowers on the wall marked the city gates. There were three of them, each with a drawbridge to span the wide moat tracing its way along the wall.

Someone grabbed my arm and pulled me slowly to my knees. Charlie whispered something into my ear. Her words faded away, lost in the back of my mind as I stayed with Oona. I wondered idly if I had gotten shaky on my feet while I flew. Following Charlie's lead, I lay down in the grass. The cool blades tickled my neck.

The city crawled with people. Outside the wall, families on foot and on horseback lined up to get inside. Men and women pulled wagons and led herds of animals together, clogging the gates. The procession stretched out at least a mile. Guards stood watch at each of the gates, ushering the people through. Someone put a hand over my mouth.

Disconnecting from Oona, I found myself huddled down with Charlie and Bak in the band of trees between the town and the fields. Bak crouched in the grass, taut as a bowstring. Sam had all three horses tethered by the silo, the reins in his hand. He stood between his stallion and the mares, trying to soothe Deacon. Sweat dripped from his face. Charlie's hand covered my mouth.

"Shhhhh," she whispered in my ear. As I came back into my skin, she let go of me and pressed her hand onto my chest. "They're here. Dozens of them."

Each of the houses backed into the shared backyard with no fences standing between them. Out of sight, at the front of the houses, stood the little square with the well. A horse nickered from somewhere in the square, and a woman called out.

Two men stepped into the backyard. One turned and walked away from us, around the back of the houses and out of view. The other one stood still, watching. He had a long red beard and a thick belly hanging over his belt. I didn't recognize him. My pulse raced. This was it. I knew it. They'd found Mathan's body, and now they'd found us.

"If they came this way, they are gone from here." The man with the beard turned to speak to someone behind him.

Another man stepped into the yard next to him—he was holding a kid by the neck. It was Silver Braid, and I realized with a start that the "kid" he was holding was the munchkin man with the green pants who I'd saved from the cliff this morning. The little man wore Hollis' daggers on his belt. The scabbards reached almost to his knees. He wasn't a little person, not like the people back home. His arms and legs were proportioned and slender, not thick and stunted. He was built like an average man, only smaller.

"This one says he's been tracking them since last night." Silver Braid raised the creature into the air like a weightless toy. The little man fought to keep from swinging but was no match for Silver Braid's strength. "Says there are three of them, two boys and a girl, with a big tiger and a white falcon. He described the Sending—it's the white loragrine, of course—and said it sticks with the one boy. Isn't that what you told me?" He turned the creature to face him.

"That's the—" I whispered.

"Shh." Charlie put her fingers to my lips.

The creature spat and struggled against Silver Braid's grip. "Mal bitrun! Bitrun! Gata loon gah!"

"Yes, yes. You've told me that. They're long gone. I see no people here, although we've been tracking them on this road. They can't be far."

I didn't know whether to be worried or relieved. Maybe both. This wasn't a posse of lawmen looking for Mathan's killer—these were more of Eldred's men. But either way, they were still after us, and now there were a lot more than four of them.

"Let him go, Rand. You know he's seen them." Red Beard urged Silver Braid. "How many kids with a tiger and a white falcon do you think are traveling these woods? I don't need the wrath of the fagens on me now. Have you ever tried to sleep in the woods when the fagens are upset with you? They come close while you're deep in your dreams and steal all your belongings. Not all at once, mind you, but a knife here, a boot buckle there, a saddlebag one night and your bed roll the next. Before you know it, they've taken your horse and you're wandering the forest in your small clothes. No, it's hard enough to manage the true outlaws without the forest folk against me. Thank you much."

"Aye, but he's not telling us something." Silver Braid—Rand—released the creature, who turned and kicked him in the shin.

Red Beard flipped a silver coin to the little man. "Here you go, fagen. Something shiny for your junk heap."

A small, hairy hand snatched it out of the air, and the fagen ran into the trees a few yards away from us. As he passed into the leafy underbrush, he turned and looked right at me and winked. My breath caught and my blood froze in my veins.

"We'll find them." Red Beard turned and left the yard.

Silver Braid—Rand—lingered a moment longer. One last time, he scanned the trees, turned, and went back to the square.

# FOURTEEN

I t felt like forever before Eldred's search party left the
village. Whatever the creature—the fagen—had told
them, Eldred's men thought we were farther down the
road. I could only guess why the little wild thing chose to
mislead Rand. The fagen clearly knew we were there—he
looked right at me as he passed. I hoped he was protecting us
in return for helping him and his friend.

Charlie slept beside me, her cloak balled up for a pillow in
a bed of thick green grass. The trees, some with trunks at least
twenty feet around, towered over the houses and created a
canopy of leaves thick enough to keep the sun out almost
entirely. Even so, the air was still and warm and made it hard
to stay awake.

Closing my eyes, I tried to give in to sleep, but my mind
spun like a broken compass. The needle directing my thoughts

bounced back and forth between Eldred and the reason he wanted me dead, my mom and if she was safe, Charlie's dream vision, and Dan. It always came back and settled squarely on Dan and the look on his face when he realized he had a sword sticking out of his chest. It was pure shock, like he was seeing it and feeling it but still couldn't process it. I wondered if he regretted standing up for me. I kept seeing him fall, his eyes locked on nothing. Blood from the hole in his chest coated the gravel like spilled paint while everyone screamed that Dan was the wrong kid.

*If he takes you, it was all for nothing.*

My mother's voice was in my mind-loop, too, an endless echo of words that made no sense at all. I kept circling to that one phrase, nine simple words that taunted me and felt so heavy. What did she mean it was all for nothing? Clearly, she and Dan had worked hard to keep the truth of Bellenor from me and Charlie and Sam. Were we the only ones who didn't know? Was everyone in Sweetwater's in on it? Could they have all spent their lives playing their parts in some scheme to keep us in the dark? Why? Why all the lies? What could be so important?

And then there was my father. My father.

*Go to your father.* My mother said. *Tell no one who you are.*

The idea that my father was alive seemed too far away to grab hold of. Why was it so important to tell no one my name? The more I thought about it, the heavier the weight grew in my chest. I needed sleep. Maybe I'd wake up in the morning complaining of a crick in my neck from sleeping in the passenger seat of the RV instead of in my bed. Maybe I'd turn around and find Dan asleep on the couch, snoring like always with his headphones threatening to strangle him. I thought of all the times had I wished he'd meet some awful and untimely end. He always seemed so angry with me, so impatient. Maybe he was. Maybe he hated me. Maybe he resented me.

The only thing I knew for certain was I'd give anything to have him back. If I could have a do-over of the past couple of days, I would tell Dan not to come out when Eldred called. I'd ask my mom to keep Dan hidden instead of me. I'd make her promise. I fought against the tears, but they came anyway. I was glad Charlie was asleep.

The forest was alive with birdsong and insects. They seemed to grow bolder the longer I sat still. Bak skulked through the woods beyond the crop fields. Before he became obscured by foliage, my tiger looked back at me. Dark leafy shadows mottled his stripes. I felt him reach out to me with his mind, slipping into my head.

*Bak hunt.*

*Okay, boy. Good luck.*

Then he disappeared into the forest. It never ceased to amaze me how—with orange and black and white stripes over a four-hundred pound frame—he could camouflage himself so easily. I let my eyes drift closed. Then I realized I hadn't tapped Bak. He came to me that time. Come to think of it, he'd come to me a few times before.

Merging with Oona was getting easier with every flight. Already I could fly with her and keep my saddle, no problem. It was like my mind split into two separate halves, one in me and one in Oona, wherever she took me.

Sam arrived and knelt next to us with a huge load of berries in the front of his shirt. "There's a ton of them over behind the barn." He smiled, revealing a mouth full of purple teeth. The fruit looked like oversized blackberries.

I popped one in my mouth. It tasted sour.

"Want one?" Sam leaned over me to hand one to Charlie, still lying next to me. He froze.

"She's aslee—" I looked at her. Her eyes were open, but completely green—no whites at all. I thought she had something on her face, some weird Bellenor bug or a leaf, or a reflection of sunlight from the trees, but her eyes were open—and solid green. Her cheek felt warm and she was breathing fine.

"Dude! What's wrong with her eyes?" Sam leaned closer, his hoard of berries spilling onto the grass.

"Charlie? Wake up." My mouth was dry. She didn't respond. I shook her. "Charlie!" Panic gripped me in its giant fist and squeezed the air out of me.

When she spoke, her voice sounded airy, like she was off somewhere far away and we were an afterthought. "He has taken the heart-blood from the scholar who is not a scholar. There is no life in the mundane blood. All shall burn."

I shook her again. "Charlie! Quit freaking us out!"

She blinked as if waking from a trance. The green faded away, and her eyes went back to her own amber irises flecked with dark brown, normal and clear.

"Holy crap! What was that?" Sam said.

"Are you good?" I grabbed Charlie's hands. "Your eyes were ..."

She covered her face with her hands. "I don't know what's happening to me. I keep seeing things, visions." Tears ran down between her fingers.

I pulled her hands away. Her eyes were bright with tears, reflecting every last ray of light from the forest.

"It's okay. You're with us and you're okay now." I tried to be reassuring, but my voice shook. Another vision. After the dream she had about Dan's death. There's no way that was an ordinary dream because she saw way more than I did, and I was right there watching the whole thing. I wanted to know more about what she'd seen.

"Are all the—the visions—the same?" I asked.

She shook her head. "I think I'm going crazy—I keep seeing things, but they're all inside my head. When we're riding, these images pop in front of my eyes, like watching a movie, but it's inside my head. I can barely keep track of the road. I do my best to hold on and let Honey follow the other horses." She sobbed. "Jim, I'm scared."

I had no idea it was that bad. "I thought that one dream repeated. Where Dan died and Eldred took my mom to the black castle?"

She rubbed her nose. "No, that was the start of it. I feel floaty all the time now—like I'm not all here. It's like the back of my head is wide open, like a window."

Movement in the trees behind us made us all turn. Was the fagen back? A young deer burst into the field with Bak on its tail. With a couple of long strides, my tiger was on top of the animal, wrestling it to the ground. It wasn't as smooth and controlled as a tiger in the wild looks on the nature shows—Bak was new at hunting for his own meals. He swatted the deer, snagging its flank and dragging it down so he could go for the throat and the kill.

"What did you see this time?" Sam asked. "You spoke about heart-blood and a scholar."

"I talked?" Charlie suddenly looked exhausted. "Oh." She picked at her fingernails in her lap. "It was mostly Eldred and Dan and this weird crystal thing, like a puzzle in the shape of a small sword."

Staring into the trees, she wouldn't look at me. "They were in this room and Dan was lying on a table and his chest was—his chest was ... open." She could barely get the words out through her sobbing. "Eldred held Dan's heart. He ... he was squeezing drops of blood into a cooking pot. The blood steam rose up and condensed onto this glass sheet above the pot. Eldred had this little metal vial collecting all the drops."

Dan's heart being ripped out of him was too much to imagine. This must have been awful for Charlie to actually see.

"What did he do with it? With Dan's blood?" I had to know. Was he going to drink it? The whole thing sounded insane.

"That's all I saw. It ended there." She sighed. "Why is this happening?" She leaned her head against me and cried into my shirt. "I'm so tired." Her tears were hot on my skin.

Closing my eyes, I pretended I could mind-tap her. I knew she couldn't hear me, but I sent the message all the same.

*I'm not going to let anything happen to you. I promise.*

People still clogged the road leading to the city. Oona perched in a tall oak near the gate, hidden within the thick leaves. Through her eyes, everything was crisp and clear like a wide-view magnifying glass. Her hearing was as sharp as her eyesight. I watched and listened through Oona awhile.

While parents waited in line to enter the city, their kids ran around playing a game of tag. Two guards stood at the gates, green and gold banners and matching cloaks flapping in the gentle breeze. Flags flew above the city walls as well, deep green bordered with gold surrounding a white tower in the center.

A man in a long brown robe addressed the crowd near the gate. "Your children will be safe within the city. The Black Riders have been spotted outside the village of Corlan—two days ride from here. Their murderous trail will not reach White Tor. The good brothers will show you all to the abbey. We have room for everyone." He motioned to a table with two guards writing in a book. "Able-bodied men and women are to sign in here for the harvest. You'll be escorted back to your farms with armed guards to tend your crops. You will receive a fair price for your yield. We'll feed everyone in the city. We have room for you all. Please be patient."

Someone was murdering children? Charlie hadn't mentioned seeing anything like that.

A long row of carts and stalls had been set up on the road, separating the crowd from the wide moat snaking between the road and the white stone wall. The carts were loaded with all kinds of food for sale. One had huge red apples and bright yellow pears. Another was loaded with onions. Shouts rang of "Apples! Fresh picked! Only a half waypen each, three for a waypen!" and "Sweet corn!" and "Ale, mead, and wine here!" A man selling fish was stationed across the road, no doubt sent to his place to stay downwind of the other sellers.

A woman dressed entirely in purple, with hair dyed to match, walked among the crowd shouting, "Willem the Bard's back from his travels. He brings news from the High King and songs from court at Marren City. Only at the Plum Goose!"

Mention of Marren got my attention. Even Oona perked up at that.

Sam would have loved seeing all this. It was kind of like Sweetwater's, having a Talker on the road outside the gate. Funny being on this side of the sale, even disguised as a falcon hiding in the trees. The purple woman was a good Talker. My uncle'd be proud.

Uncle Paul was always trying to get someone to take the job of Outside Talker at Sweetwater's. He said it was more of a tradition among the carnivals of the world. "Aye, but you simply must have a Talker. That's the sign of a class show, there. Yes sir, every show worth its salt has someone to kindle the flame in the bellies of the townies while they clutch their money, itching to get in." Uncle Paul was a great Talker. If you got stuck doing the job, he'd walk with you, giving you pointers and telling you what to say and how to say it. It was so annoying.

I missed my Uncle and wondered for what felt like the millionth time if they got away after the police came—wouldn't they head to the crossing stone as well? They had to know where it was. Maybe they crossed. Maybe everyone from Sweetwater's was behind us on the road, worried about us like we were about them.

I wasn't sure about this place. What if Eldred's crew was here? Something inside me kept saying we should stay on the road and keep going. I felt jumpy sitting here with Oona. She could sit so still and watch everything.

Guitar music rang through the air from near the gate. The purple woman continued walking up and down the line of people on the road. "Come to the Plum Goose and hear all about the sack of Marren City and the hunt for Eldred, the scholar of Dorren, and his Black Riders. Will our children ever be safe from this murderer and his evil men?"

Mention of Eldred stopped me cold, and the words from Charlie's vision echoed in my head. She'd talked about scholars. Was Eldred a scholar?

Leaving Oona, I opened my eyes to find Sam with Charlie cradled in his arms. She was limp, and her eyes had gone green again.

"She's been like this since you left. I can't wake her. Oh, man, what if she stays like this?"

*Charlie sick?*

My tiger's thoughts popped into my mind. I scanned the forest until I found him standing in the trees not three yards away.

I could feel his thoughts. He knew something was wrong with Charlie.

*She'll be alright,* I told my tiger. I knew he felt my uncertainty. He came close and settled next to me.

"He has taken the heart-blood from the scholar who is not a scholar." Charlie's voice had that distant quality again. "Lashte does not live in the imposter's blood. The hunt will go on until all the true blood of Lashte has been joined and purified. The Keystone reveals all. The blood shall burn."

As her eyes cleared, Charlie caught her breath.

Sam helped her sit up. "Oh, thank God you're back."

"What did you see?" I wanted to know.

"Give her a second, Jim, jeez." Sam scowled at me.

Charlie cried into her hands, silent, heavy sobs that made her whole body rock. When she looked up at me, she looked so sad.

"Eldred's got his men hunting you, Jim. He's communicating with them somehow with that crystal, but he isn't here. He kept calling you the scholar. He needs your blood—scholar's blood—for some kind of ritual or something." She wiped her eyes. "He's really angry that Dan tricked him, and he knows that he was your brother. Eldred's done awful things to Dan's body. He's hurt your mom, Jim. Trying to get her to tell him where you are. He believes you're the last one, the last of the scholars. He's waiting for his men to signal they have you so he can cut back through the world and take your heart. He wants to burn your heart. Purify it with fire. He keeps saying that all the blood will burn."

"A woman from the city called Eldred the scholar of Dorren. How can I be the last one if he's one too?"

Charlie shook her head. Dark circles stood out under her eyes. "Eldred has a mark behind his ear that looks exactly like the one on your shoulder. I saw it when he was doing the ritual thing with the blood." She touched her neck, behind her right ear. "His mark is here. I think you are the last one—the last scholar—besides him. He's murdered the other scholars, some were just little kids. He's been threatening people all over. Before he found you in Sweetwater's, he thought they were hiding you somewhere here in Bellenor. That's why the villages are all empty. The people are fleeing to the cities for protection. They think Eldred's on a killing spree, but they don't know he's only killing scholars. You're the one he needs. You're the only one left."

"How can you know this?" My heart pounded.

She shook her head and looked from Sam to me. "I don't know. I just do."

# FIFTEEN

Oona and I perched on a tree branch outside the windows of the Plum Goose. Perching wasn't like flying at all. When I flew with Oona, I didn't pay attention to my body—everything was wind and light and delicate shifts in air temperature. But when she stopped moving, I became acutely aware of being in two places, and all I wanted was to stretch my legs and move around. Staying connected took effort, but if I let go, I wouldn't be able to get her back until she came within sight again.

Concentrating, we scanned the crowded room through the open windows. Fiddle music carried outside with the sounds of people laughing and talking. Oona froze as a man in a purple robe stepped through the door with a candle and lit an oil lamp on the corner of the building. The flame caught and somehow spread to the next lamp, and continued on until all the lamps along the back flared up. Not wanting us to be seen, Oona hopped the length of the branch, into the shadows.

A crowd stood near the bar, elbowing for space as even more people squeezed through the doors. A small stage occupied the back corner of the room, with the head of a gigantic purple goose with green eyes mounted on the wall above.

The purple lady stepped up to the stage and waited for the performance to end. Applause followed the fiddler as he made his way slowly through the throng by the bar. As he bowed, people tossed coins into his upturned hat.

The purple lady waved her arms at the crowd. "Quiet now. Quiet everyone. Thank you for coming this fine evening. Willem Goldfinger, our very own Bard of White Tor, is back from King Jonus' court at Marren City. He'll be out in a moment to bring you news and music. For now, we have ruby beer with a chicken pie for only a waypen half, until they're gone."

Hunger hit me in the gut. Oona huddled down on the branch as a tall man with stooped shoulders and long red hair shuffled onto the stage. He sat on a stool and arranged his beard so it hung straight down into his lap. While he spoke to the crowd, he strummed absently on a small guitar.

"I am Goldfinger, returned from court at Castle Marren. I bring you news." Pausing, he looked at the ceiling as if for inspiration. His voice was deep and velvet smooth. "The king has asked that I make it known: Your children are safe." He raised his hand to quiet the low talk of the crowd. "Eldred has taken three of our young ones—it is true. The search for them continues. But the king has consulted the Seers who have reason to believe Eldred sought those particular children only. King Jonus reassures you that every measure is being taken to stop Eldred and his Black Riders."

A man in the front called, "How? Where is Eldred now?" The crowd murmured agreement with the questions. Goldfinger sat quietly and raised his hand for their attention. When they were quiet again, he continued.

"As terrible as the loss of those boys has been, there has been another, more troubling development. Eldred has stolen the Keystone from the Sisters' Grove."

The low mumble of the crowd erupted into shouts. Below Oona and me, a door swung open and a man wearing a brown leather hat with a wide brim stepped out of the pub and lit a pipe. Puffs of sweet tobacco smoke wafted up to us in the tree.

The man on stage continued, "The Sisters of the Grove have ..."

The man below drew on his pipe. Listening to the news, he leaned against the wall outside the window. "I knew I heard your song again."

The familiar voice sent a zing of adrenaline through me. Oona looked down at the man in the hat. At least we were too high for him to reach us.

"And what are you doing *here*, beauty?" Mathan's smile was pinched in one corner by the brown eye patch cutting into his cheek.

"Are you in there, boy?" He waggled his fingers up at Oona. "You can't hide from me. You know that, don't you? Nothing but death will keep your falcon from you. You see, she can't resist the pull of you. And the strength of that pull?

Well, that is what I hear. It's like a little bird song from her little bird heart. I'm bound by my vow to deliver you alive to my Lord. But he said nothing about needing you whole. And now you and I have some business together as well. A debt, eh?" He lifted the patch and showed me his empty eye socket. "An eye for an eye, isn't that how they say it in the Modern World?"

*Oona, fly. Far away.*

As she took off, I separated from my falcon. Then I was sitting next to Charlie as she fed twigs into a small campfire. My heart raced, each pulse threatening to make it jump out of my chest.

My mouth went dry. "Mathan's alive."

We rode hard. Bak raced alongside the horses, darting in and out of the trees. With every empty village we passed, I thought about the people running to the city for protection from Eldred and his men. Eldred was kidnapping kids? Why? Were these the same ones Charlie said he'd killed?

*Tell no one who you are.*

Had my mom known what Eldred was doing? Was she afraid that villagers would turn me in to Eldred in order to get their kids back? I had hoped for some answers from the Plum Goose, but instead I got more questions. I couldn't wait to reach my father and finally see what the hell was going on.

Charlie rode on Sam's horse so I could hold the map while I rode. With her horse tethered behind me, we thundered through the forest, bringing us ever closer to Marren City. If we could get to Marren ahead of Eldred's men, we'd be safe. We had to keep going.

"Slow down! Charlie's losing it!" Sam shouted. As she slipped into another one of her visions, he slowed Deacon to a trot and struggled to hold her. We came to a narrow stream and slowed the horses to a walk, but they refused to cross. I tapped them and tried to coax them into the water, but they wouldn't budge. They were sweating and exhausted. We wouldn't be able to ride any farther tonight.

Sam held Charlie as she slumped off the horse and into my arms, her feet landing in the icy water. The whole time her green eyes stared at nothing, unblinking. I pressed her eyelids closed.

We didn't make a fire.

Sam wanted to take first watch.

"You sure you're not too tired?" I asked.

"Like you're not? We're all beat. Whatever. I'm fine." He leaned against a rock and looked up at the moon and the other thing peeking from behind it like a huge glass ball. "What do you think it is? Another moon?" Sam yawned. "Or another world, like Bellenor."

"Maybe. I don't know." *And right now, I really don't care.* I curled up on the ground next to Charlie. She lay on her back in the same position Sam and I had placed her. This vision was the longest one by far. Bak settled next to me, and I pushed myself into my tiger's fur, letting his warmth come over us like a blanket. When I closed my eyes, they burned. I was so freaking tired.

Sam said, "You really think everyone's going to be there? When we get to Marren?"

I yawned. "Yeah, I'm sure of it." *Well, not everyone.* "And once we get there, my father will help us get my mom back." I kept trying to imagine what my dad would look like now. If he would still resemble the image from my memory. Was he strong and athletic like Dan or thinner like me? He was a falconer—that much I did know. I wondered if he'd want Oona back when we got there.

"Weird to think he's really alive. Your dad …"

"Yeah." I played over in my mind how it would be when we met. Should I hug him or let him make the first move? Maybe I should shake his hand. Would he want to know all about me at once or would that have to wait until after we got Mom back? How would he take the news about Dan?

I felt Oona coming closer as I drifted off to sleep.

"Jim, wake up," Charlie whispered. She shook my shoulder.

"Mmmm?" My eyes refused to open.

She nudged me again. "Sam's asleep. We need to talk."

I moved Bak's paw off my chest and wrapped my cloak around me. As I followed Charlie, I felt Oona off somewhere to the south. The tug of her at the back of my mind made me want to turn my head and look for her even though I knew the forest filled the night sky between us. Bak opened one eye.

*Jim going?*

*Go back to sleep, I'll be right here.* My tiger yawned huge and curled up next to Sam.

Charlie took my hand, leading me through a break in the trees. The ground sloped steeply down into a wide grassy meadow. Dozens of huge boulders peppered the field below. We sat on a bed of fallen pine needles and sparse grass. As Charlie turned toward me, moonlight caught her face.

"You look terrible," I said.

"Please. Have you looked in a mirror lately?" She nudged against me.

"Sorry, I—you look tired."

"I can't remember the last time I actually slept. These visions are coming all the time now." She took my hand. "Promise me you won't say anything to Sam about this, alright? I don't want him to worry. You know how he gets. But we need to be really careful from now on."

"Why? What? Did you see something?" Part of me didn't want to know. Part of me wanted to turn around and go back to the crossing stone and California and pretend none of this had ever happened. But the other part, the part that had watched Dan die, the part that saw my mom get kidnapped— that part of me wanted to find Eldred and rip his heart out with my bare hands. And to do that, I needed as much information as possible. I had to know what Charlie saw.

She glanced at me and then up at the sky. "It's ... I don't know. I'm getting pieces of things. Most of it doesn't mean anything." She wrapped her arms around her knees. "It's like a jumble of all kinds of stuff. Some of it's totally off the wall. I saw Eldred walking into this tiny house in a hill. It was surrounded by a flower garden where the flowers glowed like Christmas lights. He was visiting a woman called Alonna, she was about his age. She was sick, sitting in a wheelchair in this room. She looked shrunken and weak, skin and bones, you know?

"And then I saw this beautiful place in the middle of a huge green meadow with all these women in long flowy dresses. They were chanting by a pond. Then there was this super-tiny woman with green skin sitting on this crazy throne made of tree roots. She pointed off to the side, saying, "Go!" And then ..." Her voice broke.

"Don't cry," I wrapped my arms around Charlie and pulled her against me. "It is going to be okay."

She shrugged my arm off her and sat up straight. "That's the thing. You can't say that. Not anymore. Not to me." She covered her face with her hands. "It isn't going to be okay. It's—I saw ... I saw Sam."

"Saw Sam what?" A wave of fear rippled through me. "What's going to happen to Sam?"

"I don't know. I only saw him after it had already happened." She let her tears fall without even trying to hide them. "He lay on the ground in the woods, screaming his head off. Covered in blood. His own blood. His leg was cut really bad. But you and I weren't there. When it happened, he was alone. Let's make sure we stay with him, alright? Make Bak stick with him, too. I don't know. I feel like we need to stay close to him. From now on. Promise?"

"I promise. Of course." Movement in the valley caught my eye. "My God."

"What?" Charlie sat up straight.

"Did you see that? The boulder, it moved." I pointed to one of the huge rocks in the field below.

Charlie smiled. I couldn't remember the last time she'd done that. It was nice to see her face relaxed, if only for a second.

"I guess you can't hear them?"

"I don't have x-ray hearing, remember?"

She pushed against me. "They aren't boulders. They're some kind of animal, like giant buffalo or something." She got up and pulled me to my feet. "Let's get back."

Once the camp was in view, we stopped to sit under an evergreen tree, its low branches like a pine-scented umbrella. I saw Bak snuggled up close to Sam, both of them asleep not ten yards away.

Charlie leaned her back into me. I leaned my cheek against hers and somehow we ended up in a kiss. We sat together under my cloak as the incredibly bright moon above kept watch over us. After a while, Charlie's breathing became slow and steady. I checked her eyes. Not green, thank goodness. She was asleep. I sat still, not wanting to wake her.

The moon had started its descent, and with the moonlight coming from behind me I saw that what I'd mistaken for boulders really were huge, elephant-sized buffalo. There must have been two hundred of them grazing in the valley. The feeling of having stepped back in time struck me again. I let my eyes slip closed.

Charlie startled, waking me. The morning was not quite full yet—the sky was a deep blue and orange through the trees as the sun prepared to rise.

"What?" I asked.

A branch snapped in the woods, close by. Charlie cocked her head to the side, listening.

Then something flew through the air in a blur around the tree where Sam and Bak slept.

Bak roared.

# SIXTEEN

"Oh. Please, no," Charlie whispered. She crawled to the edge of the evergreen canopy.

Oona landed on a branch above us. She clicked and rocked from side to side, a move I now recognized as her distress signal. I tapped her and urged her to stay quiet. *I know, girl. Quiet down.*

A man, dressed entirely in black, led our horses away. Deacon was having none of it. Sam's horse nickered and pulled, snapping at the guy's hand when it got close enough.

Charlie pulled her short sword from its scabbard and crawled ahead of me.

"I don't see Sam," she whispered, frantic.

I got on my knees and tried to get a good look. Stiff pine needles poked into my scalp. My stomach clenched. Sam wasn't there. "Me neither," I said.

Bak writhed on the ground, caught in a rope or something. I felt my heartbeat in my fingers as they tightened into a fist. Charlie hadn't mentioned Bak in her visions. I couldn't think. *Please be safe, boy.*

"I'll take the tall one with the horses," Charlie whispered. "You get the one over there." She looked to the left, where Sam and Bak had been sleeping.

I gaped at Charlie. "What? You'll take the tall one?" I whispered. "Are you insane? What are you going to do?" I'd lost my dagger in the barn with Mathan.

"I don't know. But if we wait, they'll be gone." Exploding from under the trees, Charlie startled the two men. The one with the horses dropped Deacon's reins and hopped on Darla. He took off riding into the trees. Charlie fought to get on Deacon to give chase.

The other man rode off on his own horse, heading in the opposite direction. As he passed in front of me, I saw a flash of brown cloak covering a bundle on the back of his saddle. A pair of dark blue Chuck Taylors stuck out underneath. My stomach dropped.

"Sam!" I ran after them and tripped. Landing on my face in the dirt, I looked back to see what I'd fallen over. It was Bak, tangled and writhing in a net. He'd pushed himself up against a tree. Every time he struggled against the net, the ropes grew tighter. The guy with Sam was getting away.

*Jim help Bak. Bak need air.*

I pulled at the ropes, but it didn't help. Loosening one made another tighter. The thunder of hooves grew more distant with every second. I needed a knife. A third man stepped out of the trees.

"No need to fuss. Our orders are to take him unharmed," the man said. He had a high-pitched voice and a long, curved knife in his hand. He pointed his knife at me, but he wasn't near enough to reach me, yet. I stood and backed away. I'd managed to get Bak's face free.

Deacon burst through the trees with Charlie. She flipped her leg over the saddle and jumped, tackling the man to the ground. He must have outweighed her by a hundred pounds. Standing up, he grabbed her around the waist, lifting her off her feet. Her eyes went wide with surprise. She fought against his hold. When he put his knife up under her chin, her eyes flashed milky green, and she went limp. I saw her struggle against the vision that wanted to overtake her.

"No! Charlie!" I yelled at her. Willing her vision to stop. I couldn't hear the horses any longer.

Charlie blinked once, and her eyes were her own again. She tried to wriggle free of his grip, but he was so much larger than her. Instead, she pulled out her short sword and turned it to point at her own chest. She pulled it around her side with two hands, stabbing the man in the ribs—a self-defense move Hollis had taught us almost every day since we started weapons drills. The blade went in up to the hilt.

With an agonized groan, the man crumpled like an empty sack and pulled Charlie down on top of him. She rolled and pushed herself away, kicking him to get herself free even though he wasn't moving anymore. Her hands were red with his blood. Spatters dotted her face and her clothes. She stared at her hands.

"Help Bak! I'm going to find Sam." I had to get to him before they could ... I didn't want to think about what Charlie had seen.

"Oona!" I scanned the trees twice before I spotted her. She chirped once and bounced on a low branch behind me. As she waited, I dropped to my knees and tapped her. We soared through the top of the woods into the sky.

Oona found the forest road almost instantly. We traced the thin line as it flashed in the shafts of morning light slicing through the trees. Shooting higher into the sky, we scanned the ground until we spotted Sam's kidnapper racing through the forest about a mile ahead. Oona dove.

We sailed above the treetops. I saw Sam wrapped in his cloak. Facedown, he lay limp against the horse. Thin ropes bound his arms and ankles around the horse's belly. The horse's hooves drummed a constant beat below us. As the rider turned north, Oona let out a shriek.

Three more riders joined the man who carried Sam. Their pace didn't slow. One of the men looked up and saw Oona. From this distance, his eye patch looked like a black hole boring through his face. Mathan let out a whoop. He shouted something at the riders.

The path forked and the group split. Two riders went west. Mathan stayed with the one who had Sam. They took the eastern fork. Oona followed Sam.

*Good girl, Oona. Stay on them.*

Something whistled by Oona's face with such surprising speed that it took a moment for me to register what it was. An arrow. Oona twisted and dove, spiraling down toward the trees to avoid the attack. When she opened her wings to fly up once more, we were shot right out of the sky.

Our connection broke instantly. I sprang to my feet back at the camp.

"Oona!" I screamed.

"What happened?" Charlie cut the rest of the ropes from Bak. Some of the blood from her hands now smeared my tiger's fur. He pulled his paws away as she freed them. "Stop, Bak, let me get it," she said, trying to soothe him.

I hurried to help her with the last of the netting still caught on Bak. "I found Sam. Oona's hurt. We have to go." I grabbed the reins and tapped Deacon as I jumped into his saddle.

*No fighting, Deacon.*

I pulled Charlie up behind me and kicked the horse to go. Bak ran with us, limping.

"Jim, slow down." Charlie squeezed my waist. I wouldn't slow the horse, not for anything. Not now.

"We have to find them!" I couldn't leave Oona to die alone and injured. And what if Mathan found her first? After all she'd done for us. I knew she would wait for me. In the same way I knew Bak would come for me if I were lost. Oona needed me. The two of them, Oona and Bak, they were the purest things alive. Nothing but plain honesty and loyalty and always being there.

And Sam. How would I ever face him again if something happened to him? Was this what Charlie had foreseen? But why did they take Sam?

Surprised to feel tears on my face, I dug my heels into Deacon's sides and folded myself lower. My best friend. And Oona. What would my father say if I lost Oona?

I followed the forest path. It seemed a much longer distance on the ground. We turned north and then took the eastern fork. There was no sign of Oona or the riders.

"She must be right around here," I said. My breath caught. "They kept going that way with Sam," I said, indicating the road ahead.

"What happened?" Charlie and I jumped down and started looking through the scrub.

"An arrow." I pressed my hand into my right shoulder. "We were tracking Sam, and it knocked us out of the sky."

"Oona!" I called. She had to be nearby. If she was still alive. *Please, God, let her be alive.* We hadn't flown much beyond the eastern fork, and the ground sloped steeply to the water about twenty yards ahead. The riders hadn't crossed the creek yet when we got hit.

Keek kek kek.

"Here!" Charlie called as she crawled into a patch of shrubs.

"Oona?" On my hands and knees, I dug through the leafy ferns growing thick around the base of the trees.

She chirped softly when Charlie pulled her from the leaves. Relief pressed in on me like something physical.

Oona held her right wing outstretched, the arrow still lodged there, wobbling as she moved. There was only a little blood around the shaft. But it was clear she couldn't fly any time soon.

"Is it broken?" Charlie turned Oona so I could inspect her wing.

I touched the edge of the fletching.

Oona squawked.

"I don't know. Let's get the arrow out."

I pulled the fletching from the back of the arrow and pushed the shaft the rest of the way through. We helped Oona fold her wing. I dug the backpack out of Deacon's saddlebag and pulled it on, pouch forward, tucking Oona inside so her head poked out the top.

We rode east, following the road where I'd last seen Sam. I wondered how far they could've gotten in the precious minutes it took to find Oona.

"Stop." Charlie pointed into the woods to our left. "I hear something," she whispered.

Oona let out a little chirp. Her feet scraped against the inside of the pack. Tapping her, I saw immediately that she'd found something in the distance. Something shifted in the grass.

"There," I said, pointing. My mouth was dry.

"Oh my God. It's Sam," Charlie whispered.

I kicked Deacon and we jumped off the road into the woods.

Charlie slid from the saddle and ran to Sam. "Oh no. No. No, God, no. It's exactly like I saw."

The ground sloped down toward a creek where Sam lay on his back in the dirt, his breath coming in bursts. Blood covered the ground around him.

Charlie ran to him and inspected his wounds. "Sam? We've got you. You're safe now." She wiped dirt from his face and mouth. His skin was impossibly pale. Silent tears rained from her eyes into Sam's hair. Blood pulsed bright from a huge gash in his thigh.

I knelt next to him and peeled back the fabric on his jeans looking for the wound. "What do we do?"

Charlie moved to Sam's side. "He's losing too much blood." She pressed her palm onto his thigh, trying to stop the flow.

Sam screamed.

"Jim, press here." Charlie moved her hands to make room for mine.

I put pressure on Sam's leg, praying for him to hold on.

"It's alright. You're going to be alright." Charlie tore a strip of fabric from her cloak and wrapped it around his leg.

"Jim ..." Sam croaked.

"Yeah? I'm here, man." I bent down and put my ear next to his mouth.

Sam's breath smelled metallic. "They thought I was you."

His words chilled me. I looked at my friend. My best friend since forever. Had they left him for dead once they realized they had the wrong kid? Mathan knew what I looked like. Had he told them to get rid of Sam when he joined them on the road? Sam didn't deserve this. Were they trying to send a message to me? The weight of Sam's words hit me.

This was my fault.

My brother was dead, and now Sam was going to die. And it was my fault. Sam wouldn't even be here if not for me. We'd convinced him to come.

I didn't know what to say. "I'm—I'm sorry, Sam. I'm so, so sorry." The words caught in my throat.

"He's passed out." Charlie's tears mingled with the blood on her face. "Something's wrong. He's bleeding from somewhere else. I can't stop it."

We rolled Sam over and found another cut around the back of his thigh. Blood seemed to come from everywhere.

I took off my belt and helped Charlie pull it tight around Sam's leg.

"Oh, Sam," Charlie whispered through her tears.

I remembered where we were on the map. "We're too far. I think we're still a day—maybe two—from Marren. Even if we could ride with Sam, we'd have to take it slow with him like this."

"I'm so stupid." Charlie said. "I—I saw this." Her breath stuttered.

"You didn't do this. You didn't know how it would happen."

She tore another strip of fabric off her cloak and tied it around Sam's leg. "He can't die, Jim. He can't." Her words came out in a rush. "What good are these stupid visions if they don't help us at all? I knew this would happen, and I couldn't even stop it."

Sweat mingled with my tears and stung my eyes. "It isn't your fault."

"But it is. Don't you see? He's going to die because I was too damned stupid to see what was totally obvious. I pulled you away from him so he wouldn't overhear and get worried and that's when they *took* him. He was alone because of me."

Sam groaned.

None of this was Charlie's fault. Visions or no, she wasn't responsible for Sam being here. She wasn't the reason why they took him and then threw him away. She wasn't the reason they left him for dead. No, that was all squarely on me. I was to blame. For every last bit of it. For everything. I didn't care anymore what happened to me. I swore then that no matter what happened, Eldred and Mathan were going to pay for this.

# SEVENTEEN

I cinched my belt tighter around Sam's leg. It didn't seem to help. Charlie tore more fabric from her cloak, and we fought to tie it around Sam's leg. She moved her hands to make room while keeping pressure on his wounds. No matter what we did, we couldn't get them tight enough to stop the bleeding. Sam's words echoed in my mind.

*They thought I was you.*

This was my fault. "This isn't working." I looked at Sam. His skin had gone waxy and looked even more pale than before. He couldn't die here. Not like this.

Charlie leaned hard on Sam's thigh. "Maybe if you braid them or something, make the strips stronger?"

I nodded. "Okay." I didn't know how to braid, and my hands were sticky with blood, so I twisted them together and made a thicker rope.

Oona chirped from the backpack, which hung from Deacon's saddle. It swung a little from her movement. Bak huddled on the ground nearby, watching us.

*Jim save Sam.*

*I'm trying, buddy.*

"I can barely feel his pulse." Charlie pressed harder. "Sam, can you hear me?" she shouted. "Stay with us!"

"He's gonna be fine. We'll get it stopped." I would not give up on him. "You're going to be okay, Sam. Dude, you have to hang on. Just hang on." *Please be okay. Please be okay*, I prayed to anyone who was listening.

The forest came alive around us with a rustle of leaves. My stomach lurched thinking Mathan was back. Then I thought Bak had somehow left without me seeing and was returning. But when I looked up, I saw three tiny green girls wearing dresses made entirely of leaves. They walked toward us, taking tiny footsteps on tinier green feet. They were like living dolls with jet-black hair that brushed the ground behind them. I blinked the sweat out of my eyes.

"Charlie. Tell me you see them."

"I—yes."

The fagen I'd rescued stepped into the open, followed by another, this one taller and with long red hair. A female.

The one with the red hair spoke. "I am called Kira. Let us help your friend?" She sounded like a cartoon chipmunk, only softer. "Our Good Mother has said we might intervene on behalf of our young one called Grono. A life for a life." She waved her small brown arm to indicate the fagen I'd saved from falling over the cliff. The creature bowed to me, the hint of a smile on his face.

I nodded to the fagen. "Grono."

"C—can you save him?" Charlie asked.

"We have leave to try. I fear it may be his one hope," Kira said.

"Please help him," I said.

Kira motioned to Charlie. "You must step away from the one called Sampson."

Charlie nodded and lifted her hands from Sam's leg. The blood pumping from his wound was slower now, but still coming bright red and constant. "You know his name," Charlie said.

"Yes. And yours, Charlotte. And James. We bear witness to all that happens in the forests." She held her hand in the air over Sam's wounded leg. The bleeding stopped. "It is rare that we are called to intercede in the matters of your kind," Kira continued. She turned to the three green girls. "Sellahun veen." The tiny creatures walked over to Sam like they were floating above the forest floor.

"Lisora," the three said in unison to Kira. She smiled. Their musical voices sounded impossibly small, like rainfall and birdsong and delicate wind chimes heard from a distance.

The one in the middle held something wrapped in leaves. The second girl unwrapped the bundle, revealing a lidded stone jar. She placed the lid on the ground and then hopped up on Sam's waist, lying down across him with her arms spread wide. She started whispering.

My heart pounded.

The third girl laid her pointy green chin on Sam's good knee and spread her arms up and down his good leg. She whispered as well. Her words joined with the sound of the other one and conjured thoughts in my mind of campfires and childhood, of warmth and home.

Charlie sighed.

The one holding the jar knelt and placed it next to the foot of Sam's injured leg. She could barely see over the top of Sam's size elevens. Her black, almond-shaped eyes focused on the jar. The sound of the other two was sweet and constant, an earthy forest hymn.

"They're so ... beautiful." Charlie grabbed my hand.

I felt like my heart would burst with all the love I felt at that moment. I threaded my fingers through hers and pulled Charlie to me. She turned and wrapped her arms around my waist. I kissed the top of her head. We watched the girls as they worked on Sam.

"He's going to be okay," I said. And I knew it. Everything in me was assured and calm. The forest people knew what they were doing.

The girl at Sam's foot waved her hands over the jar as if coaxing something from inside it. "Alfundia. Styfus. Lee." She never let her gaze leave the jar.

From inside the stone vessel, a green vine rose. It hovered in the air in front of the tiny green girl. She stepped toward Sam's foot and waved her hands in front of the vine, guiding it to his leg as if she were a snake charmer. The vine touched Sam's sneaker. She made circles in the air with her hands. The vine wound itself around Sam's shoe and then his ankle. It wrapped its way upward, still connected to the endless vine that continued to slither from the jar.

Sam screamed as the vine constricted around the wounds on his thigh. My friend was in agony. I knew it. I could see him writhing on the ground, fighting against the pain. But warmth and good thoughts overwhelmed me. I knew that no harm was going to come to him, or us. When he finally passed out, beads of sweat stood out on his forehead.

The two green girls—one at his waist and one on his good leg—kept weaving their words together, watching the progress of the vine as it wound around his leg. Every time the vine tried to veer up his hips, toward his torso, or to jump to the other leg, their words urged it away, keeping it on his wounded one.

The narrow vine covered every inch from the top of his thigh to the tip of his toe. Not even a hint of his jeans or navy sneaker was visible between the tight green cords. The bleeding had stopped. Standing together at Sam's feet, the green girls said something that made the vine stop winding. It fused itself end to end and hugged itself down tight, so there was no longer a loose part that could grow and reach out. Their singing stopped abruptly, and the mood in the forest felt as if a bucket of cold water had been thrown on us.

"Lisora maloon," the green creatures said in unison. They picked up the stone jar, replaced the lid, and wrapped it back up in the leaves.

All the certainty I'd felt about our safety and Sam's well-being a second ago disappeared.

Kira clapped her hands twice, and a dozen more fagens stepped out of the bushes. They walked over and stood on either side of Sam. I recognized one of them as the other thief who woke me trying to steal our daggers. He smiled and winked at me. He had perfect white teeth. Together they lifted Sam's body off the ground. They didn't seem to mind all the blood that dripped on their hands and stained their rough clothing.

"Your friend called Sampson does not have a wealth of time. The fairy vine will not hold forever. Come now, and we will do what can be done. A life for a life."

Fairy vine. Were the green girls fairies? I watched them walk single file into the trees. The fagens followed in two rows, shoulder to shoulder, carrying Sam between them like pallbearers in some whacked-out funeral procession. Arm outstretched, Kira waited for us, urging us ahead of her.

I didn't like this. A minute ago, I was completely sure they were here to help us, help Sam. But my confidence faded into the forest with the echo of the green girls' song.

Charlie stopped and pulled my arm back. "Wait. Where are they taking Sam?"

A fagen grabbed Deacon's reins. For once, the horse didn't fight.

Kira nodded at the fagen. "The horse cannot follow where we must go. We will make sure he is brought safely to where others from this world dwell. You may bring your bird and your great cat, Bakeneko. We must make haste. Time works against your friend called Sampson."

Mention of Sam got me moving again. I pulled Oona's pack from Deacon's saddle and strung it on, wondering if we were making a mistake.

As Charlie and I followed, the small group wove its way through the forest. They waited for us at a moss-covered boulder nestled into a low hill. The tiny green girls walked right through the stone and disappeared.

The fagens carrying Sam followed them without so much as a pause in their march. The moss swallowed them up like it was a curtain covering a cave, but I could see the solid rock underneath.

Bak watched them disappear into the stone and stopped short.

"Bak, it's okay. They're helping Sam." But I knew he could tell I wasn't sure.

*Bak afraid. Strange people.*

Kira touched Bak's shoulder. "Indeed, we must appear quite strange in the light of day to a creature such as you. You have the right of it, great Bakeneko." Kira smiled at my tiger.

"You can hear him," I said, stunned.

"He is not like other animals of his kind. Much in the way you are not like others of your kind, James." She reached up and touched my shoulder where my mark lay hidden under layers of clothing. Her touch was electric, sending a jolt through me down to my toes.

She knew about me.

"You must maintain physical contact with me as we pass through the toran. Should you let go before we are through, you will be lost forever inside the stone." Kira took my hand. It was soft and warm, like the hand of a toddler.

Charlie wove her fingers through mine. "Don't let go."

"You too," I said. I gripped her hand tight.

Keek kek.

Oona rocked inside the pack against my chest.

Kira reached out for Bak. "Come, allow me to grasp your tail."

He moved away from her. *Bak not go. Bak wait here.*

Kira smiled and shook her head slowly. "Our path drives us forward, dear Bakeneko. We will not be returning to this place." Reaching up, Kira waited for him to lower his tail for her. He backed away again.

Charlie pulled away from me. "Wait, you mean we won't be coming back *here*, right? You mean not to this part of the forest?"

The fagen woman didn't answer. She seemed to be concentrating so hard on Bak that I couldn't tell if she hadn't heard Charlie or if she was ignoring the question. We'd never asked where we were going, actually. How stupid. She said we were walking through a toran, whatever that was. But nothing about our destination. My stomach twisted. The last time I saw the fagen I'd rescued, he'd been hanging by his collar with Mathan's guy, Silver Braid. What if the fairies were working for Eldred?

I swallowed. "Where are we going, Kira?" I fought to keep my voice steady.

She didn't answer me.

*Bak afraid.*

*It's okay, boy ...* I said.

Feeling Kira inside my tiger's mind made me anxious. I couldn't read her thoughts, but being with her inside Bak's head felt as real as standing next to her by the boulder. She looked at me, her face serious, unreadable. I couldn't shake the feeling we were making a mistake.

Then Kira started to sing. Her words rang into Bak's mind as her voice rose. Her song seemed to weave its way around us and through the forest like a blanket of goodness. Calm returned like a welcome breeze. Were we being lured in? Lured into what? No. These people—these creatures—they were *helping* Sam. Repaying me for saving Grono. They were doing us a favor.

I felt Bak relax as his thoughts went back to that day in the Alberta zoo when we first met. The first time I fed him as a newborn cub, and the first time any animal had ever talked back to me. Love swelled inside my tiger's mind. Pure, gigantic love. Every fiber of him lifted with sheer adoration—devotion to me. His love was so complete and unconditional it made my heart ache. He let Kira take his tail.

My own mind went to my father. To my one memory of him with me as a child. I felt the tall grass tickling the backs of my knees in my memory. As it always did. But this time it felt like real life, the present:

*My father looks down at me and smiles, his blue eyes and white teeth framed by dark brows and the hint of a beard. A small scar cuts a white J into the edge of his beard just under the right side of his lip. He takes my hand in his and squeezes gently. He bends over and scoops me into his arms, hugging me to him.*

*"I love you, son. I can't wait to meet the man you've become. I'm so proud of you." His eyes sparkle as he smiles.*

This isn't right. This isn't how my memory goes.

I shook my head, knowing it wasn't real, and yet everything in me yearned for it anyway. Tears welled up in my eyes. I rubbed them on my arm, too afraid to break contact with Kira or with Charlie.

Charlie squeezed my hand and smiled, making the skin on her nose wrinkle. I wanted to know what she was thinking about. I gripped her hand tight as Kira stepped forward. We walked toward the stone, none of us able to resist the pull of Kira's song.

# EIGHTEEN

U nder normal circumstances, walking into the boulder would go against every instinct I had, but here, with Kira, it seemed natural. I was aware that Kira's singing made me feel at ease, and even though I knew the feeling of calm and sureness was some kind of spell she had woven over us, I couldn't bring myself to care. The part of me that would normally pull away and protest was silenced by an overwhelming sense that walking through this boulder—Kira called it a toran—was exactly what I had always wanted to do.

Bak was already through. Kira led me by the hand, pulling me into the stone while Charlie trailed behind me, her grip now full-vise. I expected to feel the moss tickling my face and then the hard rock crushing my nose. Instead, it was like walking through a hologram. The granite didn't disappear, though. I could see it all around me: speckled veins of lighter stone twisting through the dark rock—a rainbow of smoky grays—but without substance. It was like granite air, dark and thick. Smelling of earth and fresh black soil, it filled my senses completely. I couldn't see my hands or Kira or Charlie.

Once through the toran stone, I found myself on the edge of a rock cliff overlooking an enormous underground cavern. The roof of dirt and stone arched smooth overhead, with pale roots poking through from above. The floor was a valley of green. Giant tunnels opened in the walls of the cavern, leading off somewhere deeper into the ground.

"Incredible." Charlie gazed down into the cavern.

Kira was no longer singing and she'd let go of my hand. I kept hold of Charlie's.

A river snaked through the meadow below us. Fagens and tiny green creatures busied themselves, oblivious to us. Some hauled water from the river while others picked fruit from bushes and vines and loaded them into large woven baskets on wooden wheels. Music rang through the air. Voices sang. Flutes and tiny whistles played while little green children—so small they were completely obscured from sight once they ran into the grass—played some kind of a game like hide and seek. As a bird sailed slowly by, a little green boy on its back waved and smiled at us. Kira waved back at him.

"They're singing. Do you hear it?" Charlie leaned into me. "Gosh, I could listen to that forever."

*Bak want to go. Leave bad place.*

"Yeah," I said, wondering what would happen if the music stopped in here.

"Come, we must hurry. Time is everything now." Kira led the way down a narrow stone ledge protruding from the wall. I followed Bak and Charlie. Ahead of us, the fagens carried Sam on their shoulders. The three green girls were far in front, leading the way. Sam wasn't moving.

"Where does the light come from?" I asked. There was no sun down here, and yet the cavern was as bright as if we were in daylight.

"Many plants here create light of their own. And we have some insects that fluoresce, and the fairy flame, of course. Please, you have no time to linger." Kira stepped off the ledge onto a dirt path and hurried behind Sam's body. "Our Good Mother awaits."

We were inside one of the tall tunnels. It curved around to the right, making it impossible to see too far ahead. Vines grew up the walls. Glowing flowers, like drops of water, hung white and blue and pink. The blooms filled the vines and the tunnel with soft light but did nothing to ease the chill from the damp.

Kira didn't slow down. "This way. Come," she urged us on.

The tunnel ended at an archway opening into another cavern. This one was larger than the one where we'd arrived. Moss covered the ground rising upward into a hill so steep I couldn't see the top. All around us, half-buried treasure crusted the land. Gold rings, silver platters, and pieces of armor glinted everywhere. Swords, some with hilts of plain steel and others with gemstones and elaborate designs, stuck out here and there as if they were thrown down during a battle and forgotten. Still more ground was covered with silver and gold eating utensils, mugs, pots, and what looked like diamonds, rubies, and emeralds. Some gems were the size of baseballs.

"Wow." I bent to take a closer look.

"Touch nothing," Kira warned.

I pulled my hand back.

She hurried up a narrow path in the grass, created by years of tiny feet. Bak sidled up next to me.

*Jim leave. Bak leave.*

*Soon, Bak.* I hoped he couldn't feel my doubt.

Guitar music echoed through the room. A soft male voice sang a sad, weary song. It wasn't like the music Kira sang. I couldn't make out the words, but the melody was heavy and mournful.

Kira followed the fagens and the three fairy girls up the hill. "Quickly," she whispered. "Do not speak unless she addresses you first."

We rounded the top of the hill and arrived at an elaborate throne made entirely of tree roots. The roots were still alive— connected through the dirt roof of the cavern presumably to trees growing somewhere above. The roots were braided and bent to form a nest-like chair in which sat a tiny green queen, surrounded on both sides by tiny guards with shiny little swords. All of them wore clothing made of leaves. Sparkling jewels and random things of gold and silver decorated the throne. Behind the tiny woman, a tarnished teapot hung in the roots. A branch threaded through the top of the pot and snaked out through the spout, the silver edges had split as the branch had grown thick with rough bark.

The queen wore a golden crown on her head that would have been too small for Charlie to wear as a bracelet. It had tiny rubies and diamonds woven into the gold with sticks and leaves forming a wreath.

Charlie took a step back, her face pale. "I've seen this."

The woman on the throne was no larger than my shoe. Her green skin and black eyes made her almost indistinguishable from the three girls with the stone pot who had saved Sam with their fairy vine. The three bowed to the queen and stepped to the side, waiting.

As we approached, an old man with a guitar stopped playing. His hand froze over the strings, and he shifted on his wooden bench to stare at me. He was human—or maybe Bellenorian—a full-sized man. I wondered if we looked as out of place as he did, a giant among all these miniature creatures. The musician watched us, his shaking mouth set in a thin line, but his eyes betrayed deep sadness as if he might burst into tears. Then he dropped his guitar and pointed at me. He opened his mouth and moaned. Shock or maybe disbelief on his face, he looked at the queen, then stared at me again.

The fagens carrying Sam knelt on the ground before the queen. Sam lay across their shoulders breathing steadily—asleep or passed out—I couldn't tell. At least he wasn't bleeding.

The queen addressed the three green girls. "Bitora falsa?"

They responded in unison, "Magna salinda. Bitora falsa morgala. Lisora maloon." They bowed together.

The queen stood up on her wooden throne. Her bare feet were impossibly small. "James, scholar of the Wales clan. Your place is not here."

Hearing her speak English startled me. Hearing her call me scholar made me shiver.

She went on, "For the life of our young Grono, you have my gratitude. His wish to pay tribute to me with your great sword nearly cost his life. I have given my leave to help your friend Sampson. However, there is no place for you here. You will not stay." She glared at the fagen, Grono, who blushed and looked down at his hairy feet.

Her voice was like soft flutes and burbling water. Part of me wished I could curl up at her feet and listen to her talk forever. The other part of me wanted to run the hell away. The sound of tiny voices singing rang through this place, making me feel calm and competing with the silly voice inside me that screamed for escape.

The queen waved a hand in Sam's direction. "Your friend's injury is grave. His wounds are beyond the magic of fagen or fairy. We have summoned a healer from your world who awaits you at this moment. Your friend's life may yet be spared. Before I give you leave, you must agree to my bargain."

I cleared my throat. "Bargain?" I felt my insides go cold.

All eyes turned to me. Kira had said they were allowed to help us because I helped Grono. A life for a life. This made us even. "What bargain?" The music tugged at me from some unseen place, soothing and mellow.

Kira touched my arm. "I am sorry, James, but you must."

I pulled my arm away from her. "What's the bargain?"

"Scholar James, you will acknowledge there is no debt owed to you and your party." The green queen's face, which seemed serene only a moment ago, looked fierce and angry now. "Acknowledge our gift as payment, a life for a life." She looked at Oona, and I felt her eyes blaze into my mind, as if the queen could tap me through my falcon. I shut my eyes and shook it off, forcing myself to concentrate. Wasn't that what Kira said? Her help for my help. What was the big deal with agreeing to that?

"In addition, you swear to be bound forevermore as a protector of our realm."

I steeled myself. "I don't know what that means," I said.

The queen turned and snapped a twig from her throne and held it out for me. I reached for it more out of reflex than anything. "Eldred has taken possession of Shihorren—the Keystone. No one, in any world, is safe while he wields it. You must retrieve Shihorren from him. And should you be called upon to aid our people, you must forever hold true to the bargain you have made this day. Or your friend's life—should he live—and your own, will belong to us forevermore."

*Forever.* I looked at the guitar player. He was crying now and staring at me. I wondered if he ended up on the wrong side of a bargain and got stuck here. I wasn't ready to agree to anything for forever. My brain told my arm to pull back, but my hand reached for the stick, my fingers extending as if they had already made up their own minds to betray me.

"Do you agree, Scholar James?" She offered the twig.

My hand stretched for it. And stopped.

"Sam does not have time," Kira whispered.

*Bak leave this place. Jim leave with Bak. We go now.*

I looked at Charlie. Her cheeks glowed as she smiled and rocked to the music that had grown louder somehow. It was coming from everywhere.

My chest was full to bursting with a sense of righteousness and purpose. What was the big deal? It wasn't like I was planning on doing anything to these people anyway. I nodded my head.

"The words are your bond. Speak the words," the green queen urged, her wicked smile as dark as her black eyes.

"I swear it," I said. "There is no debt owed." I nodded.

"And you will return with Shihorren, the Keystone." She took another step toward me.

"I'll return with the Keystone, Shihorren."

"And you pledge your protection to all from this realm …" she added.

"I pledge my protection."

The twig leapt from the queen's hand and wrapped itself around my fingers. It crawled up over my palm to my wrist where it grew longer. As it circled and curled itself into a knotted cuff, I thought of the vine wrapping itself around Sam's leg so tight it could stop his bleeding. But the bracelet wasn't tight at all. I tried to pull the wooden cuff over my hand. Thorns appeared on the thin branches and stabbed at my skin. Gasping, I let it go.

The little queen sat back down on her throne and lifted a tiny wooden staff. "It is done." With a satisfied smile on her face, she nodded to Kira and the fagens who were still holding Sam. She pointed down the hill, back the way we came. "You may go."

The fagens stood, lifting Sam's body. They marched in their little procession down the path.

Charlie stopped. "Wait. What about Sam? What about the healer?"

I raised my arm with the wooden cuff to the queen. "What is this?"

"Go!" She pointed down the hill. Her eyes flashed.

Kira stepped between us and the queen. "Charlotte, say no more. James, we must leave," Kira whispered as she pushed me forward.

She hurried us through a series of tunnels that grew smaller as we went. Smooth dirt gave way to rocky ground and eventually we had to crawl through earthen tunnels so tight the fagens had to pass Sam's body through.

Glowing green spiders with dozens of legs ran for cover as we passed. A small brown rat with white antlers hissed at Bak from its hole high in the tunnel wall.

Water dripped from the ceiling and seemed to seep up from the ground, forming puddles on the floor. As I crawled, my knees squelched in the mud. Pretty soon we were all soaked through. The fagens stopped at a bend in one tunnel. It looked like the rest of them, a dirt wall with roots sticking out and fat beetles digging in.

"We must hold together again while we depart, " Kira said.

"We're leaving?" Charlie asked. "Where are we going? Why can't we stay? It's so wonderful. The music."

I wanted to be far away from this place so much I could taste it. But I could also feel the pull of the songs. A nostalgic yearning—deep and aching—but for what, I had no idea.

The fagens stepped through the wall with Sam.

Kira turned and took my hand, reaching out with the other. "Bakeneko, your tail."

My tiger slapped his tail into her hand, he was so eager to leave.

I grabbed Charlie by the wrist, afraid she'd let go and try to stay behind.

As we emerged in the forest again, I noticed three things right away. First, it was nighttime. Second, it was raining.

Third, we weren't alone.

# NINETEEN

A woman crouched over a small cook fire, stirring a steaming pot. The smell of onions hung heavy in the air. I became aware of the cavernous feeling in my belly, and couldn't remember the last time we ate. The woman stood up and stepped toward us. Mud and bits of leaves and forest rot clung to her sodden robe.

"Thank the good, I thought you'd never arrive." She pulled her hood back to reveal a smiling face with bright eyes and long sandy hair. "I am Lurine."

Keek kek kek kek. Oona jumped inside my pack, the top of her head tapping against my chin.

Kira walked over and clasped Lurine's hands. They almost looked like mother and daughter with Kira standing barely to the woman's waist. "You look well, dear one. We came as quickly as we could. My Good Mother insisted on speaking to young James." Kira indicated my wrist, wrapped in the wooden cuff. "I regret you were kept waiting."

"Kept waiting?" I asked.

Bak sidled up to me, and I scratched the fur between his ears. He was soaked. I didn't understand. From the time we found Sam until now, it couldn't have been much more than an hour, ninety minutes, max. I figured we'd only been in the underground for maybe half that. "What's the big deal? We didn't take that long getting here," I said.

Charlie slipped her hand into mine. She was shivering. Oona chittered. Her talons snagged the fabric inside the pack against my chest. She'd tear through it soon.

Lurine touched Oona's head, peeking from the pack. "Hello, little Oona. You found him. Good work." She smiled at my bird. "I am sure it did not seem long to you, James. Time moves quite differently in the fairy caves. Or, rather, it hardly moves at all. A fagen came to the Grove seeking a healer for young Sam. I was told to bring a litter to carry your friend because he was so badly injured. I am bound to heed the call of the Good Mother—as you are." She pulled her sleeve back to reveal a wooden cuff like the one now woven onto my own wrist. "One comes when one is called. And I was called more than three weeks ago, right after the full moon. Now the moon is almost full again." She looked up at the overcast night sky. She didn't seem to mind the rain falling on her face.

The moon wasn't visible through the heavy clouds. Could that be possible? I thought of Charlie and me, last night on the hill with the buffalo creatures. The moon was only a bit past full. That was only hours ago.

"Three weeks?" Charlie looked at Kira.

Lurine's voice was kind and soft. "Sam would have been lost to his wounds without the help of the Good Mother. He is alive. Let us keep him that way, yes?" Lurine whistled.

A young girl with a long blonde braid led a horse and wagon over to Sam. The fagens lifted his still body into the wheeled litter and left him there. Then they walked back to the hill. One by one, they disappeared through the wall without a backward glance.

"How does he fare?" Lurine felt Sam's forehead and leaned down to listen to his chest. Her face softened as she listened. Was that relief or resignation? She looked at his leg. "Fairy vine. Was this truly the only way? The poor boy."

"He was near his end," Kira said. "His wound is grave."

"What's wrong with the fairy vine?" Charlie asked.

Lurine nodded at Kira. "His heart is strong. I will do what I can for him." She pulled a blanket over Sam's legs. "Give the Good Mother my regards."

Kira smiled at Charlie and touched my shoulder, my mark. "Be well, scholar." I watched as she disappeared through the hillside and back into the underground world.

Lurine lifted the cooking pot and poured the contents onto the fire. The flames licked out in a puff of pale onion smoke. My stomach growled. She nodded at the blonde girl, who led the horse and Sam's wagon away. Lurine followed behind on the muddy path. "This way."

The going was slow through ankle deep puddles. I fought to keep from losing my boots in the sucking mud. Bak padded behind me. He hadn't left my side since Sam got taken and almost killed.

I walked up next to Lurine. "I'm sorry you had to wait so long for us," I said. "Do you think Sam'll be okay?"

Lurine looked ahead at Sam in the wagon. "He will live. He is young and his heart is strong."

Charlie caught up with us and took my hand. "We're lucky they came to help him."

Lurine glanced at Charlie. "Luck had nothing to do with that, to be sure. The fagens and fairies don't care much for our lives, only their own."

"Then why did they help us?" I asked.

"I imagine that has more to do with you, James, than any good will on the part of Queen Aulsana. As a scholar, you pose a particular problem to them, given what that fiend Eldred has been doing. I imagine the Good Mother from below saw an opportunity when she … found you. She certainly seized the chance." Lurine grabbed my wrist, raising it up to look at my new wooden accessory. "With this bauble, they can be assured you will forever be on their side," she said, fingering the knots in the wood.

"Their *side*? Why would I be against them after they've helped us, helped Sam? And what the hell is so important about being a scholar?"

She arched her eyebrows at me. "Can you truly not know? Damn your mother for shielding you from this."

"Don't talk about my mother." I snatched my arm away.

Lurine stopped walking. "I am sorry. You've got the right of it. I shouldn't have said that about your mother. Truly." She pulled her hands into her sleeves and started walking again. "What do you know about the scholars?"

"Nothing. Never heard of them. Had no idea." I didn't like admitting it to her.

She shook her head. "It has been an age since the last scholars walked in our land. Scholars, when they come into the world, always come as a group of twelve, never more, never less. They are always male, born in families of all kinds. Each bears the mark of Lashte, like your own, and each possesses a certain energetic ability, quite distinct from the others, yet linked."

"Linked?" I asked.

Lurine lifted a low branch and held it for Charlie and me to walk by. "Yes, linked. In that way, I suppose you could say the scholars are like the mages, although there are many more than twelve mages in the world. When a mage is born, she— they are always female—has innate abilities for magic and spell wielding. Each mage has a focus, if you will, an area of expertise. Like potions, spells, foretelling, and herbs, and— physical healing, which is my gift."

"You're a mage, then?" Charlie asked.

She nodded. "I am a Sister of the Grove, yes. By ourselves, our abilities are very useful, yet limited in their way. When brought together, as a collective, each of the mages becomes quite powerful. Some say all-powerful, in a magic-wielding sense. The same can be said of the scholars."

"But why is Eldred after me? What happened to the old scholars?" I asked.

Lurine sighed and glanced sideways at me. "The ancient scholars were the ones who discovered the power of the collective. They formed an order—a brotherhood—and built Castle Dorren in the North. They lived there for centuries together and were renowned for their longevity and wisdom. People came from the farthest lands to be healed and educated by the brothers. One could live among them as a disciple, serving alongside the scholars and learning. Much like our novice girls do with us in the Grove." She pulled her hood back as the rain lightened. "It is considered the highest of honors to be chosen for such a life."

"Sounds boring." I watched Bak prancing through the grass next to the road. Mud covered him.

Lurine tsked. "The scholars were far from boring, I can assure you. They studied the elements and how their ability to manipulate the energy of the material world could be used to help all living beings. They wrote great works that have educated the world. In fact, some of their discoveries laid the foundation for many advancements in the Modern World."

"What happened to them?" Charlie asked.

Lurine shrugged. "No one knows what happened to the ancient scholars. History tells us a group of disciples returned to Castle Dorren from pilgrimage to find the scholars slain. The secret of their demise died with them more than a thousand years ago. Though the castle remains, waiting, I suppose, for the world to bring forth new scholars.

"All of Bellenor thought we'd seen the last of your kind until a boy named Eldred Ward Cathern was born with the mark of Lashte—the mark of the scholar—on his person, here." She pointed to a spot behind her right ear. Exactly where Charlie said it was.

"After him, there were eleven more scholars born over the course of the next quarter century or so."

"And I was the last one? To be born?" I said.

"No, actually, you were eighth or ninth to be born into the world. But you are the last one living—save Eldred, of course."

None of this made sense. "But why is he killing all of them? All of us?"

"We did not know it at the time, but the murders started about fifteen years ago, when you were just a babe. For a time, no one realized the deaths were related. You see, the murders happened years apart and across the distant lands of Bellenor. Then about ten years ago, a mage—one of the Sisters of the Grove—had a vision in which she saw Eldred in the act murdering another scholar. He did certain things to the body, things that connected him to the other deaths. That's when we knew. That's when we sent all the living scholars into hiding. And since you were already on Earth, we asked your clan to stay and protect you, there. I still wish they'd prepared you for the worst ... it was only a matter of time before Eldred found you and attempted the same gruesome acts he did with the others."

The hairs on my neck prickled. "What gruesome acts?"

Lurine grimaced. "The mage saw him dissect the body of another scholar and remove the man's heart from his body when it was still warm."

Charlie gasped. "And then he boiled the blood and collected the drops from the steam, right?" she said.

Lurine stopped walking and gaped at Charlie. "How could you know that?"

"I—I've been seeing things," Charlie said, blushing.

"What else have you seen?" Lurine was all business now.

Charlie pressed up against me, clutching at my hand. "I don't know. Random things, really. Um—one vision was of Eldred attacking us at Sweetwater's, and I saw him afterward, doing that thing with the heart-blood. Then I saw that Sam would get hurt. It's all a jumble really. I don't know. I want them to stop. I can't even sleep." Charlie started to cry.

Lurine turned to me, her blue eyes boring in to mine. "Have you been with her when a vision comes upon her?" she asked.

I nodded. "Yeah, she goes blank, like a trance. She fell off her horse once into the river. The water was freezing, but it didn't even wake her up. And her eyes go green, even the white parts. One time she talked."

"Oh." Lurine's eyebrows shot up. She looked genuinely surprised.

Charlie grabbed Lurine's arm. "What does that mean? What's wrong with me? Is it serious? Can you make it stop?"

"Oh, no, no. Not to worry." Lurine patted Charlie's hand and started walking again. Did she turn away to hide the concern in her face? "I didn't mean to alarm you. We … we didn't know you were a seer. This is unexpected, that is all. Does your family know this about you?"

"A seer? I don't see how they could. It only started the other day, after we crossed the bridge into Bellenor," Charlie said.

Lurine didn't say anything in response to that.

"Why is Eldred killing the scholars?" I asked.

"Only Eldred knows for certain, but I have long wondered if perhaps it has something to do with the power of the collective," Lurine said.

"How do you mean?"

"Some of us believe Eldred has found a way to assume the powers of the collective on his own. By killing the others and taking their heart-blood—as we believe he has been doing—he somehow becomes the collective."

"But why?" Charlie asked.

"What happens when the all the scholars are together?" I said.

"No one knows really, aside from what has been recorded in the histories. Those archives are a chronicle of healing and study of the natural world. Scientific discovery."

Thunder rumbled in the distance, rolling across the sky. The rain fell double time. If Eldred could grow his powers by killing the others, what would my ability give him? Did he think he could use my power to round up an animal army or something? I wondered if he'd be disappointed to learn that I could only tap a couple animals at a time. Well, that was something he'd never find out, for sure. My father would protect us.

We continued on the muddy path until the girl leading the wagon turned onto a cobblestone road near a stream. The stones were light gray, almost blue. Water flowed over the stream's banks, swollen with the heavy rain. Charlie and I followed Lurine, with Bak behind me. We walked behind the horse and wagon carrying Sam. The wooden cart ambled up the path, away from the rushing water.

Oona shifted in my pack. Keek kek kek.

"You know Oona," I said to Lurine.

"Yes. I was … It was I who forged her … made her into your Sending."

Realization buzzed through me. "Then you must know my father."

Lurine nodded. "I do."

We crested the hill. A city spread out across the valley below. From the distance, it looked like something you'd build around a model train set. If they'd had trains during medieval times. A pale stone wall surrounded the city, tall and imposing even from where we stood. In the center of it all stood a castle built of the same faded stone. On one side, a tower had collapsed, and the remains appeared black and sooty as if from a fire.

"It's gigantic," I said.

"Welcome to Marren City, Skystone Castle," Lurine said. "Welcome home."

# TWENTY

Home. The idea of this place being home was both strange and thrilling. Home for us was always somewhere new. Home had always been our caravan of RVs and big rigs rolling into the next small town. Home was the yard behind a maze of old dusty tents and rows of concession stands smelling like spun sugar and hot dogs and funnel cakes. Home was Bak and Cotton and the Dueling Knights of Mysteria. Home was Chef's iced orange juice and Mrs. Mercer's steaming apple cakes. Home was Hollis and Uncle Paul and Mom. And Dan. For the first time, I wondered if they all felt the same way, or if they all had lived in Sweetwater's and longed the whole time for Bellenor. Had this place, with its weird sky and its huge trees and this amazing castle been home for them all along? Was it still?

I had so many things to ask them and wondered if I'd ever get the chance. Like whose decision was it to keep me in the dark about Bellenor, about Eldred, about who I really was. Like what Dan knew that made him give himself up for me. Maybe in the three weeks that flew by this morning in the fairy land, the others had found a way to cross and get here ahead of us, and now they were waiting. Maybe they were thinking about how to apologize to me—to us. Maybe they were wondering how to explain—and how to gain my trust again.

The rain eased to a drizzle. Thick clouds hung low, an oppressive ceiling over the valley that made everything look flat and dreary. Overcast as it was, the sky looked flat and monochrome, almost like the Modern World, almost normal.

"It's not far now," Lurine said. She pulled a glass lantern from the wagon and lit it, waving it back and forth over her head as we walked.

"What's my father like?" I asked.

Lurine gasped and clutched her wrist. "He is an old friend. A good man. You look nothing like him, by the way. What would you like to know?"

Oh, how about everything? Why didn't he ever make contact before now? Did he know that I thought he was dead? I swallowed. "I don't know. Why does he live here? I mean, why wasn't he with us, with his family?"

"Your father does very important work here, in Bellenor. He leads the Science Guild, working to repair the damage caused by the Great Shift."

I stopped walking. "Wait, so the Great Shift really did happen?"

"Indeed. Ages ago. Generations. The scientists have been able to make some measure of progress over the years to repair our connection. Now, at least, it appears they've stopped us from drifting. I don't pretend to understand it all. But I do know that everything depends on his success. I'm sure your father wanted to be with you. I do know that he misses you very much."

*Misses me.* Present tense. Could it be? I was afraid to admit how badly I wanted it to be true. I reached behind me for Charlie's hand and brushed against Bak instead. I turned to find her, but she wasn't there. "Charlie?"

She stood on the path behind us, at the top of the hill, transfixed. I couldn't see her face, but I knew her eyes had gone green again. I ran back to her.

"Is this what's been happening? Her visions?" Lurine hurried after me.

I nodded. "She freezes and blanks out. And her eyes …" Her eyes were the freakiest part. They didn't look like eyes anymore. I shuddered.

"Help me." Lurine took Charlie's arm over her shoulder. I took her other arm and we carried her to the wagon. I closed Charlie's eyes and laid her next to Sam. Looking at them side-by-side like that, they almost looked dead. I pushed the thought away and touched Sam's chest. He was breathing. Charlie was fine. We were all fine. We'd made it. After passing through the fairy lands, we had to be weeks ahead of Mathan. And we were together. We would be safe now.

Keek kek kek. Oona spotted something on the road.

A group of men on horseback approached us at a gallop. Soggy banners hung limp on their poles despite the biting wind. When their horses got near Bak, they reared and whinnied.

"By the good, a tiger!" The man in front drew his sword.

Bak hissed, making the horses rear again, their front legs kicking the air.

*No Bak, get behind me.*

*Bad men hurt Sam. Bad men not hurt Jim.*

"Put away your steel, man!" A second man dismounted and bowed to Lurine. "It's Sister Lurine."

"Lord Cranston," Lurine said, nodding at the man. "The beast is no threat to you and your men, I assure you."

"Sister Lurine, I didn't know you in those robes," Lord Cranston said. "Your pardon, please.

"Aye, I'm sure I look a sight. Please, dispatch a man to summon the sisters. We have two injured children with us."

Cranston sent a man off, his horse racing back on the dirt track lining the cobbled road toward the city.

"We've been keeping watch for you. King Jonus's orders. We expected you to return weeks ago. He'll be glad to know you've arrived safely." He mounted his horse and reached his hand down to Lurine. "Care to ride the rest of the way?" Grabbing hold, she let him swing her into the saddle behind him.

Nobody offered me a ride. "I'll walk, thanks."

"This one has a mouth on him, then," Lord Cranston said. He spun his horse and looked me up and down as if I were some sewer rat.

"Let him be," Lurine said.

Lord Cranston glared at me as he urged his horse to walk ahead of the wagon. Several of the guards moved behind me, careful to keep their horses away from Bak. The two with the wet banners led the way.

The city wall had to be three stories tall. Its heavy iron gate rose as we approached. Inside the gate, a group of women in flowing white robes met us. Lurine dismounted and walked over to Sam and Charlie in the cart. The sisters gathered around her. "Tend to the boy at once. Make sure to tell Sister Manda that his leg is wrapped in fairy vine, and she must take the proper precautions before removing it." She turned to another woman. "Bring the young lady to my chambers. See to it that she is changed into dry things. I will be with you very soon."

The blonde girl led the horse away with the sisters walking alongside the wagon. Each of them had a hand on Charlie or Sam. I watched them until the wagon was swallowed up by the crowd of guards surrounding us. They wore thick leather armor and light blue cloaks. Swords hung from their belts, sheathed in leather scabbards. For a moment I felt like I was back in the yard at Sweetwater's getting ready to do battle with Sam. But these guys weren't in costume. And not one of them smiled.

"Take us to the king," Lurine said. "His Grace will want to see his grandson straight away."

"His grandson?" Cranston looked at me.

"Grandson?" I said.

"Aye, this is young James Wales, Lord Vernius' second son," she said.

Cranston dismounted and knelt before me. "Forgive me. I didn't know you. Your pardon, please, my lord."

I gaped at him on his knees in front of me. "It—it's fine. Don't worry about it." The King's grandson? No way.

Keek kek.

Inside the wall, the streets were pretty empty. We passed a few shops and houses with windows dark and shuttered. A few people were out, setting up for the day, I supposed. On the way to the castle, we crossed two bridges with dark water rippling below.

"The king is my grandfather?" I asked Lurine.

"Yes, and I should be calling you 'my lord'. Quite. But don't worry, you are twenty-first—no, you are twentieth in line for the throne."

"Please, don't call me that."

"What? My lord? Fine. James, then." She said my name like she was trying it on for the first time. Lingering over it. "If you wish, but only when we are not in the company of others … my lord." She smiled.

Another wall, lower than the one that encircled the city surrounded the castle. Towers stood tall and imposing, their pointed turrets like witches' hats which seemed to stretch upward as I got closer to them. Pale flags way up on top touched the overcast sky. The burned tower seemed wilted, like melted wax. The tang of charcoal and burnt wood clung to everything.

"Eldred's handiwork," Lurine said, eyeing the tower.

I tried to imagine what force would be able to burn a tower made of stone.

A wide wooden drawbridge lay open across a moat. At the gates, guards stood with swords on their belts and double-sided long axes in their hands. They were dressed like our escorts—in brown leather and blue cloaks. They didn't even glance at us as we passed.

A group of boys hurried out to meet us. They circled around Bak, who crouched and let them pet him while we passed.

Lurine stopped me once we crossed the bridge. "I must tend to Sam and Charlie. I will send for you later," she said. "Good luck in there. Remember, your father is as nervous as you are, my lord. James." She squeezed my arm, smiled, and was gone.

My father.

I followed Cranston and his men up a flight of stone steps and into a great hall. Tapestries as large as some of Sweetwater's tents hung on the walls. A crackling fire filled a stone fireplace so big, I bet Hollis could have stood up inside it. In front of the fire sat an empty throne on a raised platform. It was made of multi-colored wood, braided and twisted in the shape of a chair. It reminded me of the nest-throne of the fairy queen. Sky-blue banners hung from the ceiling. Below the throne platform stood a long wooden table with seating for at least twenty. Every seat was taken, and even more men and women stood behind it.

"By the good, you've made it," a man at the table said. He pushed his chair out behind him as he stood.

Cranston and each of his men got down on one knee and bowed.

The king wore a small gold crown. I searched his face, trying to find some kind of resemblance to my family—to me. He had pale blue eyes and a sharp thin nose. His white hair was close cropped. His beard hid the rest of his facial features. Was this my grandfather? He was a complete stranger.

Cranston nudged me. "Kneel before your king."

I was the only one of our group still standing. I got down on my knee.

*Bak, down.*

My tiger crouched next to me, causing the people at the front of the room to laugh. Oona chittered in my pack. Looking at the floor, I wiped my palms on my jeans.

Boots on stone, coming my way. "Rise, rise, everyone, please."

*Bak, you can get up, boy.*

"We've heard much of your tiger. You have trained him very well. What do you call him? Block, Brock …?"

"Bak," I said.

"Your Highness," Cranston whispered at me.

"Bak, Your Highness," I said. I felt the heat rising in my face.

"Bak, yes. Of course." The king stood next to my tiger, his hand out. "May I?"

"Yes, sir. He likes it if you get between his ears." More laughter from the front of the room.

"Leave us," the king said to the people at the table.

They stopped laughing and filed out a side door while Cranston and his men went back out the way we'd come.

Oona went crazy in my pack, chittering and bouncing, her head bobbing.

Keek keek keek keek.

*Settle down, girl. You're going to hurt your wing.*

"Hello, Oona," the king touched the top of her head. Then he nodded back toward the table, and I realized there was one man who'd stayed behind. "Someone has been waiting for you." The king smiled and then left through the side door.

I blinked. My father. He looked older than I remembered. His hair was gray at the temples. But the familiar scar still cut a pale J into the edge of his beard, under the right side of his lip. It was surreal seeing him there. I'd played the scene over and over in my head forever. My one memory of him. The field. The tall grass tickling my legs. His smile. His words. *Look there, son.* I realized now that a part of me had always wondered if he was real or if I'd imagined him after all. If I hadn't recognized him from my memory, his eyes would have given him away. They were dark blue and familiar. Dan's eyes.

He stood. "Son," he said, his hands at his sides.

My father's voice was exactly as I remembered.

# TWENTY-ONE

My father walked around the table and pulled out a chair for me. He sat in the one next to it. "It is … very good to see you," he said.

Oona shrieked and began tearing at the pack with her beak.

I touched her head. "Settle down. You must be excited to see him, too."

"It has been quite a long time, son."

I nodded. I didn't know what to say. "I remember you." I felt shy. My voice sounded like it was coming from someone else. Outside of me.

You do? How curious. What do you remember?"

I swallowed. "We were standing in a field. You were showing me something. Holding my hand. Telling me to look where you were pointing."

"You must have been very small," my father said, he tilted his head as if trying to remember.

"Yeah. I've tried forever to remember what you were pointing at, but I can't. It's always the same, though. You tell me to look, and I turn to follow where you're pointing, and that's it. Nothing." I felt stupid telling him my memory. Maybe it wasn't even real. But I remembered his face, his voice.

He smiled. "Well, now. I do remember."

"You do?" Every muscle in my body went taut. I felt like I might snap if I moved.

"Aye, it must have been right before you left for the Modern World. We were in the foothills outside of the city called Denver. Do you know a place there called Lookout Mountain?" he asked.

I nodded. "Sweetwater's always stops there. The fairgrounds entrance has this crazy sculpture of a wild horse." I could picture it perfectly. If you stood at the right spot and looked at the statue from a certain angle, the horse appeared to be jumping over Lookout Mountain. We'd ridden our motorcycles up to the top a hundred times. From there, the view was unobstructed all the way across the eastern plains to the horizon. It's so completely wide open, I used to imagine I could fly up even higher and see the curve of the earth. Funny to think I could do that now, with Oona.

"That's right." My father stood up behind me. He put his hands on my shoulders and squeezed. The tension in me melted away.

"Well, when you climb to the top of Lookout Mountain, there is a shrine and a park," he said.

"I know it," I said.

He walked around the table. His profile reminded me of my brother. Dan looked like him. *Looked*. Past tense. How was I going to tell my father about Dan? I swallowed hard. I didn't want to be the one to break it to him. I had to keep telling myself that I was actually here. My father was actually alive and this conversation was real. This wasn't a memory from years ago. It wasn't a dream. My father was alive.

"Up in the park beyond the shrine is a crossing stone, a bridge marker. I was showing you the way home, son," my father said.

My chest tightened. Bak pressed up against me. I stroked the fur on his back.

*Jim sad.*

*I'm okay, Bak.*

My father continued, "Of course, now I remember it all. As clear as yesterday. I told you that I would always be here, waiting for you. That if you wanted for anything, anything at all—you need only find the crossing stone and come back to Marren. Back to me, my son." He squatted next to my chair, looking up at me. "I've been waiting a very long time for this day, James. Welcome home."

He touched my shoulder, tentative.

I couldn't help myself—I grabbed him and hugged him hard. Tears fell hot on my cheeks, and I didn't care if he thought I was a wimp for crying.

"All this time. I thought you were dead," I mumbled into his shoulder.

"Oh, son, no. I am very much alive and so very glad you're home."

Oona bumped against my chest, squashed between us. I'd forgotten she was there.

My father felt her too. "And who is this?" He looked at Oona, peeking out of my pack. He reached to touch her and pulled back. "May I?"

"Of—Of course," I said, surprised he thought he had to ask.

He moved his hand closer and Oona nipped at his finger, hard. She cut him.

He pulled back and sucked the blood.

"Whoa. Wow, I'm sorry. She's injured. Her wing," I said, reaching for my bird—my father's bird—and pulling her from the pack and placing her on the table.

*What was that about, Oona?*

She keeked and bobbed her head.

"Will you want her back? Now that I'm—here?" I couldn't bring myself to say that I was home.

Keek kek kek. Oona watched me and hopped back and forth on her feet.

"Would I?" My father arched his eyebrows at me. "No. No, thank you, son. She is yours."

I extended her wing to show the hole where the arrow had struck. "It's a clean wound. I don't think any bones are broken."

Keek kek.

My father snapped his fingers, and a guard stepped out of the shadows behind the throne. I hadn't realized anyone else was here.

"My lord?" the guard said.

"Take the bird away, my father motioned to Oona. "To the aviary. See that the master tends to her wing."

"Right away, my lord." The guard laid his arm out in front of Oona and waited for her to grab hold of his leather sleeve. She wouldn't go. I lifted her onto his arm.

*What's gotten into you, girl?*

He walked out through the side door holding Oona against his chest. She kept her eyes on me the whole time.

*It'll be okay, Oona. You'll be flying soon.*

She shrieked as she moved out of sight.

"Where is everyone?" my father asked. "We were told there were only three of you with Lurine. We expected the lot of you. What happened?"

"Then they haven't returned yet?" I asked.

He shook his head.

I told him about the attack on Sweetwater's. Everything I could remember from the first time I saw Oona. How Hollis disappeared and how Charlie was knocked out by the lightning weapon. How it must have been Mathan tracking Oona that brought them to Sweetwater's in the first place. The whole time my father paced the floor, nodding and listening. I told him how mom had been held at knifepoint and how Eldred had called for me to come out and show myself.

My father stopped. "Eldred was there? Himself?" he asked.

I nodded. "When Dan came out of hiding, Mom totally freaked. She cried for Eldred to let her go and for Dan to run.

The whole time she was mind-tapping me, telling me to stay hidden." I watched it all unfold again in my head. My mother's screams filled my ears. Everyone in the cages was shouting and crying. I could taste the black smoke billowing through the air as the tents burned. "Then Eldred." I cleared my throat. "Eldred ... He kil—he did it with his sword."

"Oh, James! That must have been terrible to see." My father knelt next to me, his hand on my knee.

I nodded and wiped my nose on my sleeve. My cloak was still wet from the rain. "I didn't think he would really do it. I don't think anyone really believed he would. I mean, it didn't make any sense. It happened so fast. And Mom was screaming. But I don't think it hurt, actually." In my head, I watched Dan fall to his knees, touching the point of the sword poking out of his chest as if he really didn't believe it either.

"A quick death can be a blessing, in its way," my father said.

Closing my eyes, I watched Dan fall face first on the gravel, his blue eyes staring. All the blood. "I can't believe it. I mean, I watched it with my own eyes, and I can't believe that Dan's dead."

My father stood. "Dan?" He seemed confused.

"Wait, wh—who did you think I was talking about?"

"Forgive me. It's all quite a shock. You were saying? You are sure it was Eldred?"

"Yeah." As if I could have been mistaken. I'll never be able to get those images out of my head.

He paced again. "That is not ... is not ..." He turned to look at me and stopped. He took a deep breath. "I thought—

yes, I thought you were talking about your mother. I thought that your mother had been killed."

He said it like he was talking about someone else's dog instead of his wife. My insides clenched.

I watched him pace the room again. "As far as I know, Mom's still alive. Charlie saw it."

"Then we shall rescue her."

"Eldred traveled without a bridge. He cut a hole in the sky. Ripped it right open and disappeared through it. Took Mom and Dan with him. Charlie said later, when Eldred did this thing with Dan's ... with Dan's heart, he knew that he had the wrong kid. He knew Dan had tricked him. But we were long gone by then." My tongue felt too big for my mouth. I tried to swallow.

Was my father even listening anymore? He paced back and forth, talking to himself. "No. Not like this. Not like this," he kept repeating. He walked to the side table, shuffling papers as if he could change the past if he found the one he needed.

I sat up in my chair. "I'm going to get Mom back. Charlie thinks she's being held in a dungeon at Eldred's castle."

"This can't be. It's not ... Curse the depths! He'll lose his head for this!" My father grabbed the hair at his temples. He searched the table again, frantic, swearing. He threw a book at the wall, his anguished cry echoing down the stone hallway. The book tore apart, and the pages fell like feathers at his feet as he stormed out through the double doors.

*Man angry at Jim?*

*I don't know. Don't think so, buddy.*

I didn't know what to think. Unsure what to do, I sat by myself for a while until the king came back in.

"You've been through an ordeal getting here." He sat in the chair next to me. "I'm sure you're hungry and would like a bath, perhaps?"

"Is he … is my father alright?" Looking at him, I couldn't say "Grandfather."

"This has been very trying for him, this business with the Keystone. There is so much at stake. And now to have you caught up in all of it … Your father has not been himself in quite some time."

"I want to get my mom back," I said. And deal with Eldred, I thought.

The king nodded. "We will find your mother. Try not to worry. Eldred has many talents, but a warrior? He is not. When he set his men to Marren City, it was an unconventional attack. We couldn't understand it. His men set fires along the city walls and flung pots of darkfire all over town. Tower Gate was burned to ash, yet there was no advance, no army waiting to strike. It was not how a warrior—a man of strategy—would have staged an attack on this city. Of course, later we realized it was a diversion, a trick.

An older woman in a apron and cap came to the side door, carrying a tray with a pitcher and glasses and a plate of little pies. The king waved her in. She laid out china cups and plates for us, then bowed and left the room. My mouth watered at the smell of food.

The king continued, "While everyone was dealing with the fires, it seems Eldred slipped right through our guards and into the Grove. Your father insists Eldred must have thought we were hiding *you* there. The Grove is beyond the reach of most people. We don't know how he knew to find it, let alone get in. It is protected by the old magic." The king walked over to another table near the wall. "While he was there, Eldred stole this." The king searched through the papers on his table until he found the one he wanted. He walked back and handed it to me.

It was a drawing of what a looked like a short sword made from four crystals in red, green, blue, and white with rainbows shining through them like prisms. A fifth sketch showed how they fit together to create the sword. These were the images engraved on all of Hollis' blades.

The clear, white crystal formed the blade, and the other three formed the pommel, hilt, and hand guard. "What is it?" I asked, reaching for a pie and trying not to shove the whole thing in my mouth. It was still warm.

"This is the Keystone. It is what makes travel between the worlds possible, anymore. There are four keys in the stone, the diamond, emerald, sapphire, and the ruby. The three colored stones have been in the Grove since the time the ancient scholars placed them there. The scholars kept the diamond stone, the location of which was lost when they perished. These stones serve to fortify the connection between us and the Modern World. The Keystone is the only thing keeping Bellenor— and all the worlds connected to us, for that matter—from drifting into nothingness."

*All the worlds?* "How do you mean?" I asked.

He waved me over to the table near the window. "Look, here."

The table was covered with books and loose pages of maps and diagrams, some of them annotated in weird languages and characters that looked like code.

He moved a sheet to the top of the pile. It showed a spiral with circles strung along like a pearl necklace. "This is a map of the known worlds." He pointed to the circle in the center of the spiral. "This is the Modern World, where you've been living for the past dozen or so years. It acts like an anchor, holding the rest of the worlds together." He slid his finger to the next circle on the chain. "And this is Bellenor." He pointed to the next few circles. We are all connected, or, I should say, we were once all connected. Until the Great Shift closed the worlds off from one another. We really can't be sure."

I tried to get my head around it. "What happened with the shift?"

"The Great Shift. We don't know exactly what caused it, but hundreds of years ago, something caused a cataclysmic disruption—a shift—in the energy that keeps our worlds aligned and connected to the Modern World.

"The ancient scholars sensed it was energetic in nature, and they used their ability to harness similar energy and created the Keystone—a very powerful vessel that helped correct some of the damage caused by the shift. It works to keep the crossings connected. It is the one thing that keeps us from drifting away entirely."

"What? You mean Bellenor is going to like ... sail off into space?"

He nodded. "Something like that. Or collide with one of these other worlds as happened with Sorcallarant." He pointed to another circle on the map. "We survived that event, but only because our world is so much larger. We don't really know what could happen." The king walked back to the table and poured the contents of the pitcher into our cups.

I sat and sipped my tea and let the steam tickle my nose.

"But we *are* certain Eldred has placed us in imminent danger by removing the Keystone from Bellenor."

"Why is that dangerous?

The king frowned. "We depend on our link to the Modern World for our connection to the sun and moon rhythms, to the seasons, and the tides." He waved his fingers through the air. "To life itself."

I nodded.

"The scholars created the four keys of the Keystone, three of which have been kept safely hidden in the Grove here in Marren since that time—more than a thousand years. The fourth key—the diamond key—they kept with them, we assume at castle Dorren. When the last of them died, its location was lost. But even if we knew where it was, we could never retrieve it."

"But why?" I asked.

"Because only a scholar may lay hands on the Keystone. The energy channeled by the keys on their own is quite strong. Many have died trying to wield them. That is why your father called for you to return to us. We suspect Eldred has found the lost diamond key. And now he has stolen the three other keys that make up the Keystone. As long as Eldred has the

Keystone, we're all in danger. Should he leave Bellenor with all four of the keys, our world—all the worlds—could start to drift again until we are lost. Eldred must be stopped and the Keystone returned to the Grove. And you, James, are the only one left whom we can trust to make that happen."

The magnitude of it awed me. "Is that why you sent Oona for me? So I can save Bellenor? Even though Eldred wants to kill me?"

*Bak keep Jim safe.*

I reached down and touched my tiger's head. *Thanks, buddy.*

The king grimaced. "Yes and no. But if we hadn't brought you here, you'd probably already be dead. You see, someone revealed your location to Eldred. Our only way to protect you now is to help you stop him."

"But what about the thing with the powers, the collective?" My hands shook.

"How did you know about that?" the king asked, taking another sip.

"Lurine talked about it. She had a theory about why Eldred was after me."

"Of course. Well, we believe she is correct. We know that when brought together, those with certain abilities, like the scholars, grow more powerful. We suspect Eldred has found a way to harness that power—the collective—on his own."

I took a sip to stop my cup from clanking on the saucer. "My friend, Charlie, she saw that. But how did you find out?"

"It seems your father had a man in Eldred's camp for some time. He was discovered several months ago while sending a message to your father. The man was killed, but not before he sent his message that Eldred had already found the other scholars and had acquired eleven of the twelve abilities by murdering them. Now that you're here, the winds have changed in our favor. But if he manages to ... obtain the final power of the collective from you and retain the Keystone, then there is no hope. Not for anyone in any world, modern or otherwise." He slammed his empty cup on the tray, and it rang like a death knell.

# TWENTY-TWO

My father stormed back into the room, carrying a wide sheet of paper scrolled under his arm. He smelled of rain and the outdoors. I lifted my cup as he unrolled a large map and spread it out on the table before us.

He pointed to a spot in the center, at a pale blue castle in the area marked Marren Lands. "This is Skystone Castle, Marren City, where we are. Eldred is here, with your mother." He moved his hand to the very top of the map where another castle was drawn in dark green. "Castle Dorren. My men are making ready. We leave at dawn."

I felt my shoulders relax. "Thank God."

A guard stepped into the threshold. "Sister Bette to see you, Your Grace."

The king nodded and the guard stepped aside to reveal a stout woman with curly blonde hair. She stood with her plump hands clasped together at her waist.

Sister Bette bowed. "Sister Lurine has sent me, Your Grace. The boy, Sam, is awake. He asks for James."

Sam was awake! I pushed my chair back and stood. "Come on, Bak. Let's go." I couldn't wait to see Sam.

My father pulled me aside. "James, there is something else we should talk about. Something important. My men and I can rescue your mother. But Eldred … It must be you. By your hand. Are you prepared to take Eldred's life for what he's done? It is not an easy thing—to kill a man."

I'd been imagining Eldred's death since California and Sweetwater's, but in a general way. And after what happened with Mathan, the way I freaked out thinking I'd killed him myself, I wasn't so sure. I wondered if—when it was really down to him or me—if I could actually do it. Could I really go after someone with the intent to kill them? We weren't talking self defense. But this was bigger than that. Bigger than me. Eldred could potentially kill everyone. Could I kill one person to save billions? "I think so."

My father moved the map aside. "We aren't certain exactly how it works. We do know that Eldred has discovered some method by which he can take on whatever abilities the scholars he kills possess."

I nodded. "It's the blood," I said. I explained how, in Charlie's vision, she'd watched Eldred boiling the blood and saving the drops in the jar he wore around his neck. I didn't mention that it was Dan's heart he was draining.

"And she saw all this?" my father asked. "How curious. Son, you are the only chance we have at stopping Eldred. When he is dead—by your hand—the chain of the collective will be broken, and the Keystone can be returned safely to us."

I followed Sister Bette down the stairs and out into a courtyard. Bak loped ahead of us, happy to be outside again. We followed a path, the cobbles cut from pale blue stone. Everything here was built of this blue stone. I thought of the map my father had shown me with the blue castle and the green one where he said Eldred was.

"Excuse me, Sister? Do you know anything about Castle Dorren?"

"Aye, Castle Dorren is in the north. It was built as a shrine to knowledge and learning, not for defense in battle. The castle itself is tall and slender, looks almost delicate. The stones shine in the sun, when the sun chooses to shine up there, that is. Dreary weather in the north country."

"Do you know what color it is? The castle?" I looked down at my feet and the stones weaving a path through the garden. Like the walls and the castle, everywhere I looked was this light blue stone. Sky blue. Skystone.

"Oh, aye. Most of the stone there comes from the ground in the most striking shade of green. Emerald, almost, but not a jewel, you see. It is stone, to be sure. Everything thereabout is built from it. Quite lovely."

I thought about Charlie's vision and how she'd described the black stone castle where Eldred held my mom. With a start, I realized they were going to the wrong place. I had to tell my father.

"Wait here. I'll be right back. I have to tell them …" I ran through the garden and across the courtyard to the stairs. At the castle door, I passed the guard who waved me through. I took the stairs two at a time and had to stop and catch my breath before I barged back in to tell my dad that Mom wasn't at Dorren. I bet he would know where Eldred was hiding her based on Charlie's description. When I heard my father's voice echo out into the hall, I stopped.

"You think it matters?" he said.

A woman responded, her voice low. "Of course it matters. Don't be a fool. If it doesn't matter now, it will in the near future. He will learn the truth."

I crept closer to the door. It was open partway. I couldn't see who was in there talking with my father.

"Do not chastise me. He seemed satisfied," my father said.

"Well, you are his father, Vernius Wales. Of course he was satisfied. Do as you will. I care not. My concern is for the boy once Eldred is dead. We will need him and he will need our guidance. Are you sure he said Eldred escaped by slicing open the sky? If that is the truth, it confirms he has the Keystone," the woman said.

With my heart pounding in my chest, I leaned closer.

"My duty was to get the boy back here, and he is back. It did not go as planned—I grant you that. But he is here now. I should be released of my vow.

"That was not all you promised. You were fool enough to pledge the boy, the Keystone *and* the power to wield it." The woman's voice was like a hiss.

"Ow! Damn you, woman!" my father growled. "Very well. I shall continue as planned. I will even help the boy rescue his damned mother, though as far as I'm concerned she can rot."

"You can't bring his mother back here, she'll know."

"I said I'd help rescue her. I don't plan on being successful. Once James relieves Eldred of his life *and* the Keystone, as promised, I shall be free of them all.

"Agreed," the woman said.

My father's words—the cheating bastard—were like a kick in the gut. They were using me. I steadied myself against the wall. I had to think. I had to get out of here. I had to go get the guys and tell them. We had to leave Marren.

Running down the stairs, I dried my eyes with my sleeve. I found Sister Bette in the garden, waiting. Bak had rolled onto his back and the Sister was scratching his belly, laughing quietly.

"There you are. Shall we go find your friends?" Sister Bette said.

*Something wrong with Jim?* Bak rolled to his feet and sidled up to me.

"Yeah," I said.

# TWENTY-THREE

How could I have been so stupid? It was all an act and I fell for it. I totally fell for it. I'd been so caught up in having my father back that it made me blind. I thought about all the times my mom had cried over my dad. I didn't get it. Didn't she know he hated her?

This couldn't be happening.

Bak and I followed Sister Bette across the courtyard and through a winding flower garden. At a stone wall, the path hit a dead end. The sister produced an iron key from the folds of her gown and touched her forehead with her fingertips. As she waved the key in front of the wall, a keyhole materialized in the blue stone. She inserted the key and it turned with a heavy thunk. The door opened to reveal a narrow dirt path curving into the forest. The air felt instantly tight, like something pressing on my chest. Like when the mist bridge formed in California.

"This way." Sister Bette walked through the gate.

The path wound through the trees and continued deeper into the forest. I tripped over my boots trying to see the tops of the trees, but Sister Bette didn't slow down. If the trees in Bellenor looked ancient, then the ones here were primeval. They were so tall I couldn't follow the trunks all the way to the top. My boots sank into cushy moss and a carpet of moist, dead leaves. We emerged from the forest into a meadow and the sun beat down on my back, warming me. I hadn't realized how cold I was.

In the distance, a cluster of small wooden houses with sloped roofs sat on a hill. Sister Bette walked toward them. "Welcome to the Sisters' Grove of Marren."

Everyone we passed was female. And they all wore light-colored robes. Sister Bette kept on walking until she reached a small house with a plain wooden door. She pulled a cord and a bell rang softly from inside.

Another sister opened the door and her eyes went wide when she saw Bak.

"Aye, the big cat takes the breath away at first." Sister Bette smiled at the woman. "Greetings Marrie. Where is Sister Lurine?"

"I left her in the herb garden with Sister Clary. They are harvesting sweet linchkins for the boy's wounds. Shall I fetch her?"

"No, thank you, sister," Bette said. "I've got to bring Bak to the butcher at the castle. I'll find her on my way."

Sister Bette touched my hand as she stepped into the house. "Come, Charlotte is eager to see you."

The house was clean and very plain—white walls and unfinished wood furniture worn smooth with use. I followed Sister Bette through the house and into a back yard. Charlie sat on a blanket in the sun. She wore a long white dress, and her wet hair hung loose down her back. Her eyes were closed and her face turned toward the sun. She looked so relaxed.

I stopped a few steps from her blanket, not wanting to disturb her. "This place agrees with you."

"Jim!" Charlie jumped up and hugged me. She smelled of sunshine and fresh picked everything. "How did it go? Sister Lurine told me you met your father. Was he nice?"

The last time I saw Charlie she lay in the wagon next to Sam. The two of them looked like corpses heading for burial. Now, she was so awake. So alive. "Uh, yeah," I said, not wanting to say anything in front of the sister.

"I'll leave you two here while I take Bak to the kitchens. Someone will fetch you when Sam is ready. When I return, I'll see to your bath and some new clothes, my lord."

"Thanks," I said.

"Of course." She bowed slightly and turned to Bak. "Come, kitty, let's see if cook has some mutton for you."

*Bak go with nice lady?*

"Go, boy. I'll find you later," I said.

As soon as the sister left, Charlie kissed me. "It feels like I haven't seen you in days."

"I know what you mean." I felt like I'd aged ten years in the last hour. The revelation that my father wasn't all that glad to have me home stabbed through every other thought in my mind. "Have you seen him?"

She shook her head. "I wanted to wait for you. They said he's awake. Asking to see you."

"Good. Okay."

Charlie studied my face. "Something's wrong with you. What's happened?"

I wanted to lie. I wanted to tell her how perfect my father was. That he was going to help us find Eldred and get my mom back. But I couldn't do it. I told her everything. About meeting my dad and how kind he was. How he said he'd remembered the time from my memory when I was little and had finally filled in the missing pieces. About Eldred and the Keystone, and the power of the collective. How—now that I was back— we would go together to get Eldred and put an end to all of this. Out of breath, I stopped. No. I stopped because it was hard to admit he'd fooled me.

Charlie studied my face. "And then?"

"And then he said Eldred was at his castle in Dorren. I saw a picture of it on a map and I asked Sister Bette about it. She says the castles in that part of the country are built out of green stone."

"But your mom's in a castle built from black stone. Not green. I'm sure about that," Charlie said.

"I know. I remembered that after I left. So I went back to tell him about your vision and I overheard him talking to someone. A woman." I couldn't look Charlie in the eye. "My father ... he's pretending. He's only pretending to get Mom back. It sounds like he hates her. What he really wants is the Keystone."

I ran my hands through my hair and crouched down. It was hopeless. "Assuming she even *is* still alive, I've got to get to her before my father does."

"Jim, she is alive. I saw it. When I first got here, I was having a vision. The sisters helped me wake from it, and they said they could teach me to control when they come, and what I see, and for how long. But I saw your mom. She's alive. She's being held prisoner in a cell in that black castle. It has three broken towers and huge tall doorways, arched like mushroom tops. She's there, I know it."

"Did your vision give you any clue where the castle is?"

"No, I—I didn't see anything but the castle. I'm sorry," Charlie said.

"There's got to be a way. Maybe my father has a map of it. The table was covered in maps."

Charlie grabbed my arm. "The map! Jim, do you still have the glass map? The one that got us here?"

"Yeah, but it stopped working when we got here. I've checked it a few times. Nothing is blinking."

I dug in my jeans pocket and pulled out the purple marble. As the map engaged, it drew my current surroundings. The *Sisters' Grove of Marren* was in the center, surrounded by a hazy border. The words *Castle Marren* hung at the bottom of the map, which showed the back of the castle and the garden wall. There was no path to the Grove, no secret door shown in the castle wall. There were no blinking dots. No dots at all. The map was useless.

"Maybe you have to do something to it. Tell it what you want, like the coin. Maybe it seems like a one-way map because that's what it was made to do—to get us here," Charlie said.

I hadn't thought about it like that. "What, so you want me to talk to it?"

"Why not? The sister that helped me stop my vision said all the magic and abilities are about energy and intention. You have to *will* it to happen, concentrate."

"I don't know," I said.

"Ask it to find your mom," Charlie said.

I pictured my mom in my head. "Show me where my mom is." I felt stupid.

We watched the orb for some sign of change. Nothing happened.

"Maybe you have to show respect or something, like we did to open the bridge?"

"Maybe," I said.

We got on our knees together, and I cupped the map between us in my hands.

Charlie held my hands in hers. "Picture your mom."

I imagined my mother, her long brown hair pulled back in a ponytail. The collar of her t-shirt wide enough to show the tattoo on her collarbone: the wispy tree with the curling branches seared into my mind's eye.

I closed my eyes and spoke in a whisper, half expecting the air to start humming. "We are humble before this map. We ask you to show us the way to Jane Sweetwater Wales."

"Say it over again, like we did at the bridge," Charlie said. Her hands were warm, warmer than the orb.

"We are humble before this map. We ask you to show us the way to Jane Sweetwater Wales."

Nothing happened.

"I'm sorry. There has to be a way," Charlie said.

This close to her, I could count the flecks of brown in the amber of her eyes.

"You'll find her, Jim. I know it. I believe in you."

I touched my lips to hers. They were soft and full and fit perfectly in mine. God, I could kiss her forever. I shoved the map into my pocket and slid my hand around her back. Her dress was light and I could feel her skin under the fabric, still warm from the sun. She let out a little sigh as I pulled her toward me.

Charlie grabbed my hips. I walked in on my knees until we were touching. It seemed there was nothing between our bodies but our own breath. I put my hand on her cheek and willed time to stop. Right here, in this weird place, surrounded by all these strangers—I knew I was home. I felt it like I'd never felt anything before in my life. This place was foreign to me. But here, with Charlie. She was my home.

Pulling away, Charlie looked into my eyes. She reached her hand up and laid it over mine, cupping her face.

"I love you, Jim," she said. Her eyes were brimming with tears.

"I love you, Charlie," I said. Every single piece of me welled up with the truth of it. We were still on our knees with our foreheads touching when a throat cleared behind us. Charlie and I jumped apart. The sister's face was so red, she might have been holding her breath for three hours.

"I'll take you to the infirmary now, my lord. Sam is asking after you both," she said.

As we followed the sister, Charlie reached for my hand and we wove our fingers together. She bumped my shoulder and smiled.

"I can't wait to see him," I said.

The infirmary was a two story building surrounded by sprawling gardens. We were ushered through an iron gate and down a garden path. We passed a group of sisters gathering fresh picked fruits and vegetables in baskets, and carrying armloads of leafy herbs and bunches of dirt-covered roots. The air smelled of dark loamy soil that dotted their clothing like chocolate sprinkles. Even more women were on their knees, weeding and pruning the rows. The building itself was cool and clean, the sound of our footsteps muffled by the tapestries hanging from every wall.

The sister stopped at a door near the end of the hall on the first floor. "This is Sam's room. You're welcome to visit as long as he is awake. Please keep your voices down." She bowed her head and left, walking silently back along the hallway.

Sunlight poured through the window next to Sam's bed. He was propped up a little, the sheets pulled up to cover his chest. Sam was looking out the window when we came in, seemingly oblivious to the sharp scent, like rubbing alcohol, that hung in the air and burned my eyes. Against the side wall, a table held a pair of stone mortar and pestles and an assortment of clear glass bottles holding liquids in every shade of the rainbow.

Several small jars of pills stood in a row, lined up by someone with an eye for order. I read *willow bark*, and *poppy*, and something called *blood flower* handwritten on white labels in a smooth cursive hand. There were no machines here, nothing beeping, and no tubes or IVs. No television or magazines, nothing plastic like the hospitals back home. Everything here was wood, glass, or metal. It was immaculate.

"Hey, Sam." I stopped in the doorway.

Charlie moved to the foot of his bed. My best friend turned our way, his eyes unfocused, as if he still clung to whatever thought we'd distracted him from.

"Hey," he croaked, sounding parched. He locked eyes with me.

Charlie stepped to the side table and poured him some water. She raised it to his lips. "Here, drink something."

Sam ignored her and turned away. He looked out the window again. Charlie looked at me, uncertain. She placed the glass on the side table.

"Sam? What's wrong?" I stepped closer to his bed.

"They said you gave the okay, Jim." His words came out as a whisper. He looked at me, accusation in his eyes. I didn't understand why he was so upset.

"They said you told them they could wrap that stuff on my leg." He threw his words at me like darts.

I grabbed the foot rail and stared at my hands. "I ... Mathan's guys. They cut you, bad, man. You were bleeding all over the place. They said the vines would save your life."

"You had no right." Sam spat the words through clenched teeth.

"What are you saying? You would have died," I said, sure that he would have done the same for me.

"Look at what you did!" Sam pulled the sheet off his body to reveal the bundle of gauze and bandages left behind where they had amputated his leg.

"Oh, Sam," Charlie's hands flew to her face. She started crying.

Speechless, I stared at the place where Sam's leg should be. I had no idea.

"Look at me," Sam said.

It was hard to look him in the face.

Angry tears streamed from his eyes. "They thought I was you. Those men who took me. They thought I was you. And then, when they realized their mistake, they decided to let me go. I was so relieved. Can you imagine?" He laughed. "I knew they were lying, I could feel it hanging all around them and I was relieved anyway. I was so stupid." Sam's gaze bored into me.

"They tied me to a freaking horse so tight I couldn't even breathe. One minute we're racing down some road that I can't see because they have my freaking head in a bag, and then they stop and the guy with one eye—was that Mathan?—he pulls my hood off and takes one look at me and knows they got the wrong guy. So they put the damned hood back on while they discussed what they should do." Sam blew out his breath. "I thought they were going to just drop me on the road and leave me. But no. Oh, no. They couldn't do *that*." Sam punched the bed. "They wanted you."

"I'm sor—"

"Shut up! Just shut! Up!" Sam gripped the sheets. "The one-eyed guy said you were coming. That he heard the friggen bird getting closer. So they had a little fun first. They pulled off my hood and cut the ropes and told me to run. Told me to tell you they were coming for you. I took one step. One single damn step before they wrapped a sword around my leg. I think I passed out, I don't know. Everything is blank. I don't even know how long I was there. I thought I was dead. I wish I were."

Charlie sobbed. "It's my fault, Sam. I could have—"

But Sam ignored her. He glared at me, unblinking.

"They thought I was you." Sam didn't wipe the tears from his face.

"I—I'm sorry," I didn't know what else to say. I wiped my own tears from my face.

"This is on you, Jim. You did this to me." The look on Sam's face was ice. "I wanted you to see this. And now I want you out."

"But Sam, I—"

"Get out. I never want to see you again."

"Please, let me—"

"Just leave."

# Twenty-Four

I ran through the hospital gardens and out the iron gate before Charlie caught up with me.

"He's upset, Jim. He didn't mean it," she said, huffing for breath. "He's in shock. I mean, can you imagine? My God, it's awful. His poor leg."

I felt her arm around my back, but my head was still in that room with Sam. Of course, now I was full of all the things I could have said to Sam when I was standing there watching him unravel. I should have fought back. Our friendship deserved a fight. But I couldn't do it. Not like this. Not now. Not while Sam was so angry. Not while he was so hurt.

All the things I could have said felt weightless and trivial in the shadow of all he lost. It didn't matter that I didn't choose this. It didn't matter that I had no idea about Eldred until he and his men came after me. It wouldn't mean a thing to Sam that I wished he'd been with me so he could have felt my father's lies, could have warned me. He wouldn't care. He *couldn't* care. He couldn't see it, not now.

Telling him that I wanted nothing more than to be sitting around planning the next duel for the Knights of Mysteria back home would be like rubbing his face in it. Everything was different now. Everything. There weren't going to be any more shows at Sweetwater's. That was gone. Everything was gone. And nothing could ever bring Sam back his leg.

Trying to put myself in his place, I imagined waking up in a strange room to discover someone had cut off my leg. But all I could see was the searing look in Sam's eyes when he told me to leave. Like a wounded animal.

"He trusted us," I said. The words were like dust in my mouth. Trust. What a joke. "We convinced him to come."

Charlie pulled me to stop walking. "We didn't know this would happen to him, Jim. He'll come around. Somewhere inside him, he knows. He loves you. You're his best friend."

I rubbed my eyes. "He can't believe I wanted this for him. That I knew they would take his leg." I leaned in and touched my forehead to hers and closed my eyes. I was in over my head. This was too risky, too much.

"Of course he doesn't believe that. And in time he'll see. Don't worry." Charlie's skin felt warm against mine.

Opening my eyes, I looked down her freckled nose. I pushed my open palms against Charlie's and lined our hands up, finger to finger, bending the tips of mine over hers. Her chipped polish had been removed and her hands were clean and perfect.

I realized how deeply grateful I was that she was here, safe and whole. I saw now how lucky we were to be alive. And even though he couldn't see it now, Sam was lucky, too.

And right then, I knew: I had to do whatever I could to keep them alive. Eldred wasn't looking for Sam or Charlie. He wanted me. Sam was right, this was on me. With Dan's death and my mom missing, and now Sam ... I knew.

I had to do this alone.

"I'm going. I have to find my mom. I'll leave tonight, after dark, before my father goes in the morning."

Charlie pulled away. "Wait. I'll get changed. My clothes are inside."

Half an hour ago, I would have agreed that we should go together. Hell, I wanted her with me. But now, I felt like I was seeing things through different eyes. Realistic eyes. And reality was too dangerous.

I pulled her back. "No. I think you should stay here."

"What? Why? Don't be stupid. I'm coming with you." She looked confused.

I shook my head. "If something happens to you." Pushing her away felt like I was falling apart. Like a sandcastle washing into the sea at high tide. "You should stay here. What if ..."

Now she was angry. "What if what? What if I get hurt?" She pushed me away. "What about you? What if you get hurt? Or doesn't that matter?" Charlie set her chin and looked into my eyes. "I'm going with you. I can help you. I've seen the place where your mom's being kept."

"What about your visions? You don't know what it's like when you get like that. You disappear. You're not even there.

You can't control this. Not yet. Being here—being in the Grove—it's the first time since we crossed into Bellenor that I've seen you calm."

"Please don't do this alone. We'll figure it out," she said.

"What if you leave the Grove and the visions start up again? You could end up like Sam, or worse—you could get killed." I hugged her to me. "I'm sorry. I—I'm … I can't."

Brushing my lips in her hair, I breathed in the smell of her. I wished I could freeze time in this moment. It hit me how I'd never really thought any of this through. I never really pictured it. Pictured me with Eldred. Fighting him. Killing him. Could I really do it? Right now, I wanted to like nothing else. But what if Eldred won? What if I never made it back? What if I never saw Charlie again? And Sam? What would happen to Bak?

"I feel like I've let you down." She looked up at me, tears in her eyes. "Jim, I …"

I took Charlie's face in my hands and kissed her. I forced everything else out of my mind until it was only us, in this moment. Right here and now, Charlie and me. I might never get the chance to kiss her again. I might never again look in her eyes and know real trust. Wherever we are, she is home, and I might never feel that again. "I have to go." I could barely whisper.

"I …" Charlie's face flushed.

I walked away. I didn't stay to hear the rest of what she said. Another second and I would never be able to leave.

I ran back through the Grove, past the little white houses and the sisters busy with whatever errands they were on. I followed the forest path back to the castle. When I got to the wall, the gate appeared and opened for me without a key. I stepped through it and back into the courtyard behind Skystone Castle.

I needed a plan. If I went to the stables for a horse now, someone would tell my father and he'd track me down. Did anyone else know he was up to something? I had to put some time between us. I needed a head start—enough for me to get my mom out of that castle. I wondered again if Mom knew how my father felt about her. I needed to find a map. Then I'd wait until it was dark, take a horse from the stables, and slip away unnoticed. Away from everyone.

I wanted to put Sam and his blame behind me. I had to get Charlie out of my head even though my mouth still pulsed from our kiss.

Crossing the yard on the way to the castle's main gate, I walked past the kitchens and a group of boys playing with wooden swords. Watching them reminded me of Sam, which reminded me of Charlie. I wanted my friends with me. I'd never pictured myself doing this alone. And now even Oona was hurt and unable to fly. I felt like I'd been tossed overboard, left to drift and fend for myself.

With every step I felt my resolve grow stronger. I would not let Dan's death be for nothing. I would not let my mom stay in the hands of that monster. I didn't need my cheating father. I didn't need any more lies. I didn't need them. I didn't need anyone.

*Jim need Bak?* My tiger's words wisped through my head. The feel of him was so natural, I barely noticed he was nearby. The tension left my shoulders in a wash.

*I'll always need you, boy.*

"He's with you, then?" I turned to see Sister Bette leaning out the open upper half of a two-piece door. "He's fed and brushed, such a good cat. Come back later, you grand kitty." She twiddled her fingers at my tiger.

I waved at Sister Bette and kept walking. "Fed and brushed, are you? Hope you don't get spoiled now." I scratched the fur between his ears as we walked.

We followed the city wall, my hands brushing the rough blue stone as it glistened in the afternoon sun. A crowd gathered at the wide gap in the wall that must have been where the Tower Gate stood before Eldred burned it to the ground.

A pair of boys dangled above in harnesses hung from a scaffold on the wall. They had buckets and brushes and scrubbed black soot stains from the upper stones where the flames had licked them. It must have been some fire to bring down a gate that size.

One crew used ropes and pulleys to hoist gigantic logs into place while another team attached the logs to a thick iron grate, nailing them in place with metal spikes the size of my arm. Other logs lay on their sides in a row as a man brushed them with something thick and oily. More of the big logs were being hauled to the wall on immense wagons pulled by teams of red draft horses so huge, a full-grown man could stand underneath one and still not touch its belly.

Bak and I wound our way through the piles of debris littering the yard. I lost sight of my tiger near a stack of new bricks. Splintered wood, broken and twisted pieces of iron, and more logs had been organized into mounds along the wall. One pile contained broken blue bricks that appeared to have melted. I held my hand over them. They were cold to the touch.

"Darkfire," a man said. "Melted some of the stones clean away."

"Darkfire?" I asked.

"Aye, wicked stuff. Burned the iron braces clean off the gate. And where it dripped onto the stone, it did this." He motioned to the melted bricks and pavers.

"Smell's awful," I said. Bak caught up with me and sat down to lick his paws. The man was taken aback at the sight of my tiger.

*Bak's paws all dirty now.*

*Don't worry about it. I'll brush you again, princess.*

"You're him. Beg your pardon, my lord." He took off his hat and tipped his head. "I didn't know you. Though I'll wager you'll be the only one with a tiger in the city." He smiled.

I felt my face go hot. "His name's Bak. And—it's fine. You can ... Stop that, please," I muttered, wishing he would stand up straight and put his hat back on. But it was too late.

One of the other men looked up at me, saw Bak, and his eyebrows shot up into his hat, which he promptly pulled off. He shouted, "Oi!" without taking his eyes off us. You could almost see the progression of the news as it crept through the crowd. Work slowly ceased and faces turned to stare at Bak and me. They all bowed. The silence felt out of place in the previously busy yard. Whispers of "Bak" and "scholar" and "grandson" found my ears, though I had no idea who uttered them. Sweat dripped between my shoulder blades.

Bak took one look at the crowd and, as if on cue, bent into his best Knights of Mysteria bow. With one paw stretched out, and the other folded to his chest, his face looking down and his tail waving overhead, my tiger managed to charm them all. Smiles and laughter moved across their faces. I waved and started walking.

"My lord. Tiger Bak," a guard said with a smile as we passed. He tipped his head in a nod. I rubbed my hands on my shirt. This whole royalty thing was going to take some getting used to. It couldn't make up for my dad's betrayal, but it made me feel a little less alone.

Beyond the wall, the forest had been cut back, leaving a wide-open field between the city and the trees. I followed Bak as he left the road and chased some small animal through the grass. He bounded over the stalks and around a boulder before he lost track of the creature and picked up the scent of another. Bak turned toward the woods, stopped short of the trees and froze. He was looking at something.

"What is it, boy?" I called.

*Someone watching.* Bak skulked into the trees.

*Bak, no! Stay!* "Bak!" I shouted, and ran after him.

It was colder in the shade of the forest. The quick switch from sun to dark made it hard to see. "Bak, where are you?"

Leaves rustled to my right. "Chikoo renda. Renda! Staying back!"

Bak had pinned something against a tree. I crept closer and found a pair of familiar green eyes, wide as saucers, pleading with me over my tiger's head.

"Grono? Is that you?" I asked.

*He has knife.*

"Please." The word sounded small coming from the fagen.

"Let him go, Bak," I said, grabbing some fur and pushing my weight into my tiger's side. I moved him away from the creature.

"He's afraid you're going to hurt me with that," I told Grono, indicating the blade.

His speech was slow, as if the words were new and he was still getting used to forming them. "Not hurting you. Grono gifting. Returning." He held the blade in his open hand. The handle alone was too large to fit in his palm. It was one of Hollis' stolen daggers. Grono bowed his head.

I didn't take it from him.

"Grono insisting." He handed me the leather sheath for the dagger.

I thanked him and took the blade, slipping it into its cover and into my pocket. My finger traced the images of the Keystone etched into the grip.

"You speak my language," I said.

"There being safety now with Scholar James." Grono touched the wooden cuff on my wrist.

Oh, right. That. "What is it with you people? Don't you trust anyone? You were safe with me without this." I waved the cuff at him. "Or was saving your life not enough proof for you?"

"Grono not permitted before. Scholar James forgiving Grono?" he asked.

I didn't want to be angry. "What difference does it make now? It's done," I said. "Don't worry about it."

The fagen smiled.

I followed Bak along a game track, walking deeper into the woods. Grono followed. When Bak took off into the trees, tracking something, I sat down on a fallen log. Grono plopped onto the ground next to me.

"Now what?" I asked the fagen. He smiled back at me, studying my face.

"Scholar James hungry? Grono hunting and feeding?" He stood up and pulled the other of Hollis' daggers from his vest.

"I wondered about that one," I said, looking at the knife.

The fagen batted his eyes. "Grono not resisting. So beautiful." He stroked the hilt and moved it to catch the sun that filtered like liquid through the trees. "Grono keeping this one?"

"Grono keeping." I agreed.

Smiling, he pulled a stone from his pocket and rubbed it down the blade, honing it.

I took the marble map from my pocket and studied it, wondering how to make it work again. No dots blinked. It was like a regular, plain map now, showing Marren City, the Grove on the far side of the castle, and the woods surrounding it all. I willed the map to show where my mother was. Pressing it to my forehead, I prayed for some help.

"Scholar James seeking places?" Grono asked, nodding.

"I need to find my mom. She's a prisoner of Eldred's. He's keeping her in the dungeon of his castle."

"Grono helping!" The creature jumped to his feet. "Grono and Scholar James to Dorren. We going." The fagen tugged at my hand, urging me to go with him.

"No, I don't think my mom is in Dorren. Eldred hid her in a different castle. A black one. With big rounded doors." I moved my arms over my head, making a mushroom shape with both hands as Charlie had described.

Grono dropped his grinding stone and stared at me. "Mitun Sorcallarant?" he asked. "Sorcallarant tritun deesun," he said. "Sorcallarant." He nodded.

"I don't understand. Do you know it? The black castle?" A thrill ran through me. I didn't need a map. I needed a fagen.

Grono threw his hands in the air. "Sorcallarant Hall. Black Castle. Grono naming."

"Sorcallarant Hall? Are you sure?"

"Yes. Yes. Coming," he said, holding out his hand as if I should take it. I didn't. He gave up trying and grunted at me. "Come. Scholar James following." The fagen walked off deeper into the forest.

I followed.

# TWENTY-FIVE

"Eldred doing bad. Taking many lives." Grono ducked under a log that I easily stepped over. We'd been walking for at least an hour though it was hard to tell since I lost a view of the sun in the thick forest.

"He killed my brother," I said. "He took my mother."

Grono stopped and gaped at me, his green eyes impossibly wide. I had to stop short or walk right into him.

"Eldred killing my brother," he said, tapping his hand to his chest.

"I'm sorry to hear that. What was his name?"

"He is Strato." Pride beamed from the fagen as he spoke his brother's name.

"My brother was Dan. Danston," I said, pushing the images of my brother's last moments from my mind. The way he fell … "I'm sorry for Strato."

*Bak sorry, too.*

*Thanks, buddy.*

"Grono sorry for Dan Danston." He held out a hand for me and we shook. The fagen's child-sized hand felt callused with thick hairy knuckles. I wanted to tell him all about my brother and hear about his. But thinking about what I would say, where I would begin, made me realize Dan's story was over. He'd already done everything he would ever do. There wouldn't be any more to tell about him, ever. Guilt squeezed my heart as I kept quiet and followed Grono uphill. Knowing Dan died crushed me. But knowing it was because of me made it that much harder to bear.

As we hiked up a steep incline, the trees gave way to a wall of black rock rising like a skyscraper out of the ground. Grono picked his way over the smaller stones as he climbed to a ridge on the rock wall. He stepped into a narrow crevice barely wide enough for Bak to squeeze through. My face brushed against the stone. The split in the rock led us to a small room formed by the spaces between boulders. Thick grass grew over the mound of the floor. Dappled sunlight fell through the vines growing over the open roof.

"Eldred wielding Shihorren. Cutting through the worlds," the fagen said. He knelt and brushed the grass with his hands.

*Shihorren.* "I watched him do it," I said. The mental picture of Eldred slicing a hole right into the sky was something I'd never forget. Was the world really so fragile? "My grandfather calls it the Keystone. It's how Eldred took my mother."

"Keystone, yes." Grono held up his dagger, showing me the etchings on the grip. "Shihorren. Eldred using Shihorren

Trespassing into fairy lands. Eldred breaking bargain with Good Mother.

*Bargain?* My insides turned to ice.

"Good Mother keeping lady wife of Eldred until he returning with her healing. Lady wife of Eldred very sick." Grono shuffled around the small patch of grass, smoothing the blades and brushing dead leaves away from the center.

I grabbed my cuff. "Eldred made a bargain? What was his bargain?"

The fagen shook his head. "Grono not knowing this."

"Why did she agree? Couldn't your queen kick his wife out? Does your Good Mother answer to Eldred?" I asked. My blood pulsed through my body.

"Eldred wielding the power of all scholars, save one." He tipped his head to indicate that I was the one. "Eldred power greater than toran—you say door—guarding fairy land. Fagens small, fairies smaller. Toran protecting us. Toran keeping us safe."

"But why put his wife in your world?"

"Time. Eldred defeating her death. Eldred using time. Learning the ways of the old ones. Like Scholar James. Eldred learning healing. Lady wife of Eldred not dying in our world as in yours. While lady waiting, Eldred hunting scholars."

Things were finally starting to make a little sense. That's why Eldred needed the Keystone and the collective powers. He was trying to save his wife?

"How long ago did he leave his wife with you?"

Grono looked confused. "You say weeks. Grono counting two moons."

But Lurine said he'd been hunting us since I was a little kid. "And you let him go around killing and kidnapping people while you babysit his wife? How could you let that happen?"

"Grono not knowing, Scholar James. Eldred killing long time. Before he bringing lady wife. Lady wife always some sick. Now very sick. This you must believing." The fagan nodded at me. "Eldred telling of seeking last scholar and taking power—your power, Scholar James—and with it to healing lady wife. Leaving fairy lands. Our Good Mother helping Eldred to leaving fairy lands. Sending Grono to Bellenor for watching and seeking. Grono tracking Eldred and the one hearing your bird Sending call."

"Mathan," I said, wondering if he'd figured out where we were.

"Yes, that one." Finally, Grono stood up and puffed out his chest. One eyebrow raised, as if waiting for my reaction.

I looked around at the tight space formed by the gap in the black stones. "What?"

Grono threw his hands down. He looked at me as if he was making perfect sense and I was too stupid to understand.

"Mitun Sorcallarant." He pointed to the ground.

"Yes?" I made a show of looking around the small space. "Scholar James not seeing," I said.

Grono held his hand open over the grass. Bak crouched down, laying his chin on the ground between us.

*Magic place.*

"What is it, Bak? You hear something? Grono, what's going on?"

The fagen smiled and nodded. Then it dawned on me.

"Is there a bridge here?" I asked. "Is this a crossing? Wait, where exactly is Sorcallarant Hall?"

"Eldred have Shihorren going through the worlds. We having good mist. Sorcallarant of the ancient ones. Vardorden. Mountain ones." Grono threw his arms up over his head and moaned as he rocked from foot to foot, a parody of some ghoulish monster.

I tried not to smile. "What, you mean giants?" A part of me wanted to be incredulous. But then I realized that I was talking to a fagen who lived with the fairies, and if he said we had to go to the land of the giants, who was I to cast doubt?

"Exacting. Yes. Gi-yants. They are no more. Scholar James not worrying." Grono got down on his knees, placed a hand on the grass and the other on his forehead. Then he waved me down.

I knelt next to the fagen and did the same. The creature closed his eyes and started chanting.

"Lahollan vitora grun farsoon. Grono falsa vitora maladen see. Lahollan vitora grun farsoon. Grono falsa vitora maladen see."

The vines vibrated, and the air filled with the hum of the coming bridge.

Bak squeezed against me. *Not again. Bak not like this.*

My mom was over there. *It's okay, buddy. Hang on.*

Grono kept repeating the words, which were getting lost in the rumble of the vibrating rocks and vines all around us. Then the pressure changed, and my ears popped as mist poured in from everywhere. As it climbed up over the rocks, it spun itself into a spiral staircase and disappeared through the hole in the roof.

Grono stepped up onto the bottom step. "Grono helping. Scholar James finding mother."

My mom was up there. And my father was heading to Dorren to find Eldred. If I brought her back and everyone saw her, she'd be safe. And my father would see that I wasn't some stupid puppet waiting for him to use me. He could laugh at me all he liked. I didn't need him, and he wasn't going to control me.

Grono was almost to the top of the wall.

"Let's go, Bak." I took the steps two at a time.

The staircase brought us up into the treetops before it spilled out onto a landing. Wrapping through the trees, the misty platform ended at another staircase leading down. I followed Grono through the misty spiral until we stepped off the stairs and onto a grassy mound, like the one we'd left, surrounded by walls of black stone.

We inched our way through the crevice path, but instead of stepping into a forest like the one we'd left behind, we entered a wasteland. The rise overlooked a wide valley spanning flat miles as far as I could see. Far to my left, a hint of mountains darkened the horizon.

Everything else was flat nothingness. The land was dark and gray, dead and bare. Nothing grew. There were no green plants or soft grass covering the ground. What few trees still stood were black and stiff, skeletal reminders of their former selves.

Ripping through the valley like a bolt of lightning, a fissure gaped open—a cavernous tear in the earth that seemed bottomless. It zigzagged away from us, coming to an end under a huge castle made from stone so black it seemed to absorb the light, like an ink drawing on a flat paper sky. The air was thick with the acid scent of sulfur, making my eyes burn.

*Sad place.* Bak thought.

"Whoa. What happened here?"

"This world dead. This world crashing Bellenor." He clapped his hands together. "Death for all here."

I stared at the valley before me in wonder. The worlds were really moving? "You mean it actually crashed? Like it physically broke upon impact? How?" The king had said they were drifting and colliding. I hadn't thought he meant literally.

"Worlds like a chain." Grono picked up a twig and drew a diagram in the dirt. It was the same spiral the king had shown me, like a string of pearls arranged in a coil. There were dozens of them. "It going on and on. Understanding?"

I nodded as Grono poked the stick in the center circle. "This the Prinu Mittolen, First World, Modern World." He pointed at the second circle in the line. "Bellenor." Then the third. "Teernano, fairy world, fagen world. You seeing?"

I nodded again and he continued.

"We crossing to worlds coming together." He drew a line across the space where the spiral turned and the next row of circles came back around. He pointed to the circle closest to Bellenor in next round of the chain. "Sorcallarant."

"That's where we are now?" I asked, amazed.

Grono nodded. "Scholars of Bellenor discovering drifting. The old ones sending messengers to all the worlds. Each world must settling their kind in other worlds. Moving energy to other worlds. Making chain strong. Stopping from drifting. But Derlin Vardorden—gi-yant queen—not trusting. Vardorden queen fearing trick, making gold unprotected. When last warnings coming, many vardorden ignoring. And when world crashing, world dying. All dead."

I tried to get my head around it. "How many worlds are there?" Maybe he knew more than the king.

He waved his stick in a spiral over the drawing. "On and on. Not knowing. Untold numbering worlds," the fagen said. "The old ones making maps, many maps. Perhaps Scholar James soon learning the ways? Come, Grono helping Scholar James. Finding mother." He climbed down the rocky hill with Bak and me following.

Untold numbers of worlds. What did that mean, exactly? There were humans, and Bellenorians, fagens, fairies, and giants. Did that mean ...

"Are dwarves real?" I asked.

"Yes."

"And trolls?" I helped Grono hop down from a high ledge. Bak navigated the rocks easily.

"Yes."

"Goblins? And Orcs? Elves?"

"Yes, yes, yes."

"So, you've seen them?" I couldn't believe it.

"Grono seeing, yes."

"What about unicorns?" I asked, racking my brain trying to think of other creatures from fairy tales.

"Yes. Scholar James playing now." The fagen shook his head and scoffed. "What about unicorns, he wondering." Grono said it as if impersonating me.

"Seriously? That's incredible. Where I come from—all of these things— they're make believe. They're all myths. But I guess that isn't really right after all."

"Grono no myth," he said, scoffing as if offended.

"True enough." As I said it, a thought occurred to me. "Hey, I've heard of fairies but not fagens. Where are fagens from?"

Grono stopped walking. "Fagen child of fairy and Bellenorian," he said, eyeing me.

"Really?" I tried to imagine how that would work, logistically. "We're related then! Excellent. What about the Loch Ness Monster? Or the yeti?"

Grono's brows came together. He clearly had no idea what they were.

"The Loch Ness monster, it's like a dinosaur. I guess. In this lake in Scot—never mind. Wait. Okay, okay, I got one: dragons."

Grono nodded.

"No. Way!" I whooped. "Wait until Charlie and Sam hear about this. It's incredible, Grono. Can you bring me to see these worlds sometime?" Maybe Sam would want to talk to me when he heard about all the worlds and all the creatures in them.

"Scholar James simple scholar," he said, shaking his head.

"Yeah, yeah. Hilarious," I said, though I couldn't help but smile. I suddenly felt totally out of place. What did it mean to be a scholar? Was I supposed to be a major intellectual? Right. Like that was ever going to happen. Even so, my mind was completely blown by the news of the worlds—and their inhabitants.

"Pardon, Scholar James. Grono should not be joke making."

I hopped off the last of the boulders and onto flat ground. Dead grass crunched underfoot. Up close, the gash in the earth seemed impossibly huge. Heat and fumes billowed from inside. Looking down into the abyss, I wondered where it went. I tried to imagine this huge amount of rock and dirt getting dumped on the world next to it, that all of this was only a slice of air away. It didn't seem real I couldn't help but feel small, contemplating it all.

# TWENTY-SIX

The castle loomed dark and ominous before us. The wall that once surrounded it lay in a toppled heap of jet black stone. The towers themselves were reduced to jagged stumps poking into the sky like broken, black teeth.

The road that led to the castle gate was a wide swath of sandy dirt. It stood apart from the dead field only because it was so wide, as if nothing had ever grown there. In this broken world, it seemed time had frozen everything. It was all dead and dry but preserved somehow.

The setting sun glinted off the smooth stone of the castle, revealing narrow slits in the walls and a rounded double door that was easily twice the height of the Tower Gate at Marren. The giants must have been, well, giant. Black bricks, some at least two stories tall, lay strewn across the valley as if someone had taken a baseball bat to the towers and scattered them. Must have been one hell of an impact when the world crashed to do that. Some had landed at least three hundred yards away from the tower.

As Grono and I made our way to the castle, Bak explored the path ahead. We stepped around one of the flung stones and found the broken skeleton of a giant. The ribcage stood taller than me. Crushed by the impact, the skull lay hidden underground. The bones were clean and white from what looked like endless ages of decay.

One of the doors to the castle hung at an angle from its top hinge, leaving a wide opening for us to enter into the gloom. Once inside, the cavernous space filled with screeching and low moans. The sound echoed through the room.

"What was that?" I asked, shaking the chill from my shoulders. My words seemed to bounce off the walls.

Grono shrugged.

*Bad sound. Bak leave.* My tiger stepped back.

The place smelled of dust and sulfur and staleness.

*Bak, stay with us, please. Don't be afraid.* I ran my hand down my tiger's back, feeling the tension in every muscle. *Relax. It'll be okay.* I prayed I was right.

We'd walked to the center of the room when a faint shuffling sounded from the far corner. A bent-backed old man stepped through an archway so tall it made him seem almost childlike beneath it.

Grono grabbed my wrist.

I froze.

The white haired man wore a long tan robe that dragged behind him as he shambled along, his soft shoes scuffing the slate. Making his way slowly across the room, he carried a huge wooden tray, its contents too far away to see. The room was so huge that he might not notice us unless he had a reason to turn his head toward the front door.

I felt Bak's fright twisting around my own and sensed his haunches flex, making ready to bolt.

*Don't move, Bak. Don't move. Don't move.*

Bak took a single step backward. His claws clicked once against the cracked slate. The sound carried through the stone room like a pebble plinking right up onto the old man's tray.

*Bad smells, bad sound. Bak wait outside.*

*BAKENEKO FREEZE!* I screamed my thought to him. I'd never shouted to him like that before.

My tiger cringed and crouched down.

*I'm sorry,* I thought, trying to soothe him.

Bak didn't respond. Wouldn't even look at me.

The old man stopped walking and tilted his head a little, trying to gauge the direction of the sound. He turned our way.

Holding my breath, I reached for my pocket and the dagger Grono had given back to me.

The man had no eyes. They'd been cut out a long time ago, judging by the white scars spreading from his eye sockets like a pair of cheery suns scrawled by a deranged surgeon.

"Wickley, is that you?" he asked, his shrill voice like an alarm in the cavernous space.

We stood as still as the stone around us, waiting for the old man to continue on his way. And he did. Once he passed through another arched doorway into the adjacent room, we followed him, being careful not to make another sound.

He turned down a sloping corridor, leading us through a series of arched tunnels, each of which branched off into more giant-sized rooms and hallways. One room had a white stone table, the size of an RV, with chairs to match. After seeing the skeleton of the dead giant in the field, I tried to imagine anything that huge walking around this place.

The old man stopped and put his tray down, taking a break. He had to be over eighty years old, the poor guy. What was he doing here?

I crept close enough to get a look at the tray and wished I hadn't. It was full of knives, razors, and an array of shiny surgical instruments that looked like they came from the modern world. They were all laid out, clean and orderly, on a black velvet cloth. I didn't want to think about what he'd need those for. I sent a silent prayer out for my mom to be alive and somewhere close.

Looking over the side of the walkway, I saw it spiraling deeper and deeper into the earth, turning around countless times before it was lost in the darkness. Sickly sulphur air wafted from below. The old man picked up his tray and turned off the sloping walk. We entered another hallway, this one flat and narrower than the other. This far inside the castle, there was barely any light. Blind as he was, the old man didn't need it, but I worried we would lose him if he got too far ahead. We sped up and followed even closer.

Through another series of rooms, the man kept on shuffling until he came to a stop outside a tunnel, arched and huge like everything else in this awful place. Lit torches lined this tunnel, high up near the ceiling, giving the black stone an almost cozy feel if not for the smell. The air stank of rotten things and mold. And something else, something burnt.

The tunnel sloped downward and curved, making it impossible to see where it led. The old man placed the tray on a small table near the entrance and tugged twice on a rope hanging from an iron ring in the wall. Somewhere deep in that tunnel, a bell rang, its distant peal like a hint of itself as it echoed back. His duty apparently done, the man shuffled right past us. Stopping, he sniffed, and I held my breath, thinking he'd smelled us. But he coughed and walked back through the arched door to who knows where.

I almost coughed too. Thick smoke leaked from the top of the tunnel's arch, feeding a cloud hanging over the room. I was about to step into the tunnel when the click clack of hurried footsteps rose from within. Turning to Grono, I searched the little room. There was nowhere to hide.

A tall, thin man in a brown robe emerged from the tunnel and walked over to the table where the old man had left the tray. With his back to us, he couldn't see us pressed against the wall. Bak lay against my legs, quivering.

The tall man hummed to himself, a tuneless nasal sound that stopped when he picked up the tray. When he turned toward us to enter the tunnel, I saw his eyes had also been cut from his face. Grono startled, bumping against me. I braced his shoulders and held him tight. This man's face was like the other old man's—his eyes were gone, leaving a pair of shriveled empty holes framed by ghastly sunshine scars. Had Eldred done this to them? Had he used those tools on that tray to do it? Anger boiled inside me. Eldred was a monster.

We followed the tall man into the tunnel and farther into the depths of the castle. This had to be the location of the laboratory from Charlie's vision. Suddenly, I wanted Charlie. I wasn't prepared for this. I didn't even have a sword. I touched my pocket, grateful that at least I had the dagger from Grono. If Charlie were here, she'd be whispering to me all the things she'd seen in her visions. All the details. She'd be holding my hand and making me feel strong. I tried to remember everything she'd described. The small room, the shelf of books, the tables, the boiling apparatus Eldred used to distill the … Oh freaking hell.

That smell. The burnt smell. It was blood.

The thought made me retch. I turned away from Grono and Bak, afraid I'd puke all over them. My eyes watered and my vision blurred. Bending over, I tried to calm myself, to stifle the gagging with each acid heave.

"Scholar James," Grono whispered. "What happening?"

"The smell. My brother's body, his blood." I wiped my eyes, willing myself to puke and get it over with.

"Scholar James thinking well thoughts. Thinking flowers and water. Cool water."

*Jim good?*

I thought of Charlie. I pictured her as I had seen her back in the grove, sitting in the sun, wearing that long white dress. Her hair still wet from her bath. Her smell.

"I'm good," I whispered. Standing up, I steeled myself. Whatever was about to happen was going to happen. I'd see what was what on the other side.

Voices floated through the smoky air, too far away to make out the words.

"Quickening," Grono whispered. He hugged the wall and padded ahead. Bak followed. I couldn't run with my boots on—they'd make too much noise. So I moved as fast as I dared, willing my boots to roll across the floor.

The bottom of the tunnel opened into another large room, this one surrounded by doors all around. The voices were louder, men's voices. They were coming from a door on the right. One door stood open, a golden wedge of light spilling out and drawing us in like moths to a flame.

"Where is it?" a voice demanded.

We crept closer, careful to stay out of the light and against the wall.

"All in time, man. All in time," another voice spoke, trying to calm the first. The second voice sounded deep and slow. Unforgettable. It was Eldred.

If I had hackles, they'd have risen then. I felt every hair on my body tingle.

"I've grown weary of your games, Eldred. We had a deal. The boy for the stone. You said nothing of kidnapping the mother. Nothing of murder," he shouted. "What do you intend with the mother?"

Something tugged at the back of my mind. The other voice ... it was ... familiar.

"Besides, you killed the wrong son."

It was my father! How? Why was he here? With Eldred?

I stepped back from the door, my mind reeling, unsure how to proceed. What the hell was going on?

"Yes, that was unfortunate, I admit," Eldred said. "But I sensed they might have tricked me, so I took the mother—for assurances, if you will."

"Where is the Keystone? Do you have it here or someplace else? Is it at Dorren?"

"I know you plan to cross me, old man." Eldred spoke to my father as if to a child, all calm and easy. "I know you intend for the boy to kill me. She'd have the Keystone and someone able to wield it for her. Someone to bend to her will. To what end? Really, you must tell me what you were planning to achieve."

"There are no such plans, Eldred. I—I know better than to cross you." Was my father afraid? The coward. My fists squeezed shut.

*Jim okay?* Bak asked.

"I'll deliver the boy to you on the morrow. At Dorren. As was agreed. But you must tell me where you've hidden it. She requires the Keystone."

Cold rage gripped me. They were bargaining for me as if I were a sheep. Talking about my mom and Dan like they were nothing.

Eldred sounded so patronizing. "The brother, he was a strapping lad. Royal Guard, I hear. And brave, my yes, so brave. What was his name?

I couldn't help myself. I pulled out my dagger. I felt my feet walk through the door and felt my knees wobble as I stood there and eyed them both.

"My brother's name was Dan, you murdering bastard."

# TWENTY-SEVEN

s soon as I stepped into the room, my senses went
totally berserk. My eyes felt sharper, my hearing
keener—everything was turned up full blast. I saw
each leg on the baby spiders in a web on the far wall. I heard
running water in the caverns below us, sensed it moving
beneath my feet. A mouse padded on the floor, each footfall a
tiny puff in my ears. I heard the blind man's heart racing as he
sat at the desk pretending not to notice the tension in the room.
I smelled the sweat and fear coming from my father. And I felt
the energy coming off Eldred like an aura all around him,
encasing him, encasing me.

I saw it all in a moment. Even though I'd gotten a hint of
these sharp senses from flying with Oona, this was more, far
more. It took everything I had to stay on my feet as I absorbed

it all. I was aware of Grono next to me, his dagger out. Eldred flipped his hand, and the fagen flew backward out of the room.

Bak rolled on the floor, swatting at his face.

*Bad man hurt Bak.*

"Scholar James!" Grono got to his feet and ran back to the room. The door slammed shut, leaving the fagan outside, banging to be let back in.

Eldred smiled. "See that, old man? The boy feels the power of the collective."

My father gaped. "How is that possible? The ampule is around your neck, not his."

"This is true." Eldred fingered the metal jar on a chain around his neck. "And now you see." He waved a hand between me and himself. "We are the vessels of the collective, the boy and I. Our proximity is all that's required. But this—" He indicated the jar. "—is intended for another. And for that, I'll need his heart."

Power ran through me like a torrent of wind and raging water. I felt like my skin might tear from the fullness. My head wanted to explode, but not with pain, with ... more, as if my brain were absorbing everything and filling up. If this was the collective power of all the scholars, it was awful. I felt the ground through my boots, each grain of dirt and grit as it rolled under my knobby soles.

"James, son? What are you doing here? How did you get here?"

How dare he call me son. "I ..." My voice sounded huge in my head. It was too much to take in. All the sounds. And the smells. My eyes ... I was on overload. I squeezed my eyes shut and imagined myself bigger. Big enough to hold all this power. I imagined myself as big as the cavernous hallway outside the door, and then, as quickly as they came, all the powers dissipated and settled down. I was like myself again. But sharper.

"I should ask you the same thing, *Dad*." To think I dreamed of having him back. And doing what? Playing catch? Going for a ride on his horse? I'd been a fool. A complete and total fool. Everyone had me swallowing my phony life from the beginning.

"Oh, the boy is upset with you, old man," Eldred said, his smile a prim line on his gaunt face.

I squeezed my hands into fists. "You lied to me. You've all been lying to me. You call me your son? Tell me why. Father, why?" I had to know. Right then, nothing else mattered more than knowing. If I was about to die, I wanted to leave this world knowing what it was that was worth so freaking much.

"Son … I …" My father stepped toward me, pleading.

"Please." Eldred threw his hand out and my father flew back, slamming into the bookcase. Books and scrolls fell to the floor. Eldred held him suspended there with nothing more than his will.

"You want to know why?" Eldred said. "Why—a simple query with a complicated answer. But perhaps I can illuminate you."

I wanted to punch his smug face, but I couldn't move. He waved a hand at me and I felt myself being pushed back.

"The lies were woven around you in order to protect you—from me." He smiled his prune-faced grin. "And here you stand. A family torn apart by love and devotion, and fear. And yet, you're all here, well, mostly all here … father, son, other son." He tipped his head toward a hatch door built into the floor. "And mother. Isn't that the height of irony?"

"My mother's here?" I took a step toward the trap door and felt myself lifted off the ground. I hovered in the air an inch or so, unable to move. Eldred's hand was outstretched, pointing at me, pushing me back to the door. Bak stood behind me, backing up into the wall as I backed into him. The dagger was pulled from my hand. It hit the floor with a clang.

*Bak afraid. Bak not moving.*

The force of Eldred's hold on me was strong, but I could push against it. Push it back. It didn't hold me the way it seemed to hold Bak and my father. I let myself slide the inch back down to the floor.

Eldred didn't seem to notice. His gaze was on my father again. "You see, many years ago, I had reason to do some research into the ways of the ancient scholars. Their demise was a mystery, especially when you consider the scholar collective's power to heal." Eldred lifted a book from the table behind him. "While looking into some of the older texts, I discovered a secret library which contained the writings of a single scholar gone rogue. It seems that this one scholar, Barthimus, discovered that by killing his peer, he could take on the power of the one who passed. It has to do with the blood— it's all very complicated." He waved a hand dismissively.

The blind man felt along the wall as if trying to find a place to hide. Bak hissed and pawed at his ears, shaking his head. I took a step toward Eldred.

"Stay there, boy. You wanted to understand? Allow me to explain." He lifted me into the air again and pushed me against the door. "Where was I? Oh, yes. Well, judging by his notes, it seems Scholar Barthimus went a little mad. Over the course of a single night, he crept into their sleeping cells and slit their throats. Oh, he described each of those in ghastly detail, but the way he wrote of the power he gained ..." Eldred clasped his hands in front of him as if remembering how joyous he felt reading it.

"He took their lifeblood and took their power. And after each met his end, our friend Barthimus came back to his little hidden room and recorded it all in his diary. It is quite something to read."

I inched forward toward Eldred. Toward the table with the boiling blood. "You've killed children—little kids!"

Eldred didn't seem to hear me. "Alas, our Barthimus went off in search of the final scholar. All this took place at Castle Dorren, which I am sure you will never get a chance to see, young man. Of course, his little missive on the way to his last kill was his final entry because, as history reveals, something went very wrong. Barthimus and his scholar-prey fought to the death, and both lost. There must have been quite a row, and neither had time to heal themselves of their wounds. This is conjecture on my part, you understand. Those secrets went with them to the grave."

I thought about the boys, the scholars that Eldred had taken before he found me. They must be dead if we were both feeling the power of the collective. My God. "You're no better than Barthimus, you know."

"Oh, but I am. You see, because I shall be victorious." He turned to me. I could actually feel his gaze on my skin. "I find it endlessly amusing that they hid you in a carnival. Were you a performer? Yes, I wager you were. Well, I think it is time for the grand finale, yes?" I felt Eldred's hold on me turn into a pull. It wasn't enough to drag me, but I moved toward him, taking a step in his direction. He reached behind him and grabbed a long golden sword. With a jolt, I realized it was the one he'd used to kill Dan.

"Come here, boy. No sense in fighting it." I moved closer to Eldred, closing the gap between us step by step. The nearer I came to him, the less pull I felt. I was getting stronger. I felt it with every fiber in me.

Bak was unsure what was happening. Eldred was holding him back as well. I heard his breath huff through his nose in small puffs.

*No, Jim. Stop, Jim. Very bad man.*

*I'm fine, Bak. Don't worry. Stay back, he has a sword.*

"James, Son, resist him, you can do it." My father strained against the bookcase.

"Don't call me son!"

Eldred turned to my father. "Old man, spare us the ruse." Pushing his hand out, Eldred forced my father back against the wall hard enough to make his teeth click shut. His hold on me flickered. Seeing my chance, I took it.

I threw myself at Eldred, grabbing for his sword hilt. He turned, but he was too late. I was on him and we crashed to the floor. He was stronger than I expected him to be. But I was stronger than normal too. It felt almost as if I could will my arms and legs to do more than ever before. Like the power was coming from somewhere inside of my body. Eldred flipped me onto my back—but his hold on me was gone. I twisted under his weight and threw him off me. I straddled him, staying as close to him as I could so he couldn't swing that sword. I was not going to die here.

Grono banged on the door, shouting and cursing from the other side. The door vibrated under his hands.

*Roll right, Jim.* Bak's command was the same as I gave him when we were dueling in the show.

*Good boy!*

My tiger was right behind me, released from Eldred's hold as well. I threw myself backward and rolled away. Bak's paw flew over me. Eldred saw it coming and dodged. Though Bak half missed, the blow still threw Eldred back. The sword hit the ground with a clang. As Eldred crashed into the tray of surgical instruments, silver tools went flying. Bak had shredded Eldred's robe, but there wasn't much blood.

I dove for the sword. Eldred was on me, our hands like a single creature, clawing and fighting to scrabble onto the golden hilt. Touching Eldred brought a surge of power like I felt when I'd first walked in. Light blinded me. Closing my eyes, I tried to picture where the sword laid. I willed my hand to the sword—willed the sword to my hand. I needed to have it. It was mine.

I opened my eyes. The sword was gone.

My father stood over us, holding the sword.

"Do it! Kill him," I shouted.

My father shook his head. "It has to be you. You must deal the fatal blow."

Was he joking? My father turned the sword hilt-first to me. I reached for it. But Eldred grabbed it and pulled, slicing my father's hand open. Screaming, my father cowered to the wall. I punched Eldred in the throat. He dropped the sword. I felt Bak plotting his next attack. Unsure about attacking a person, my tiger was petrified of hurting me. But he knew that Eldred needed to be stopped.

*It's okay, Bak. Good boy.*

My mind and Bak's joined. As he made ready to pounce, I got ready to roll away. Then my tiger let out a strangled whine. Shaking his head and pawing at his ears, Bak ran into the wall. He barreled into the blind man, and the two of them rolled to the floor. The blind man's dead sunshine eyes took in nothing.

"You think ..." Eldred spat his words at me. "... you alone control that beast?" He punched my ribs, left, right, left. He was impossibly strong.

The wind went out of me. I grabbed his throat, squeezing with everything I had.

His words came out in a wheeze. "The collective serves us both, boy." He flicked his hand and Bak crashed against the wall, head first. My tiger fell to the floor in a heap.

"Bak!"

Eldred spread his hand over my chest, I felt pressure building inside me. Crushing me. Pressing the air out of me.

Squeezing my heart. Eldred reached out to pick something up off the floor. A scalpel. My ribcage was going to cave in.

*The collective serves us both ...*

His words finally made sense. I willed my chest to be like iron. It threw Eldred's hand off, and the man let out a howl of surprise.

"You learn quickly, boy," he said, his sweaty face twisted in a sneer.

I threw Eldred off me. He slammed into the wall. I had to end this. Distract him. Throw him off balance. Then I remembered what Grono had told me.

I caught my breath in heaves. I grabbed Hollis' dagger as I got to my feet. "I know about your wife ... In the fairy land." I showed him my cuff. "I know you're doing this to save her. They told me she's sick. The fairy queen told me everything."

Eldred's eyes were like twin moons. Shock and worry washed over him and broke whatever spell he had going on. He stood against the wall, stunned by my words.

I pulled out my dagger.

"What did you say?" Eldred asked, his panic seeping from him into me. It felt almost strong enough to overwhelm me.

"I made a deal with the fairies." I lifted my braided cuff again. "That's what this thing is all about. They helped me out when your guy Mathan almost killed my best friend, and in return, I agreed to help them. The Good Mother doesn't like you." I got to my feet and turned the dagger in my hand.

"My Alonna? What have you done?" Eldred's words poured from him like liquid menace.

"Your wife is dead. I killed her," I lied.

In a flash, Eldred was on me, screaming. His face twisted into an anguished mask. "No!" he wailed. He was like a bear going in for the kill. There was nothing left but him and me—death waited to take one of us.

Through the holes in his robe, I saw it. The glistening jewels sparkled, catching glints of firelight. I reached for the Keystone as Eldred dove. Felt it move into my hand as if it wanted me to hold it.

Eldred threw himself on me and we slammed into the door. For a moment, we stood face to face, frozen. Eldred's eyes were all watery, wide and staring at me. He staggered back a step, his gaping mouth moving soundlessly. The hilt of Hollis' dagger stuck from his chest. A single tear tracked down his cheek and fell to the stone floor.

Eldred dropped to his knees.

My senses exploded. As fast as Eldred's life drained out of him, his powers seeped into me. All the powers from all the scholars surged and pulsed though my veins and through my bones.

My father ran to Eldred and pulled the chain from Eldred's neck. He placed it on the table. "Quickly, we need his heart."

Eldred fell to the floor. I watched as his eyes found mine. He blinked once, and then he died.

Slowly, as if the sun were rising and lighting me from the ground up, I felt myself grow whole again. Fatigue and exhaustion fell away. Aches eased. A cut on my head stopped bleeding. I felt like I'd woken up from a nap. I was totally refreshed, but not quite present. I felt like the world was moving out of time, like everything was happening on a delay.

"Snap out of it, boy! Check his pulse." My father set a bowl over a flame. "It must be done quickly. Here, use this." He tossed a knife to me.

In slow motion, the knife tumbled toward me. The iridescent handle caught light from the fire. I still held the Keystone. I slipped it into my jacket pocket and reached up. The knife seemed suspended, waiting for me to pluck it by the handle. Taking it from the air, I stared at the weapon in my hand. What did he expect me to do with it?

My father called me again, "Now. It must be now."

I tried to focus on him.

He hurried back to me. "By the good, boy. Come on then. Give it to me!" He snatched the knife and knelt next to Eldred's body. Without even hesitating, he pulled Hollis' dagger from Eldred's chest and stabbed the knife in. He tore through Eldred's chest.

I flinched and felt myself snap back in to reality. Turning away, I stepped over Eldred's body to the makeshift lab he'd set up and saw what my father had taken off Eldred's neck. The silver necklace with the small metal jar—the tarnished silver ampule Eldred used to collect the blood. The jar hummed as if it knew my blood was the match for what it held. But if this was how the collective worked, I wanted none of it.

I picked up the ampule and felt my powers surge again. A thousand times stronger. The chain wound through a ring fastened to the small metal cap.

"Quickly." My father was back again. He ran around me, snatched a fallen bowl from the floor and placed it on the table. With Eldred's warm and dripping heart in his hand, blood covered him up to his elbows. The tang of blood hung in the air.

My father said something, but it was all so far away. Everything in me rang with the vibration from the necklace. He squeezed Eldred's heart over the bowl. Drops of blood sizzled as they landed on the hot surface. There was a lot of blood—it filled the bowl, growing thick. It smelled of meat and burning metal.

This was so far beyond wrong. I watched my father as if through a window. Like I was apart from it all. I tried to concentrate. "Why are you doing this?"

"So close. I have to see it through." My father grabbed the ampule from me, ripping it from my hand. The power seeped from me.

As he pulled his hand away, his sleeve rose and I saw a familiar ring of knotted wood circling his wrist.

The fairy queen. All at once, I could see it. Eldred had figured out how to capture the collective for his wife, by containing the blood in a way that she could wear. Eldred was doing this for his wife. The fairy queen wanted the Keystone and a way to wield it. And with the jar of blood and the power it contained, she didn't need me. Or Eldred.

I blinked, shaking the fog from my mind as I realized my father was working for the fairy queen. I thought back to what he'd said to the woman in the castle. He'd made a vow. It explained everything—the betrayal, all the lies. "You're doing all this for the fairy queen?"

A wet smear of Eldred's blood had stained my father's beard. He adjusted the glass over the boiling blood, letting the brown-red steam condense. It rose from the bowl and met the glass. Droplets of Eldred's blood joined and slid down the glass into the tiny silver jar.

In silence, my father counted the drops. They each made a tiny plop when they landed in the liquid already inside the small container. Ten drops.

Bak moved against the wall behind me.

*You okay, buddy?*

*Bak wake up.*

The power in the room swelled, threatening to break me open with the fullness of it.

My father twisted the lid onto the ampule, the pads of his fingers sticky with Eldred's blood. He put it around his neck and sighed with relief. "Ah, much better."

I could feel the power all around him in an aura the way it had been around Eldred. It surrounded me, pulled me in.

"And now, we can be done." My father searched the floor, digging a bag out from under the pile of fallen books. He pulled a tiny stone jar from a bag. My stomach coiled as he moved his fingers over the top of the miniscule jar and removed the lid.

Fairy song filled the small room, overwhelming me with that longing and swoony feeling from the fairy caves.

He exhaled. "Finally." He picked up Hollis' dagger from the floor near Eldred's body and pointed it at me.

*Jim down, roll right.*

*No boy! Don't ...*

In a flash of orange and black and white, Bak flew over my shoulder, knocking me aside as he crashed into my father.

"Bak, no!" I screamed.

# TWENTY-EIGHT

"Oh my God. Bak. No. Bak!" I felt suspended in time, detached. I knew the fairy song and the collective powers were doing this to me. It felt like it had in the fairy caves. I concentrated on resisting it. I needed to get a grip.

I'd landed with my back against the door. Grono's banging a tiny drumbeat that rang through my skull. I got to my knees and opened the latch.

"Scholar James!" Grono ran to me, smiling and whooping. "Scholar James living!"

"Bak." I crawled to where my tiger lay sprawled on the floor, his chest torn open by the blade still clenched in my father's hand. My tiger wasn't moving. I put my ear to his chest. His heartbeat was soft, faint.

*Jim safe now. No danger.*

Tears filled my eyes and blurred my vision. "Stupid tiger. What did you do?" I grabbed the fur at his cheeks and turned his face toward me. I needed to look in his eyes.

"Bak ... ?" I whispered.

*Jim safe now.*

Bak's eyes closed. His head grew heavy in my hands.

I blinked, not understanding. This wasn't happening. Not Bak.

Grono put the lid back on the fairy jar and the music stopped. The room seemed chillier now, despite the roaring fire.

I hugged my tiger, letting his fur fill my senses. "No!" My tiger. My Bak. Oh God, no.

My father burbled something wet and incoherent. His words lost as they spilled through the gash Bak had torn across his throat. I got to my knees.

Blood spurted from my father's wounds.

I wiped my eyes and crawled over to where he lay on the floor.

He gasped as he breathed in. "My ... vow," he said.

I wanted to scream. He lay dying and all he cared about was some stupid vow?

"Blood," he said.

*The blood.* Where was that necklace? I wanted to find it and shove it down his throat. I looked around for the silver ampule. He'd been wearing it when Bak attacked. I had to find it and destroy it. This was going to end here. I searched his collar, pulling his blood-sodden clothes away from his skin. The chain wasn't around his neck. He blinked once, his dark eyes following me as I searched for that damned necklace.

His eyes were exactly like Dan's. Anger flared inside me at all the lies and deceit. I didn't know who I was anymore. "Where is it?" I screamed.

"Scholar James."

I turned to Grono. He knelt next to Bak on the floor. In his hands he held the ampule, the chain caught in Bak's paw.

I felt myself snap back into my skin again. I felt my feet in my boots on the gritty floor. I smelled the bloody steam, filling my head with death and horror. I saw my father for the monster he was, staring at me, unable to move, and unable to let go of his quest.

I looked at my father, his eyes now half-closed. "You see that?" All that power in one tiny little jar. It ends here." I moved to Bak and grabbed the ampule, tugging at the chain.

I worked it free of Bak's fur and untangled it from around his claws. Twisting the lid off the ampule, I walked to the hearth and tipped the jar over, attempting to pour the contents into the flames. Nothing came out.

The jar was empty.

I turned the ampule over in my hand and found a hole through the silver. It had been punctured, a broken piece of tiger claw still stabbed through.

"Scholar James coming here." Grono had his ear to Bak's chest. He was smiling.

"Bak?" I hurried to my tiger.

"Scholar James seeing." Grono spread the fur on Bak's chest away from his wound.

Looking at it now, I could see Bak's fresh red blood mingled with the dark blood from the ampule that had leaked all over his chest and into his wound. His fur reeked of the burned blood. The blood of eleven scholars. I touched his wound and watched the cut heal before my eyes.

Bak's chest heaved with the intake of breath.

*Jim safe.*

I nodded. *Bak safe, too.* I wiped my nose and felt tears spill from my eyes. *Bak safe, too.*

Across the room, my father groaned as he rolled to one side. He picked up a wooden stick from the floor. A lightning weapon like the one Eldred's men had back at Sweetwater's. The blast went low, hitting me square in the gut. But it didn't explode like it had in the Modern World. Instead, thick oily liquid coated me, eating through my clothes like acid.

I felt something surge within me. Starting in my groin, it worked up through my chest and down to my hands. My fingers tingled. I touched my stomach, and the acid stopped burning. It went cold as if I had somehow deactivated it.

My father took aim again, higher this time—going for my face.

Raising my hands, I felt the power surge once more. It was a righteous feeling and I knew each of the dead scholars were there with me, guiding my hands to put an end to this. Red and yellow light, like ropes of flame, shot from my fingertips and wrapped around my father, lifting him off the ground, squeezing him.

"No, choice," he cried. "I had no choice. It was her. Always her."

"Save your words for when you join the devils," a voice said. The words coming from me weren't my own. "This power is meant for those who will wield it purely. This power is unable to abide the corruption of a weak mind. This power will do away with any who would misuse it. It will always find a way."

My hands opened, fingers pointing at my father as he writhed in the air above me. A voice whispered in my mind. *Be gone from here, wicked soul. Your time is done.* It sounded like a prayer.

My hands grew hot. The light from my fingers crackled and squeezed my father tighter. His eyes bulged. Blood seeped from his torn throat. I closed my eyes.

The voice in my head spoke again. *Scholar James. Open your eyes. Bear witness to the power and the wrath of the collective.* I obeyed. My hands shot up higher, the coils turning deep orange, squeezing and twisting now, spinning around my father in a tornado of light.

As the spinning grew more intense, the skin on his face seemed to stretch away from his skull. Then it pulled away entirely—like a mask. And not only his face. The vortex stripped everything away—his clothing, his skin, his entire stature, like he wore a costume. In disbelief, I stared at a different man, an old man—much older than my father ... and *familiar.*

The old man screamed.

I heard his ribs crack as the vortex narrowed. He screamed again, a guttural wail as the vortex spun inward, collapsing into a tiny dot and dissipating in a burst of white as it exploded into the room.

The old man's body landed on the ground, stiff as a board. He wasn't my father. I stepped closer to him, trying to make sense of what I was seeing. That face. I'd seen it before. My mind rolled back to the fairy caves and the sad man on the hill with the fairy queen. The one with the guitar. Somehow, that man lay dead on the floor in front of me.

Exhausted, I slumped to the ground. I turned in time to see the blind man crawl out the door, sniveling.

Bak nuzzled me. *Jim okay?*

I wrapped an arm around my tiger's neck and pressed my face into his fur.

*I'm okay, boy.*

The room grew quiet. I stared at the dead man, trying to get my head around who he was and why he was here. And if he was here, then where was my father? I looked at the old man's wrist. At his wooden cuff. Fury rose inside me. The fairy queen did this.

I couldn't begin to put it all together. My brain was fried.

"Scholar James helping Grono. Lifting," the fagen said, struggling under the weight of the wooden trapdoor in the floor. Was this where Eldred had dumped Dan's body? I remembered the noise I'd heard below.

Bak nudged me. *Dark place. Jim stay here.*

I didn't want to look. I didn't want to see Dan stuck in some hole, his body tossed like trash. I knelt and stuck my head through the door in the floor, waiting for my eyes to adjust to the gloom.

It was a store room, like a pantry. Shelves full of baskets of tubers and gourds lined one wall. Jars of food and some tools had been stacked on a table. Had Eldred built this? The hatch wasn't giant-sized, for sure. On the other side of the room stood a cage. The meager light from the trapdoor touched the corner of its metal frame.

"Jim? Baby, is that you?"

"Mom?"

I don't remember climbing down. A moment later, I was standing there pulling a ring of keys off a hook and unlocking the cage. Then her arms were around me, and she was kissing my hair and sobbing.

"Eldred's dead." My words were muffled in her hair as she hugged me close.

"Oh, thank God. Jim, honey, I swore if I ever saw you again I'd tell you how very sorry I am. For the lies. For everything. I'm sorry. So, so sorry. Are you alright?" She pulled away and looked me over. That was when I saw it.

A grave.

She followed my gaze. "The bastard let me bury him, at least," Mom said. She wiped her eyes. I reached up and wiped her cheek with my thumb. Holding her face for a moment, I looked in her eyes.

She latched onto my mind with her own. The feel of her thoughts was cool and crisp and so familiar.

*I love you, James. So much. I never wanted this for you.*

I'd never realized until now how much I missed when she did that.

"I love you too, mom," I said.

I knelt beside Dan's grave. She'd laid out a bunch of small pebbles in the shape of a tree near his head. My brother. I touched the stones. "It doesn't seem real." I said. "Why did he do it? Why did he let Eldred take him without a fight?"

"He gave his life so that you might live. So we all might live."

I closed my eyes. "Thank you, brother," I whispered. Then I stood and grabbed Mom's hand. "Let's get out of here."

# TWENTY-NINE

As soon as we got back to Castle Marren, the king summoned the sisters. The two blind servants with the scarred starry eyes sat at the table. The king's servants brought them trays of food. Mom insisted we take the men—their names were Wickley and Grossin—with us after all they had done to care for her.

The king—my grandfather—kept his distance. "Don't put the Keystone down. People have been killed by touching the thing."

We stood in the great hall, and I held the stone in my bare hands as people gawked and whispered. I worried about dropping it, my palms were getting so sweaty.

Bak wouldn't leave my side. When the sisters arrived, they escorted us through the gardens and the secret gate that led to the Grove. We passed the place where the Keystone had been

304 | CORINNE O'FLYNN

hidden safe for a thousand years before Eldred had stolen it. We walked silently past the old hiding place, everything was black and burned.

I carried the Keystone in the small procession, feeling self-conscious about how dirty I was. Charlie was there, looking beautiful all in white, her hair loose and full of flowers, flowing down her back. She carried a candle for the Keystone's replacement ceremony.

There were six sisters and me standing in a circle. The king, my mother, Bak, and Grono made up the small audience. Sam had refused to come.

Sister Lurine stood at the altar and read from an old leather-bound book. The somber feeling of the woods made it feel like a funeral. Even Bak bowed his head.

"Into this soil we give this stone. The tether of our second world forever bound to the first. May the power of the four stones hold fast for eternity. Protector of all the worlds and all who thrive within."

Lurine nodded to me, and I placed the stone into a little niche carved into a small mossy mound. My part done, I stepped back and stood with the others and watched as the sisters—Charlie included—performed a rite of blessing and protection. While several of the sisters chanted and moved in sync with each other, Charlie and another sister waved their candles through the air in a slow figure eight.

Mist poured in from the forest, engulfing us all. I braced myself for the pressure change of a bridge opening. Instead, I watched in wonder as the sisters waved their arms and caused the leafy plants and vines all around us to grow up and out, spreading over the Keystone's niche and snaking through the trees to totally conceal everything. Watching Charlie took my breath away.

*Charlie magic?* Bak seemed star struck.

*She's awesome. Isn't she, buddy?*

"It is done." Sister Lurine was unsteady on her feet as if the magic had taken everything out of her. She wiped her hair from her forehead and led the sisters away from the now obscured niche.

We followed the procession. When I looked back, there was nothing to see except thick green forest and some hazy mist. You'd never know that the key to life on all these worlds lay only yards away.

"Amazing that anyone could have found it in the first place," I said.

"Well, unfortunately, it seems Eldred had help, in the form of an imposter," the king said. I didn't ask how the fairy queen's old man knew where the stone was hidden. I wasn't sure I could find my way back to it, and I was mere paces away.

We walked past the old hiding place. "If you can grow the forest like that, why leave the burned place as it is?" I asked Lurine.

"It is all too easy to forget, my lord. Sometimes nature's scars serve a purpose, making sure we remember the fragility of life. The forest will heal itself in its own time," she said.

After the ceremony, I went to the hospital to see Sam.

Sister Bette stopped me at the garden gate. "He's not ready to see you again, my lord," she said. I nodded and turned to go.

Charlie met me as I was leaving. Her hair was still woven through with flowers from the ceremony. She took my hand and we walked.

"I'm glad you're back," she said. "Everything that happened ... it sounds awful. I'm sorry you had to go alone."

"I wasn't alone. Grono was with me, and Bak."

"Well, I'm sorry I wasn't there."

"I'm not." I laced my fingers through hers. "The castle was like you said, though. All black and huge. That's pretty incredible."

"Yeah. I've been working on honing my visions. Sister Lurine says I have great control for someone starting so late." Charlie smiled, beaming.

When we got to the gate that led back to the castle, she stopped.

"You're not ready to leave here, are you?" I wasn't sure I wanted to hear her say what I already knew to be true.

"Not yet. But soon. I promise." Charlie got up on tip toe and kissed me.

*Charlie magic kiss*

Bak stepped from the behind the trees and bumped me.

*What are you looking at?* I scratched him between his ears.

# THIRTY

The following morning, the king asked Grono to bring a group of men to Sorcallarant to fetch Dan's body. Dan would be buried with the rest of the family. They would bring back Eldred's corpse, and the man who had posed as my father, though no mention was made of burial for them.

Dan's funeral was set for that evening at sunset. It occurred to me that I'd never been to a funeral at Sweetwater's. When old Mr. Morrell, the farrier, died, Hollis told me he'd taken his body to be laid to rest over Lookout Mountain in Colorado. Come to think of it, Hollis said the same thing years later when a cable snapped and dropped a cargo container on Foss the canvasman. I had no idea Hollis was telling me about Bellenor then. How often had he shared things like that? It wasn't quite a lie, but he knew he was misleading me. I wondered how often Hollis visited here over the years. Clearly, everyone knew him like they all knew Dan.

Sam came for the funeral. He sat in a chair on the edge of the row where the rest of us stood facing the grave. I kept looking his way, hoping to catch him glancing at me. He didn't.

Charlie touched my arm."He'll come around. Give him time."

I nodded and looked at my boots.

Of course, I'd never seen a Bellenorian funeral, either. I guess it was nice as funerals go. There was singing and leaf dancing, and an offering of food for Dan—to sustain him, and candles to guide him on the next part of his journey. There were loads and loads of colorful flowers, and music. Everyone in attendance sang incredible songs. All the while the Royal Guard stood by, in their sky-blue sashes and shoulder cloaks, watching over the grave.

One of the Royal Guard broke ranks and sang a special song he'd written for Dan. A piper played a slow haunting tune as the man sang about my brother, his friend. He said Dan was a brave knight and brother who volunteered for a secret mission for the king and was sent away as protector of a treasure. The lyrics told how Dan gave up so many things in life for his duty: friends, his love, all to protect this treasure, to protect us all. The soldier watched me as he sang. When I realized the treasure was me, not the Keystone, I felt my face go hot and had to keep looking away. The song made my mother cry.

When the funeral ended, we all walked a short distance past the graveyard over the hill. Four guards carried Sam in his chair. I couldn't stop looking at the way the blanket covered his one leg.

We gathered in a stand of gigantic golden aspen trees in the field around the crossing stone. The red rock stood almost five feet tall and pointed into the sky. The moon would be full tonight and half the city had come to witness the return of the Sweetwater clan.

Seems there were many clans in the Modern World, in other countries. Most of them spent four or five years away, like a tour of duty. But only Sweetwater's had been away for more than twelve years. Several in the crowd held signs that read *Welcome Home*, with the names of their family members on them. I studied their faces in wonder. I'd always been told this world was destroyed. That we, in Sweetwater's, were the last of our kind. I always took that at face value, never really thinking what the words meant. Looking at all these people standing here, I felt bad for accepting them as dead.

Here they were, alive and well, waiting for their families to come home. Some stared at me as we waited. I wondered if they resented me for keeping their loved ones away. Judging from the looks, they knew I was the reason for all of it. Guess they've known about me all along. More secrets, more lies. I looked at my feet.

My grandfather spoke. "The people of your carnival clan, they *chose* to stay with you at Sweetwater's. It was an honor to be given such a role."

I wondered if that could be true. "It's hard to believe that." I couldn't say if I would have done the same for them. The idea of such a sacrifice …

"Perhaps, for you, it is hard to believe. But that does not make it any less true." He smiled and looked toward the horizon. "The moon will break soon. Any moment now," he said.

Bak pressed against my legs, arching his back for a rub. I let him walk his body under my hand and slide his tail through my fingers.

Watching my grandfather, I could see a hint now of how Dan might have looked had he lived to be an old man. They had the same jaw and the same thick curly hair. The king turned his gaze east. The crossing stone was up in the foothills west of Marren City. I pictured this place in the Modern World, its rolling hills peppered with trees and grass. There, the valley spilled into Golden, Colorado. Following my grandfather's gaze, I waited for the moon to break the horizon so we could open the bridge.

Two of the royal guard stood in front of the crossing stone, waiting for the king to give the go ahead.

My grandfather put his hand on my shoulder. "We owe a debt to you, son. A hero's debt. One that can never be properly repaid." He looked me in the eye.

"Thanks." I looked back to the horizon, hoping my grandfather wouldn't notice my tears. I didn't feel like a hero. Heroes weren't supposed to be royally pissed off and totally frustrated. I grabbed the cuff on my wrist. Heroes didn't make promises they could never keep. Heroes weren't murderers. Hero? Whatever. Eldred deserved what he got. I wasn't sorry he was dead. But I was no hero. Heroes were kind-hearted— they felt remorse.

Eldred and the fairy queen's man—they would have killed me if they could. They tried. *But I'm here.* I came back. I made it. And I was standing on my own two feet. I hiked up this hill on two legs. I looked over at Sam and saw all the things he'd never be able to do again. Not the way he did before. No. I was no hero.

Keek kek.

I felt her before I saw her. A man walked over to me with Oona rocking on his arm. She looked amazing.

"My lord." He handed me a long leather sleeve.

I slid the glove on and let Oona hop over. She bowed and touched her head to my cheek.

"How do you feel, girl?" I asked.

Spreading her wings wide, she keeked. I felt her itching to fly.

The moon rose over the horizon.

"It's time," my grandfather said, nodding to the two guards at the crossing stone.

The king's men got down in front of a standing stone. We all knelt as they said the words to summon the bridge. As the air pressed in around us, the trees quaked, raining leaves onto everyone. We waited in silence. The mists wafted in, building a bridge from nothing. We watched it take form, and we waited. And waited.

"Where are they?" a woman asked, worry in her voice. "Where's my Lawtry?"

With a wave from the king, the pair of guards double-timed it across the bridge. When they got back, glistening with moisture, they shook their heads.

One guard took off his helmet. "No one waits beyond, Your Highness."

Where was everyone? I worried that I'd been mistaken about what I'd seen at Sweetwater's. Could those ambulances and police have been a ruse? Had Oona and I left too soon? I traveled back in my memory to the fairgrounds. No. I was sure of it. They had been rescued. The cages were empty.

The people in the crowd started talking and crying, wondering aloud what could have happened. We waited until the bridge melted away into a damp fog hovering among the brush and spreading over the grass.

Lawtry was one of the horse trainers. A great guy. He loved to do card tricks. Lawtry's lady shouted at me, tears in her eyes. "You said Eldred left them behind! You said there were rescuers who saved them! Well, where are they?" she demanded.

I stepped back, palms out. "They should be here," I said. "They were fine ... They weren't stuck in the cages ..." It had been a month, and that's plenty of time to get to Denver from California. Even if they had to take a bus or a train.

In ones and twos, the stunned people left the hillside, heading back to the city and Castle Marren.

"Charlotte," Sister Lurine called as she led a group of the sisters down the hill.

Charlie had been standing with the sisters, but she came over to me, stunned as the bridge melted away. "I—I have to go." She stared at the bridge and I knew she was worried about her parents, and her brother, Davey.

I'd let her down.

My grandfather addressed the crowd. "We'll send a party to find them, tonight. We'll see what's happened and bring them home." He sent his guards running back to the castle to put together a group to cross over before the full moon set and the bridge closed for another month.

The king and I stood alone at the crossing stone.

"I don't understand," I said.

"Nor do I, son. But we'll find out what's happened soon enough. We'll send a tech to cross with the guards and go to one of those computer shops you Moderners are so fond of."

"You mean Internet cafes," I said, feeling completely out of place talking about computers with a man dressed in light armor and a shoulder cloak.

"Yes, those. It makes checking on our people so much simpler. World wide web, indeed."

Later that night, I lay in my bed as the moon arched its way across my window. Oona stood on the window ledge, scanning the world for food. The moonlight cast a falcon-shaped shadow across the floor. I bolted upright.

"Holy smokes, the moon hasn't set yet!" I threw on my clothes and ran for the door. I nudged Bak where he lay asleep by the fire. Hopping through the courtyard, I pulled on my boots while looking up at the moon and trying to calculate how much longer we had. I raced through the gate, past the graveyard, and onto the footpath. Oona sailed overhead, a welcome and silent presence above me.

The footpath had seemed so much shorter before, in the dusk. I ran through the trees, tearing at the rocks and the grass as I climbed. In my mind, I pictured the misty bridge sitting there, waiting for me. As I stepped into the clearing, the moon moved westward, trying to set. I realized how it never truly stayed in one place—ever.

The clearing was empty. It was pretty stupid to think they'd have been late. I mean, if they were coming, they would have been at the stone weeks ago, waiting for the full moon so they could open the bridge.

*Sorry for Jim.* Bak loped beside me.

*Thanks, bud.*

I sat in the grass, unsure what to do. I wanted to talk to Charlie. To see how she was doing now that her family wasn't here, wasn't coming. I didn't understand.

I wished things could go back to normal. I missed the "us" of Sam and Charlie and me. One more thing sacrificed to Eldred's mess. And what about my father?

I tried to balance all that was lost against the idea of Bellenor turning into something like the dead land of the giants. It seemed too strange. Too unreal. I told myself that my losses were small in the scheme of things. But it didn't make my pain any easier to take. At the end of it all, I wanted my brother back and really just missed my friends.

Oona flew by, low and close, ruffling my hair. She buzzed over Bak and dropped a pinecone on his head.

Keek kek kek.

Circling back, Oona swooped into the field and dropped another pinecone bomb between Bak's eyes.

He shook it off. *Stupid bird.*

My tiger's thought made me smile. "Well, maybe she doesn't like tigers. You ever thought about that?" I could feel him mulling that one over in his cat brain.

*Everyone like tigers.*

Keek kek kek.

I turned the wooden cuff around my wrist, thinking how the fairy queen would react when she learned I'd destroyed the collective powers and wouldn't be bringing her the Keystone. I'd give anything to see her face when she heard the news.

Oona landed on the grass and hopped back and forth, taunting Bak. Nose to the ground, he slunk low as if he could hide himself. He pounced, paws raining down. But Oona was ready and took off before he could catch her. I let the cool grass settle me down as I watched them chase each other far down the hill.

"An unlikely pair, those two." Mathan's voice stopped me cold. "Honestly, I thought you'd never leave the city alone again." He stepped out from the trees, a knife in his hand. The last of the moon lit up his patched eye and his stupid smile.

He thought I was afraid of him. But I wasn't. Not anymore. All I felt was angry.

I got to my feet. "Eldred's dead. I killed him at Sorcallarant Hall. Whatever he promised you in exchange for me isn't going to happen now." I searched his face for something, surprise or fear at the news of Eldred's death. But if he felt anything, he didn't show it.

"We've moved beyond what Master Eldred wants, you and I," he said, stepping closer. "No, what we have between us is personal. I've had a long time to think about you, James Wales, the last of the scholars. And I made a decision. I don't want you dead. I want you alive, but I'll have an eye, the left one, I think," he said it almost casually. Like he was negotiating the price of animal feed at the store. "It would make me so happy knowing you woke each day and thought of me as I do of you."

"You're crazy," I said, trying to seem as cool as he was. But in my mind, I wished I was halfway down the hill, running as fast as my feet would go. I stole a glimpse down the footpath, looking for Bak.

"They're off playing. They won't be able to help you now," Mathan said.

I darted for the trees, but Mathan was fast. He grabbed my ankle and caught me. I kicked to throw him off. He dodged and slammed his knee into my back. He grabbed me by the hair. Pulling my head back, he stretched my neck and made me gag. I felt the blade on my cheek. Warm blood ran into my mouth.

Squeezing my eyes shut, I reached behind me, grabbing his wrists. But he was bigger and stronger, and he had the advantage. I threw my head down as if to head-butt the grass. A handful of hair tore from my scalp. Mathan lost his hold. His weight was still heavy on my back.

Something in the trees moved. Were Silver Braid and the rest of Mathan's crew here after all? As my ears popped, he said something I couldn't make out. I imagined myself made of stone, hard and impenetrable, heavy and forever-thick. I heard Mathan shout, felt him pull the knife up over my left eye. Then everything went white and cold.

I always likened blindness to darkness. But maybe things were light when you couldn't see. That might not be so bad. I felt myself slip away. My vision narrowed until it went totally black.

When I opened my eyes again, I knew I was dead because Hollis was there, a disembodied face trying to communicate with me from the other side. The sky swirled dark purple and navy blue behind him, getting lighter.

*Wake Jim, wake Jim.*

Was Bak here too? How had Mathan managed to kill my tiger?

It was so good to see Hollis again. I missed his happy face.

"Quit your smiling, goofball. Wake up. It'll never do to let people see you keeled over like this. What'll Charlie think if she hears that you pass out every time you do your fancy trick?"

Keek kek kek.

Oona perched in a shrub, watching me. That didn't make any sense either.

I looked around but couldn't see well. "Are we all dead?"

Hollis stood up. "I sure hope not. I had one heck of a time getting back here, but I don't think I died on the way." He gave me a hand and pulled me up. That's when I noticed he was leaning on crutches, and his left leg was in a cast to the hip. I had to turn my head to see him. Only one of my eyes worked.

"I can't see," I said, reaching for my eye. "Mathan—" I looked around for the one-eyed man.

"Yes, I saw what happened. He cut you good, though he didn't get your eye."

I touched the skin around my eye. It was swollen and numb. When I pulled my hand away, it was dusted with dried blood.

"I'll be damned if I know what it was I saw, though," Hollis continued. "There I was, minding my own business, hobbling across the bridge—which wasn't easy to get to on my own and with these crutches—by the way. I was thinking about my Aunt Jinnie here in the city and her exquisite rabbit stew with her famous fluffy dumplings when I come around the bend in the bridge to find you. The guy has you by the hair, and he's got his knife at your face. And then you smack your head on the ground and explode all blue and green light, and he takes off flying like a sack of flour. Like that." Hollis moved his hands in an arc.

I followed Hollis' arm, searching the trees. "Where is he?"

"No idea. He vanished. Right through the air. I checked. He's gone."

"I did that?" I asked, trying to remember. My eye throbbed.

"He dropped this." Hollis handed me Mathan's knife, the one he used to mangle my face. The blade was crushed, folded and bent in impossible ways. It still had blood on it.

I didn't know what to say. I'd destroyed Eldred's ampule—the blood was gone. Had the blood somehow gotten on me when I touched Bak? I didn't feel any more of that power surging in me now. But how else to explain what I did to Mathan? How the knife blade got crushed?

"Give me a shoulder, will you?" Hollis reached out an arm, and I grabbed his crutch before it fell.

Looking around, I saw nobody else on the hill. "How long was I passed out? Is everyone already back at the castle?"

"Everyone who?" Hollis asked. "Just me and you and Bak here."

Keek kek.

"And the bird," he added.

"Everybody from Sweetwater's. Didn't you all come through?"

Hollis shook his head. "I've been on my own since I woke in the horse trailer, crushed under Tess' rump, a month ago. The news reports all said there were no staff left at the fairgrounds. They had one hell of a time figuring out how a hundred people could disappear like that. I assumed you all got here under the last moon. Way ahead of me."

"Nobody's come back, Hollis," I said, my mind a whirl of worry and confusion. I tried to imagine where they could be and what Eldred had planned for them. How would we find them now?

Orange sun sliced the horizon and separated the land from the sky. As we made our way back to the castle, I could almost pretend that I'd walk through the gate and my mom would greet me with my dad on her arm. Sam would be waiting to go explore the strange city. And Charlie would catch up with us, annoyed that we tried to leave her behind when she really knew all I wanted was to be alone with her.

The skystone castle twinkled in the morning sun.

"There it is, beautiful as ever." Hollis squeezed my shoulder.

Bak ran down the hill, jumping and swatting at Oona as she dive-bombed him.

"Yeah." I looked beyond the castle into the forest that hid the Grove. A thin mist hung over the trees. Charlie and Sam were there right now—at this very moment. I wondered if she was thinking about me.

Hollis hobbled down the path. "By the sisters, it sure is good to be home."

Home. I may not ever feel like this city was home. But for now, it held everyone I loved. Mom and Charlie. Bak and Oona. Hollis and Sam, even if Sam never would forgive me. And that made it as close to a home as anything could ever be.

But now, I knew I had work to do. I had to find out more about the power of the collective and what I'd done to Mathan. I had to find the rest of our Sweetwater clan and bring them back safely. And I had to pay a visit to the fairy queen and find out what she did with my father.

Hollis huffed as he navigated the rocky path. "Can't believe we're back for good. Feels weird just leaving with a slew of unfinished business back there, know what I mean?"

Unfinished business. "Yeah. I know exactly what you mean."

I tapped Oona, and we sailed over the city. She shrieked as the glittering castle passed below us. I felt the wind in her feathers and I knew—this was exactly where I belonged.

Thank you for reading my story. I hope you enjoyed it. And if you did, please help other readers find it by writing a short review at your favorite online vendor or Goodreads.

Stay informed of future releases in *The Expatriates* series and other book news by signing up for my newsletter: eepurl.com/YNic5

*Follow Corinne at:*
@CorinneOFlynn
www.corinneoflynn.com
www.facebook.com/oflynnbooks

# Acknowledgements

Being that this is my first book and that it took many years to write, it's been touched by and shared with countless people whose feedback, support, guidance, and encouragement I have come to value deeply. The idea of saying personal thanks to everyone involved is daunting, as I am sure to leave someone out. So I apologize in advance, and hope you'll indulge me for yet one more page (or so), as I do my best to give thanks where it is due.

First, thanks to my family, especially my husband, Michael, whose support has been constant from the start. I don't know if I can ever express the magnitude of my appreciation, but I will surely keep on trying. To my kids, Conor, Rory, Liam, and Aidan, who have been an incredible source of inspiration and energy for me. They are such interesting people, cool kids, and my first fans. I hope to make them proud.

To my sister, Colleen Carr, for being tireless in sharing her insights as an early and repeat reader, plotter, late-night brainstormer, and therapist. To the rest of my Carr and O'Flynn families for being such enthusiastic cheerleaders.

I credit my mom for instilling in me a love of words and language from my earliest days. For her, I hope they have books in Heaven.

My critique group has been a inimitable source of education, guidance, encouragement, and friendship over the years. *Song of the Sending* would never have come to be if it weren't for the astute minds of Tessa Devan, Liza Frenette, Sandy Galfas,

Sharon Gelman, Dania Ramos, and Kristi Roberts. I thank my lucky stars for the day we were brought together.

To my Rocky Mountain-SCBWI critique group: Roy Hohn, Barb Lindstrom, and Ellen Mackey, who provided early insights on this book while it was still an amorphous idea. I'm grateful for the time we worked together. To Rocky Mountain Fiction Writers, where I found my tribe. To Dennis Phinney and the team at ActFourWriters, who brought a unique experience to critiquing a manuscript as a whole, and gave me wisdom I will utilize as long as I am writing.

Thanks to my amazing friends, Sandra Courtney, Mary Doner, Jenny Haynes, Cori Knol, Shawn McGuire, Lisa Ann Riccardelli, and Rebecca Thompson, who wore various hats as early readers, constant cheerleaders, courage builders, and accountability partners.

Beta readers, Frederick Lee Brooke, Jeri Elder, Madi Elder, Chuck Harrelson, Kurt Hauer, Paul R. Hewlett, Matthew McCoy, Stephen Merlino, and Zack Raulerson, shared feedback at various stages which encouraged this writer and shaped the book of today.

I am deeply indebted to those who made up my publishing team for this book: My editor, Sher A. Hart, whose thoughtful insights and sharp eyes brought this book to a whole new level; Steven Novak, the amazingly talented artist who brought the cover to life; and Ali Cross, the master formatter who simplified everything about making the interior pages beautiful.

Since making the decision to self-publish, I've found the most incredible community of authors who have paved the way, shared every detail of their learning, and left the porch light on for those of us who came after them. It is through this amazing generosity that I was able to bring *The Expatriates* into the world, and into your hands. To each of them, my gratitude.

And finally, thank you, reader, for giving *Song of the Sending* a little time and space in your heart. I hope you feel it was well spent.

If you'd like to stay informed of future releases for this series and other books, subscribe to Corinne's newsletter at eepurl.com/YNic5.

# ABOUT
## *Corinne O'Flynn*

Corinne O'Flynn writes stories with fantasy and magic, and sometimes creepy stuff. *Song of the Sending* is her first published novel. She lives in Colorado with her family and blogs about her adventures at www.corinneoflynn.com.

*Follow Corinne at:*
@CorinneOFlynn
www.corinneoflynn.com
www.facebook.com/oflynnbooks

CPSIA information can be obtained
at www.ICGtesting.com
Printed in the USA
FSHW01n0706080518
47965FS

9 780979 616907